Silenced

Also by Anne Randall
(previously writing as A. J. McCreanor)

Riven

Silenced

Anne Randall

Constable • London

CONSTABLE

First published in Great Britain in 2015 by Constable

Copyright © Anne Randall, 2015

1 3 5 7 9 10 8 6 4 2

The moral right of the author has been asserted.

A CIP catalogue record for this book is available from the British Library.

ISBN: 978-1-47211-233-0 (hardback)
ISBN: 978-1-47212-257-5 (trade paperback)
ISBN: 978-1-47211-237-8 (ebook)

Typeset in Palatino by SX Composing DTP, Rayleigh, Essex
Printed and bound by CPI Group (UK) Ltd, Croydon, CR0 4YY

Papers used by Constable are from well-managed forests and
other responsible sources

MIX
Paper from
responsible sources
FSC
www.fsc.org   FSC® C104740

Constable
is an imprint of
Constable & Robinson Ltd
Carmelite House
50 Victoria Embankment
London EC4Y 0DZ

An Hachette UK Company
www.hachette.co.uk

www.littlebrown.co.uk

For Don

Silenced

Prologue

Communication One

Welcome, friend, have you decided to read my story? I *can* call you friend, can't I? I do hope so. This is my story, my communication to you, and as you read it, we connect and it becomes our shared journey. Our place in time.

Are you excited?

I am.

I feel a delicious shiver of anticipation, which begins at the nape of my neck where the tiny hairs stand upright. Would you like to stroke them, caress the soft down? Forgive me, it's an innocent fetish of mine. I indulge myself by shaving some fine down from each encounter with a soul-mate. A beautiful expression *soul-mate*, don't you think? Unlike the harsh word favoured by the media.

We are all connected, if only on the spiritual plane. But perhaps you disagree. That's okay. For you scientists out there, we also share matter, we vibrate – oh, how I love that word – we *vibrate* at the same frequency. All humans do; it's what unifies us. *Or lumps*

1

us together in the same filthy pit. But what interests me most are our differences and how we choose to celebrate them. If we are brave then we can learn to distance ourselves from our humanity and free ourselves from its mundane constraints. Human is not *all* that we are. You do understand this, don't you?

Glasgow. I stalk the city at night, inhaling its stench and its chaos. The city and I share the same drug: we crave the low life and the lurid neon lights that outstrip the dying stars in their fading heaven. I watch as bars and nightclubs cocoon their prey until closing time when they release the wretched filth into the gutter. And the lost souls who sleep on our streets, soil our lanes, squat in deserted shells? They make their own luck, take their chances. Who cares if sometimes they lose, if their gamble backfires?

But, as ever, the city endures. Sweet, intense Glasgow. As dark as chocolate and twice as bitter.

To us. To our journey together. *Sláinte.*

Chapter 1

Glasgow was in the throes of the worst storm since records began and the name for it was Thundersnow. Thunder growled across the skyline as snow fell hard and fast over the city. In George Square, sleet fell over the stone lions that guarded the City Chambers, and the wind rapped hard and persistently on the windows. The other statues in the square remained stoic while a lone pigeon balanced on the head of Robert Burns and scrutinized the area for discarded food. The pavements were slippery and the gutters surged with water. New Year and its gaudy celebrations were long gone and only the frozen final day of January remained.

In Carmunnock, the Rose Memorial Crematorium, a low red-brick building, surrounded by a garden of remembrance, was open for business. The officiant at the service was Raymond Crook, an emaciated man who sported a slim pencil moustache. Crook stepped forward, gripped the side of the lectern, cleared his throat and began: 'We are gathered here today to celebrate the life of Chrissie Haedyear…'

3

Mark Haedyear sat listening to the description of the woman who had given birth to him. He would not think of her as mother. They had disowned each other early in their relationship, equally matched in their revulsion. Prison Officer Gerry McClure sat on Haedyear's left and stifled a sneeze, burying his mottled nose in a menthol tissue. On Haedyear's right, a second officer, Bill Irving, sat erect, stared straight ahead and kept his hands tightly clasped on his knee as a sheen of sweat spread across his bald head.

Haedyear glanced out through the snow-splattered windows and saw the trees bend to the wind's demand. He heard the wind shriek and dance and felt that somehow it, too, was celebrating the death of Chrissie. Like Irving, Haedyear's hands were clasped tightly and blue veins bulged under pale skin. The sleeves of his jacket only partly concealed the handcuffs. Haedyear felt the excitement rise but fought it down. Not yet. He forced himself to remain calm and to think mundane thoughts. He imagined the furnace and the flames that would consume first the coffin, then the body within, knew that the heat would be blistering, maybe even 1000 Celsius. It would devour everything, leaving only a residue of ash. Haedyear had calculated the amount: there would be as little as four pounds of her left. Four pounds of dirt to dump on the earth outside.

'Now let us remember...'

The eulogy had come as part of the cheapest funeral package available, a generic, fill-in-the-deceased's-details type of thing. Her name they already had. That he was the next of kin was the most important detail he had provided. It meant that he was in charge. He closed his eyes and

4

listened to the deceased being described by a man who had never met her.

'Chrissie Haedyear was a devoted wife and a loving mother.'

Well, the first part was true. His childhood had ended the day his father died. When he was five, his beloved father had been dead a year and it had been Haedyear's first day at school. A milestone. Chrissie had knelt before him and placed her hands on his shoulders. For a moment he had hoped for a mother. Instead he heard her usual refrain, her shrill voice, hoarse with hatred: *'You are the fucking reason I drink. Do you hear me?'*

He had gone to school, face covered with vodka-soaked spittle. She had kept on at him until he was seven, when he'd grabbed the steel poker and turned on her. The blood had silenced her and she'd never touched him again. At twelve, thanks to his father's legacy, he'd gone to Oakwood, which he'd left at eighteen to attend university. He had never visited the house again, had never even seen Chrissie. And now she would be incinerated.

'...and Chrissie, a woman who surely did her best all her life, will indeed be sadly missed.'

'Come here, you little shit. I want to kill you.'

'...a woman who cared greatly for her husband and child.'

'I wish you had never been born.'

'...but she will live for ever in the thoughts of the loved ones she has left behind.'

'You'll never be loved. Who could love a fuck-up like you?'

Haedyear opened his eyes and scanned the mourners. There were five in all. They were all old neighbours from Clarkston. Chrissie had had no friends who would grieve over her death. No one to hear the news that she had finally drunk herself to death. Haedyear knew that Chrissie had wanted to be laid to rest beside her adored husband in the graveyard. 'Cremation,' he'd told them at the Rose Memorial, 'and scatter her ashes in the garden of remembrance.' He glanced at his watch: there were a few more minutes to kill.

Eventually it was over. Haedyear watched the coffin disappear and the curtains close. He turned to McClure. 'I need a quick trip to the Gents and then we can head back. I just want to say how much I appreciate you coming all the way out here just to let me say goodbye to my mother. She was a wonderful woman and I'll miss her very much.' McClure and Irving grunted their condolences and the trio walked out of the room and headed for the toilets. The sweat on Irving's head had solidified, like a film of skin around a hard-boiled egg. He went ahead and scoured the cubicles for unlocked windows, a false ceiling, a concealed exit. He returned and told them, 'Nothing, all okay.'

He lied.

McClure sneezed loudly into a crumpled tissue. 'Christ, Haedyear, be quick. I'm dying here.'

Haedyear smiled. 'Will do.'

And he was.

Chapter 2

In his badly lit office at the *Glasgow Chronicle*, Graham Reaper sat at his desk eating a lukewarm mince pie. Flakes of greasy pastry and minute grains of salty meat floated onto the keyboard of his computer until finally he noticed, leaned down and blew hard, dispersing the tiny shards. The reporter's pallor was as grey as the pastry and his eyes were bloodshot. He glanced at the clock: in an hour he would have another liquid break. A pint of heavy. Sustenance. Just the one. He'd only have the one. Aye, right. Mibbe. When his mobile rang he dumped the pie on his desk and checked the number. He spoke quickly: 'Aye?' As chief reporter he didn't have to trouble himself with manners – it was enough to be efficient.

'Grim?'

Reaper listened to the wheeze, recognized the tremor in the voice. Jimmy Westcott, kitchen porter at the jail, badly needed a drink. Reaper knew that Westcott was also a heavy smoker and keen gambler and lost more in a month than he'd ever earned. He wasn't quite the poster boy for healthy living. 'Okay, Westie, what've you got?'

'I've got a cracking wee story for you, Grim.'

'Well, spit it out.'

A pause. 'The thing is, I need the money upfront. I owe a bit here and there and the guys I'm talking about, well, you don't mess with them. I'm serious, Grim, they're not reasonable…' His voice drifted off.

Reaper kept his tone the right side of bored. 'Not my problem, Westie. '

Silence.

Reaper gave Westcott enough time to consider his severely limited options. He heard the rattle of a cough. A spit. A sigh. Then Westcott began to wheeze out his information in short, secretive bursts. Reaper grabbed a pen and took quick, urgent notes. Five minutes later he switched off his mobile and knew that he had the lead story. He hammered the digits into his mobile – his next call was to the police media liaison officer. Their conversation was brief but throughout it Reaper typed furiously. Then he called the crematorium. Unsurprisingly it was closed. He called the emergency contact and got a number for the officiant, Raymond Crook. Reaper knew that Crook would be with the police, but he'd get to him later. He also knew that it was useless to try to contact Gerry McClure and Bill Irving, the two prison officers involved. They would be suspended while the investigation was conducted. Reaper's gut instinct told him that at least one of them had been complicit in the escape. At this point he didn't know which one or why, or what Haedyear had on him. He guessed that serious threats would have been made, perhaps to a family member, but unearthing that story was for another time. Right now he had the scoop.

Outside, the weather raged against the building and the wind spat hail at the glass windows. In a few minutes he had finished the online news. He sat back, picked up the last bite of pie and scoffed it while reading his work.

Murderer Escapes

Police are today hunting for a murderer who absconded from prison while temporarily released on compassionate leave. Convicted killer Mark Haedyear, 38, escaped in what can only be described as an audacious act while attending a service for his mother, Chrissie Haedyaer, at the Rose Memorial Crematorium in Carmunnock. After the service had concluded, Haedyear managed to escape through a window at the rear of the building.

Haedyear, originally from the Clarkston area of the city, was a former pupil at the prestigious Oakwood School and had served only three years of a life sentence for the abduction and murder of Amanda Henderson in 2011. Mrs Henderson, 35, was an art historian who had been invited to deliver a lecture at Southside College, where Haedyear also worked.

After abducting his victim, Haedyear kept her prisoner in an underground chamber in a woodland area close to his home. During an intensive police investigation, Haedyear had been interviewed with the rest of the college staff but was subsequently released. It was only after police received an anonymous tip-off that his home, car and the adjoining woodland area were searched and Amanda Henderson's body found.

Police are appealing for the public's help in tracing Haedyear, and earlier a police spokesperson had this to say: 'Mark Haedyear is an extremely dangerous criminal and should not be approached. If you have any information at all about this person, please call the number below. I can assure you that all calls will be treated in the strictest confidence.'

Haedyear is described as white, five foot nine with a slim build. He has cropped fair hair and green eyes.

Earlier today a member of staff at the crematorium said, 'I'm extremely shocked by this incident and hope that it does not reflect badly on the Rose Memorial Crematorium. When prisoners are on compassionate leave they are usually heavily guarded and their entry and exit from any area is closely monitored. I can't imagine how this happened.'

It is thought that Haedyear escaped through the window and scrambled across open countryside to make his getaway. While he could have been acting independently there has also been the suggestion that he may have had an accomplice in order to facilitate the speed of his escape while wearing handcuffs. The two officers who were supervising the prisoner have been interviewed by the police and released. They will, however, be suspended from duty while an inquiry is conducted.

Reaper typed up the telephone numbers the police had issued and sat back in his chair. Decided the piece read well enough. Job done. He glanced at the clock. Time for a pint. Just the one, he told himself. Aye, mibbe.

Chapter 3

Tollcross Road. The road was deserted, the lights from the small shops and cafés had been extinguished, metal grilles and shutters dragged across doors and windows. Alarms had been set and their red eyes winked in the dark. In an alleyway the wind gusted salty chip wrappers around doorways as an ancient grey rat risked a foray into the blue skip parked behind Lou's Place. It was overflowing with plastic refuse bags, polystyrene cartons, crisp packets and scraps of meat from discarded kebabs. Soiled paper napkins bled crimson sauce into the mess. The rat sat on his hind legs, two front paws in the air, as if begging, but he was sniffing for danger. His nose quivered for a moment as he paused before sensing that it was safe to proceed. He gnawed quickly, feasting on bits of meat while his rheumy eyes scanned the street. He watched. Listened. He stayed alert but he was safe for the moment. There was no one around and the foul-smelling skip was unremarkable, except that on the road beside it the tip of a scruffy black trainer protruded. It was cheap and well-worn. The old rat nibbled on his dinner, his half-blind eyes darting from the alleyway to the road and back until he heard rather than saw the gritting truck approach.

Although still hungry, he abandoned his meal and, trailing his mangled leg behind him, crawled into the safety of darkness.

Clive Hill was at the wheel of the truck. He was forty-seven. A born introvert, Hill craved the solitude of the permanent night shift. He was unused to crowds and noise and had worked alone for thirty years. Every winter he gritted the roads, driving steadily through the night. In his free time he walked the city, tracing the old lanes and alleyways, the abandoned factories and deserted buildings. He knew Glasgow intimately, had uncovered the city's hidden gems. He walked in the early hours of morning, around dawn, when foxes slunk through the streets, their amber eyes the eyes of wolves. Hill had watched animals who lie hidden and watchful during daylight hours, venture out under cover of darkness. He'd seen bats sail through the night air, their nocturnal dance witnessed only by himself and an indifferent moon. But if Hill had uncovered gems, he also knew what the shadows of the city concealed, its hidden shame. He'd seen rain sluice blood and hair from the streets and had felt the violence linger in the air. But Hill loved Glasgow, and over the years he had accepted and understood just about everything that the city had offered. Sometimes he had even excused it. Until now.

When the lights from his truck had picked out the outline of the trainer, Hill had braked sharply, switched on the hazards and jumped onto the frozen ground. He had landed awkwardly on the icy pavement and had to steady himself against the door of the truck. He glanced around but there was no one in sight – he double-checked before he approached the body. He knelt on one knee at the side of the skip, felt the snow seep through his trouser leg and spread a cold, damp stain over his skin. He shivered, looked at the man lying before him and stared into a face he recognized. 'Shit.' He leaned towards the body, checked for breathing but heard nothing, only the wail of a far-off siren fading into the night. He took out his mobile and pressed the same digit three times. Then he began speaking. Slowly at first, so that the woman at the other end of the line could understand what he was saying. He was asked to repeat himself and did so until the police had been summoned.

He stood in the snow, heard thunder roll across the city. Watched the flakes falling silently. Waited. Hill did not touch the body, did not look at it. He would not allow himself to wonder what had happened. He told himself that the police would come and that they would take over. He wondered briefly about the tracks his truck might have obliterated, saw the snow grey and compacted by the vehicle's tyres. Hill closed his eyes and let the storm wash over him. He allowed the snow to cling to his face, his eyes, his mouth. He allowed it to still him.

Chapter 4

'So, you're saying I'm fucked.' It was more of a statement than a question. Detective Inspector Kat Wheeler sat on a banquette in the alcove furthest from the stage and tried to make herself heard. Her blonde hair was shorn at the sides and longer on top, making a little quiff. She lifted a large glass of Chardonnay, took a sip and surveyed the food on the table in front of her. It was fare more suited to a wake. Scotch pies sat in pools of grease, fat bridies and sausage rolls hummed heart attack, and bowls of chips, with three types of mayonnaise, nudged the chances a little higher. But she had to eat. She decided the chips were the least toxic and speared a fat one with her fork. Around the room, the karaoke lights flashed green, red, blue and yellow on a continuous cycle. Acting Detective Inspector Steven Ross sipped his pint and reached for a piece of greasy garlic bread. He munched it before looking at her, blinking his long dark lashes over pale blue eyes. He waited a second before asking, 'So, Stewart told you to forget it?'

'Yep. Case closed.' She glanced at a group of police officers huddled in front of the stage, the karaoke crew. 'They'll have hangovers from hell in the morning.'

'Aye, but tonight's the night to forget it all. Besides, it's a celebration. Boyd got engaged and we solved the case.'

'I'm not sure we're celebrating the right result, Ross.'

'We're celebrating a result, a pretty good one in the circumstances.'

She looked at him, kept munching. Took another sip of wine. Waited.

He sighed. 'You know the score, Wheeler. Sure you've photographic evidence, which may, just may, link Andy Doyle to James Gilmore but it's a bit of a long shot.'

She finished the chip and reached for another. 'It's shit. Do you think I should take it higher?'

'Come on, you already know the answer to that and, anyway, you'd get no support.'

She didn't contradict him.

'It would ruin their stats. From their point of view, the case is solved. Maurice Mason killed James Gilmore. Case closed. Two bastards are now off the radar, the heid-high yins are thrilled.'

'Right. An ex-con was found dead.' She speared another fat chip from the basket. Dipped it in the garlic mayonnaise. Ate. 'And he was conveniently—'

Ross cut her off: 'Wearing a St Christopher medal, which had been stolen from a murdered paedophile. You can see how it makes sense.'

'It's too neat, though, isn't it?'

'The top brass are delirious. The case is resolved. Big fucking result. You saw how Grim wrote it up in the *Chronicle*...'

'Yeah, I remember. *Carmyle police should be justifiably proud of their investigation.*'

15

'Just leave it, Wheeler. Pastures new and all that, and for starters that lunatic Haedyear's done a runner.'

'I know,' said Wheeler. 'You think he'll head back to his old stomping ground, in Clarkston?'

'He'd be a fool if he was even still in the city. My guess is he'll be long gone,' said Ross. 'You think the two prison officers were in on it?'

Wheeler sipped her wine. 'They've both been inter-viewed and released, but suspended from duty while the inquiry's ongoing. Even if they're not involved, they might end up losing their jobs.'

'Seems a bit harsh if it was done by an outsider.'

'But they weren't thorough enough. I mean, Haedyear scarpered.' Wheeler paused. 'Anyway, should you be out on the ran-dan tonight, given that you're going to be a dad?'

Ross shifted in his seat. 'It's all off again.'

'The pregnancy?'

'No, she's still going ahead with it but it's over between us.'

'Again?'

'Again.'

'Because?'

'She went into fantasy La-la Land.'

'That'll be the hormones kicking in.'

'Wanted me to leave the force, get a nine-to-five. Be there for the kid.'

'What did she suggest?'

'Insurance.'

'Right. I can just see you in insurance,' said Wheeler.

'She wanted the whole cartoon dream. Even the picket fence.'

'Roses round the door?'

'Exactly.'

'But you'd miss the glamour of this job.' Wheeler looked round the room. The Belter Bar and Grill was all about cheap booze and even cheaper artery-clogging deep-fried food. Even the humble vegetable had been coated in batter and deep-fried in fat. Tempura. Their boss DCI Stewart hadn't turned up, but those who had were either swaying to the cheesy karaoke or looking distinctly glassy-eyed.

Ross sipped his pint. 'I'm quite nervous about becoming a dad. Being a role model and all that stuff.'

'You'll be okay.'

'Since we're on the subject, did you ever want kids?'

Wheeler studied the contents of the chip basket. Speared a chip. Chewed. Said nothing.

Ross took the hint. He glanced across at the stage and changed the subject. 'Look out, Boyd's going up.'

Wheeler watched as Detective Constable Alexander Boyd lumbered towards the stage. 'Nightmare. How does Boyd not even know how shit he is?'

'Classic denial.' Ross shuddered. They settled themselves for the trauma as Boyd took the stage and began comprehensively to strangle every note of Bryan Adams's '(Everything I Do) I Do It For You'.

A police sergeant in a too-tight shiny black shirt roared from the back of the room, 'Get them out for the boys!' Boyd duly complied and opened his shirt to expose a generous expanse of flaccid flesh and tufts of thick dark chest hair. The team yelled and applauded as he gyrated and sang with no discernible talent in either department. Finally he finished and, flushed with success, left the stage to make his way to his fiancée. The upstairs function room in the bar was heaving, but not everyone in the place was drunk – the staff on the whole were pretty sober.

'So, if not the case, at least let's celebrate Boyd's engagement.' Ross raised his glass. 'The happy couple look delirious.'

'And stocious.' Wheeler lifted hers.

'That too.'

'Has no one mentioned the fact that Boyd's still married or would that just be inconvenient?'

'It definitely would seem that way. Anyway, his wife refused a divorce – he'll need to sit it out.'

'That the lucky woman?' Wheeler looked across to Boyd's fiancée. Took in the tight red T-shirt, the short black skirt and the fishnets.

'She looks like she's dressed for work,' said Ross. 'Subtle she's not.'

'Tell me what she does again?'

'She's a burlesque dancer at Foaming Frothies. Boyd's in Heaven.'

'I'll bet,' said Wheeler, as the screen on her mobile lit up. She glanced at the number, headed to the far corner and pressed the phone to her ear. She listened carefully before making her way back to Ross. 'New case.' She went behind the bar, switched on the overhead lights and killed the soundtrack. She ignored the yells and waited for the boos to subside before she announced, to a silent room, 'A body has been found in our area.'

A slurred prompt: 'Go on, Wheeler.'

'All I know at present is that we're looking at a murder in the Tollcross Road area.' She grabbed her coat and made for the door. Ross stood, pulled on his leather jacket and stared after her. 'Guess I'll be paying, then.' But she was gone.

The music was switched on again, but the party was over. The atmosphere in the room was subdued. Officers who were on duty in the morning either finished their drinks quickly or abandoned them. No point in going in to a murder inquiry with a hangover. Jackets were collected. Wives, husbands and taxis were called. It was home time.

Outside, the weather raged around them. Thunder growled across the skyline as lightning flashed. 'Thundersnow,' muttered Wheeler, pulling up the collar of her coat as a taxi turned into Byres Road. She flagged it down.

'So much for a night off and a wee break.' Ross opened the door for her.

Wheeler climbed in, gave the driver instructions and, once on their way, turned to Ross. 'Quit whining. Don't you know—'

'Aye. Your usual refrain, "Some poor sod has been battered/shot/strangled to death", delete as applicable, and here I am whining about the weather/timing/ football results. Am I right?'

Wheeler skelped his arm, then ignored him, preferring instead to stare out of the window as they started their journey across the city, from the West End, where red-sandstone tenement flats began around the hundred-thousand-pound mark, to the East End, where similar flats facing Tollcross Park went for half that.

A few minutes later the driver broke the silence: 'You polis, then?'

'Yep,' said Ross.

'So I suppose you'll not be able to tell me what this is about?'

'Right,' Ross replied.

'I'm guessing you're not uniform, so you're CID, plus you're leaving a night out by the looks of it, so I'd guess there's been a death?'

Silence.

'And you can't talk about it?'

'Have you been working all evening?' asked Wheeler.

'Just came on about half an hour ago.'

'You get any fares take you across the city to Tollcross?'

'Sometimes, but not the night. Tollcross Road, though, near the park? That where we're heading? The wife loves that park.'

'That so?' said Ross. 'She use it a lot?'

'Christ, aye. During the summer she's never away from it. It's the roses, son, she's mad about them...We don't have a garden and that rose garden's famous – must be thousands of plants, all different types, mind...And the awards they win, a Garden of Excellence. The wife keeps up with it all. Lovely wee spot. Peaceful.'

'Not tonight,' muttered Ross.

Chapter 5

Twenty minutes later the taxi pulled up on Tollcross Road. Wheeler threw open the door and stepped onto an icy pavement. Ahead she could see the flashing lights of the patrol cars and a white SOCO tent had already been erected, along with spotlights to illuminate the scene. Beside her there was a row of parked cars and she saw Graham Reaper lurking behind one. 'DI Wheeler, I need a quick word.'

'Leave it, Grim.'

'I could have it on the first page, lead with it? You might get a quick response from the public. Somebody must have seen something. What about it, eh?'

'All in good time, Grim.'

Reaper nodded to the police and SOCO vehicles. 'I see that the Beamer's not here. The Professor not on duty, then?'

'Apparently Professor Callum Fraser's not on duty,' said Wheeler. 'Well spotted, Grim, but I'm sure they've provided another pathologist.'

'Fraser's taking his sweet time getting back,' Reaper complained. 'If the Professor was here he'd give me the scoop.'

Wheeler and Ross ignored him and walked on.

'You reckon Grim had a point?' asked Ross. 'If Callum was on duty, he'd give him the heads-up?'

'Callum wouldn't give Grim a cold,' said Wheeler. 'And since Callum's not here, let's go see who's replacing him.'

Ross walked on, his head bent into the weather. 'A guy called Matt Elliot's been seconded into the post.'

'I'm impressed, Ross – and you know this because?'

'I bumped into Laura in the pub last night. She says he's some arty-farty type.'

'Thought that was your pet insult for me?'

'His hobby is photography and apparently Laura reckons he's pretty good. He's got an exhibition coming up at the Arthouse. Laura wants to go.'

Wheeler glanced at him. 'You seeing your ex Laura Mearns again? And you've just broken up with Sarah? You're a quick worker, Ross. '

'Laura and I are just friends.' Ross studied the pavement. 'Fresh snowfall. I'll bet we get nothing. The bastard got in and out and the snow covered his tracks.'

'Talk about positive thinking,' muttered Wheeler, as they arrived at the edge of the crime scene. A taut ribbon of police tape cordoned off the area, and behind it, the do-not-enter message was reinforced by the impressive bulk of Constable Gareth Wilson. He stood stony-faced and rested a clipboard on the rotund stomach that extended proudly in front of him. Behind him stood Detective Sergeant Ian Robertson, his dark hair slicked back and his suit, as ever, pristine. Robertson was speaking to a member of the public and was making detailed notes. Beyond him a group of rubberneckers were straining to get a look at what was happening. SOCOs, all wearing the regulatory white suits and bootees, were carefully searching the scene. The space had been carved into sections and each SOCO had been assigned a specific area to cover. They moved silent as ghosts in the freezing night. Ross held up the tape while she ducked underneath.

Wheeler strode across to the constable. 'What's the story?'

'Road gritter name of Clive Hill was driving by, noticed a foot protruding from behind a skip. Parked up and discovered the body.'

Wheeler looked across at a police car. Inside, a white face peered out at her. 'That Mr Hill?'

Wilson nodded. 'Looks pretty distraught.'

'Well, tell them to get him back to the station and give him a cup of tea and a biscuit. I'll be back once I've seen what's happening here. Is there a name?'

Wilson checked his notes. 'Victim was identified as Cameron Craig.'

'And we know this because?'

'Clive Hill identified him. Seems they've chatted a few times and Cameron Craig was the name he gave. Hill said that the victim was homeless and that he was living rough.'

'Anything else? Did the victim have a *Big Issue* identification badge?'

'Nothing to formally ID him...' the constable produced an evidence bag '...but this was lying beside the body.'

Wheeler held the plastic bag up to the light. Inside there was a damp business card, its edges curled. The image was of a moon reflecting on water and a line of text. She read aloud, '"What will you create today that will make your tomorrow better?"' She turned it over. '"The Letum Institute."' She glanced at Wilson. 'That it?'

"Fraid so. But at least it's something to go on.'

'True. We have a starting point. Any prints?'

'Nothing so far. The snow's been falling continually, no visible tyre marks or footprints. Think the gritter truck kind of messed with the road tracks.'

She handed him the bag and made her way past two SOCOs, who were combing the ground for evidence. She entered the tent and announced herself to the man crouched over the body: 'DI Kat Wheeler.'

Ross was behind her. 'DI Steven Ross.'

The pathologist glanced at them, 'Matt Elliot,' then returned to his examination of the body. 'I'm covering while Dr Fraser's on holiday—'

'Fraser's on honeymoon in Gran Canaria,' Ross finished for him. 'And we get to freeze out here.'

'Indeed,' said Elliot. 'As far as I know he's back in a few days, so he can recommence freezing.'

Wheeler spoke: 'So, Dr Elliot, what am I looking at? '

'Male, early twenties,' said Elliot. 'And I prefer Matt.'

Ross peered at the body. 'Was he killed on site?'

'There's nothing to suggest that he was dragged here – there are no imprints in the snow. In fact,' Elliot muttered, 'in this weather you'll be lucky to get any footprints at all. He was just dumped beside all this refuse. Apologies for the odour from the skip.'

'So, you may be kneeling next to all the evidence we have?' said Wheeler.

'Absolutely.'

'Can you estimate the time of death?'

'I can't give you a precise time but, since rigor has set in, I'd say approximately two hours but it's too early to call. I'll need more time with the body to garner the facts.'

Wheeler looked at the area around it. 'There are no blood splatters and I take it no weapons have been found?'

'Nothing,' said Elliot. 'No lucky breaks by the look of it.'

Wheeler bent over the corpse. The victim wore tight jeans, a cheap-looking T-shirt and a denim jacket. She studied the gaunt, elfin face. 'Our victim had very fine features. Almost feline.' She saw bruising around the neck and turned to the pathologist. 'So what are we looking at? Strangulation?'

'Obviously at this stage nothing's conclusive but, yes, given the pattern of the bruises, I'd say that it looks likely.'

Ross glanced at the body, swallowed. Looked away.

'Anything else?' asked Wheeler.

'There are defence wounds on one hand and some bruising but, other than that, I can't give you anything. At least, not until I meet up with him again back at the lab.'

'I appreciate it,' said Wheeler. She peered through the opening of the tent, watched the snow swirl around the scene and the SOCOs silent and precise, scrutinizing the frozen ground. 'A desolate place to die, out here alone on a freezing night.'

'If there's ever a good place to be murdered,' said Elliot. He stood and stretched, curving his spine and groaned. 'Sorry, bloody tension in my lower back.' He was around six three, lean, and his dark hair was shorn close to his head. He walked out of the tent. 'This job's not the best thing for backache.'

'Sounds like you need a break,' said Wheeler, following him out into the snow.

'I'm just back from one – a road trip around the American Midwest in a hired Cadillac. '

'And you come back to this,' said Wheeler.

'It was worth it. Detroit was interesting, although the place has its own issues.' He glanced back at the corpse. 'Every city does.'

The crime-scene photographer passed them, taking pictures of the scene, and Elliot spoke to one of the SOCOs: 'I'm done here.' The man gestured to two others, who had been waiting nearby.

Wheeler watched them carry a body-bag into the tent. 'We certainly have our challenges here in Glasgow.'

Elliot turned to her. 'The post-mortem will probably be scheduled for tomorrow, unless we have an emergency situation. Will you be attending?'

'Yep.'

'Goodnight, then, DI Wheeler.' Elliot walked towards his car.

'Night, Dr Elliot.'

Elliot turned back. 'DI Wheeler?'

She walked over, stood beside him. 'Uh-huh?'

'I read about a convicted killer who escaped, Mark Haedyear. Do you think this death has anything to do with him?'

'It's too early to say.'

'I did the post-mortem on his victim Amanda Henderson.' He paused. 'It was my first secondment here in Glasgow.'

'It was a dreadful case,' said Wheeler, 'and it's bloody awful that Haedyear has escaped.'

Elliot got into his car, pressed the automatic button to wind down the window. 'Can I offer you a lift?'

She heard Thelonious Monk's 'Bolivar Blues' drift into the night air. 'I'm fine, thanks, Dr Elliot. Good taste in music, though.'

'You like jazz?'

'Yep.'

'Great minds,' Elliot smiled, 'and it's Matt.'

'Matt.'

As he drove away, Wheeler turned and nearly collided with Ross.

'Careful, Wheeler. You feeling a bit giddy?'

'Because?'

'Elliot's dazzling talent.'

She ignored him.

He sighed dramatically. 'He had nice eyes, don't you think? An unusual colour. Would you say violet?'

'Shut it, you.'

'Okay.' He dropped the tone. 'I've organized our lift back to the station.'

'Soon. Let's hang around for a bit and try to get a feel for the place.'

'In this weather?'

'Yes, in this weather,' said Wheeler. 'What do we have? A young homeless man is killed and his body dumped. Did he know his killer or was it random?'

'Too soon to call.'

'Poor sod, what a life. But presumably he'd be known at one of the shelters or at the soup run. And this card from the Letum Institute, you know anything about them?'

'Never heard of them but we can pay them a wee visit tomorrow. Also the homeless units, if he was using them.'

'In this weather they're probably full. We'll get to them tomorrow. For now, let uniform see what information they can get. Our victim might have been sleeping here on a regular basis – maybe someone in the local community knew him. '

'And them?' Ross nodded to the rubberneckers they'd passed earlier. The group stood huddled together, their faces peering out from under brollies or hoods, desperate to get a closer look at the corpse and find out the story.

'We'll get through them all in time,' said Wheeler. 'Uniform will take statements – they can keep them up half the night since they don't seem to have any bloody homes to go to. You get anything else while I was talking to Matt?'

'We've located the owner of the takeaway and a car is being sent round to pick him up. He'll be at the station waiting for us.'

'Good.' Wheeler moved away from the tent and the cars and walked to the far edge of the crime scene. Ross followed her.

'If Matt's right and the victim was killed at the scene, what was he doing here? And was the killer waiting for him? Or did he track his victim?' she asked, ducking under the police cordon. The roads had been closed and they stood at the intersection between Tollcross Road, Wellshot Road and Braidfauld Street. 'North, south, east or west, Ross. Which way should we be looking?'

'Our killer could be anywhere in the city,' said Ross. 'Just because he has killed here means very little.'

'Does he live in the East End? Is it important for him to have killed here?'

'Or was the target here?'

'DI Wheeler, are you giving the press conference tomorrow?' Reaper shouted. 'If so, what time?'

Wheeler ignored him. 'Talk about interrupting a line of thought. Let's go.'

Ross walked beside her. 'Did you see Grim's report in the *Chronicle*?'

'No.'

'Statistics show that Glasgow has the lowest life expectancy in the UK.'

'Is that supposed to help the victim, Ross? Maybe act as a wee consolation, the idea that he wasn't long for this world anyway?'

'I only meant that he's now part of the statistics and that they're always skewed by crime. Glasgow's not that unhealthy.'

'It just the pesky dead folk messing up the stats? You worried you'll keel over before making it through the ranks? Is that it, Ross? Is this about your ambition?'

'I'm only saying that maybe the report sounds worse than it is, that if we take out the crime stats—'

'You're all heart, you do know that, don't you?' She watched the black body-bag being loaded into the van, heard Cameron Craig land on the support with a dull thud. He would be transported across town to the Southside mortuary at the Southern General Hospital complex. They watched the van drive off. Wheeler pulled her coat tight around her, shivered. 'What kind of a bloody life did the poor guy have, living rough? Can you imagine sleeping out in this?'

'Maybe he didn't have a choice.'

Wheeler said nothing. She saw the snow drift against the gates of the park and thought of the taxi driver and his wife visiting the rose gardens. Thought of Cameron Craig and heard the far-off thunder. 'It looks like we're done here.' She began walking towards the police cars. 'Come on, then. Let the uniforms do house-to-house and gather up the statements. Forensics will trawl through the skip. We'll sift through their results tomorrow. Let's get back to the station.' She strode on through the sleet, all thoughts of the earlier night out gone, replaced by an image of a pale young man who had been brutally murdered, his body abandoned next to a skip in the middle of a snowstorm.

Chapter 6

Thanks to the broken radiator, the temperature in the interview room had reached minus numbers. Wheeler sat on a bright orange moulded-plastic chair, wrapped her fingers around her mug of coffee and watched the whorls of steam curl into the cold air while she waited for Clive Hill to compose himself. As if the man hadn't been traumatized enough, she thought, he sat now in a freezing cold room. Beside her, Ross sipped his coffee.

Eventually Wheeler spoke: 'It's okay, Mr Hill, take your time. When we're finished here, we'll arrange to have someone take you home.'

Hill stared at the old desk, as if reading the pockmarks and graffiti might give him the answer to what had just happened. His coffee sat in front of him going cold. Eventually he glanced at her and nodded. 'Okay. What is it you need to know?'

Wheeler kept her voice gentle: 'Mr Hill, I realize you've had a shock but we need to ask you a few questions.'

Hill said nothing.

Wheeler prompted, 'Can you talk us through what happened tonight? Just tell us from when you started your shift and try to give us as much detail as you can remember. Anyone or anything you saw or heard. Anything at all.'

Hill's voice was so low Wheeler had to lean forward to hear it: 'I was on my usual shift. The route runs through the East End, takes in most of Tollcross Road. Just gritting the road, you understand. Nothing to it. See the odd injured animal, or stocious drunk, but other than that, nothing.' Hill stared hard at the desk.

'Can you think about just before you discovered the body? Did you see anything odd or out of the ordinary?' asked Wheeler. 'Was there anyone out on the road, walking home maybe or walking their dog? Anyone at all?'

Hill thought about it. He blinked. 'I've seen enough over the years in Glasgow but nothing like this. Not ever. I mean a body. Poor wee guy.'

'You knew the victim, didn't you, Mr Hill?'

'Knew him to speak to. He was homeless. Some of them sleep rough in doorways or alleyways, some go to squats. It's a rubbish life they have and there's an argument to say he might be better off now.'

'Better off dead?' said Wheeler.

'He might find some peace.'

'Are you a religious man, Mr Hill?'

'I believe that there's a God and some sort of afterlife, if that's what you mean. It's His people I'm not so keen on...but animals, I like animals. They don't mean no harm.' There was a tremor in his voice.

'Did Cameron say anything else about his life?' said Wheeler. 'For example, anything about where he stayed, or who he was friends with?'

'He mentioned that he had a pal. I think it was a lassie.'

'Did he mention her name?'

'No.'

'Is there anything else he told you? Anything at all?'

'Like what?'

'Did he mention if he had any family?'

Hill shook his head. 'No, he never mentioned anything about a family. I've no idea if he had one. We just exchanged a few words now and again. I slipped him a few bob, seeing as he was down on his luck. But he never said much. As I said, I'm not that interested in folk, or in their stories. I just felt a bit sorry for him.'

Wheeler placed the clear evidence bag on the table. 'Do you recognize this?'

Hill glanced at it. 'No.'

'Would you mind taking a closer look at it?'

'Don't need to. I've never seen it.'

'I'd appreciate it if you just took a look,' said Wheeler.

Hill stared at her. 'Am I supposed to recognize it?'

Wheeler heard the change in Hill's tone. 'You're not under suspicion, Mr Hill.'

'It's beginning to feel like it.'

'You're only helping us with our enquiries.'

'Right.'

'The card was found beside Cameron's body.'

Hill shrugged. 'I told you, I never saw any card.'

'Does the Letum Institute mean anything to you?'

Hill paused for a second. 'I've been to a few talks.'

'Can you tell me more about it?'

'It's just a place where they have lots of talks and presentations.'

'On what?'

'Different stuff.'

'And you attended these talks?'

'A couple over the years.'

'Can you remember what they were about?'

'Some were psychological. There was one on Carl Jung. It's interesting to sit and listen to experts. There've been a couple on the whole science versus spirituality argument. Guy called Ramsey gave a particularly good lecture on that.'

'But Cameron Craig never mentioned the Letum?'

'No.'

'And you never bumped into him there?'

'I don't think it would've been his kind of place.'

'Because?'

'Just a hunch. He never mentioned books or anything.'

Wheeler asked a few more questions before ending the interview. Clive Hill had given them all he was going to. She stood. 'If you wait here, I'll arrange for you to be taken home, Mr Hill. Once again, thank you for your time.'

When they left the room, she turned to Ross. 'Your take?'

'He certainly changed his tone.'

'Agreed. It could just be shock but I think we'll keep an eye on him.'

'Now for the owner of the takeaway, Lou's Place.'

A uniformed constable passed her in the corridor. 'DCI Stewart's already interviewed him. Then he asked me to drive Mr O'Keeffe home.'

'Right,' said Wheeler, heading into the CID suite. 'No doubt Stewart will give us the update later.'

'He's gone,' said the constable. 'He got a phone call from home, said something about his wife.'

'Adrianne?'

'Seems she's not too well.'

Wheeler sat at her desk.

Ross crossed to the kettle, made two coffees and put one in front of her. 'Long night ahead, Wheeler, for us if not for Stewart.'

Chapter 7

'He absolutely slaughtered them.'

Matt Elliot was standing in his kitchen, which, like the rest of his house, was Arts and Crafts. Oak cabinets concealed the minutiae of living while copper wall lamps cast a warm glow across the room. A dark green Aga emitted a steady, comforting heat. Outside the weather raged but the stained-glass windows, with their green and red stars set against a midnight blue background, reflected a quiet luminosity. The old stone mansion retained the heat, its thick walls a barrier to the freezing temperatures outside.

'The evening flew by – honestly, it was absolutely amazing. The guy fucking nailed it. You should've been there.'

Elliot poured his old school-friend Philip Bishop a whisky, then one for himself and dropped two ice cubes into his glass. 'I would have been there, except I had to work.'

'Some unlucky bastard got snuffed?' Bishop sipped his drink.

Elliot winced. 'If you're asking about the crime scene, then, yes, earlier this evening a man was murdered.'

'Poor sod,' said Bishop. 'Anyway, about the guy tonight, it was an outrageous set. Unbelievable. You would have loved it. The audience were dead in the aisles.'

'Where was he on – a comedy club?'

'Are you kidding me? He was on at the SECC. The gig sold out in a few days. The guy's huge. A fucking titan of comedy.'

'Right.'

'Damn right.'

'Pretty young, though, isn't he?'

'He's in his late twenties, I think.'

'The poor victim tonight was only in his twenties.'

'Aye, well, different roads and all that, but having it all at his age, the awards, the sell-out gigs, a meteoric career. The whole fucking works. He's a jammy bugger.' Bishop raised his glass.

Elliot leaned across to him and clinked. 'Jammy right enough, but we'll leave him to his fame, will we?'

'Aye, good luck to him.'

'Now, what about our show?'

'Your show. You're the talent. You took the photos.'

'Ours. You have the venue.'

'Aye, the fabulous Arthouse. Once a church and now a temple to hedonism.'

'The very place,' said Elliot. 'Let's go through to the study. They're all organized.'

The photographs had been framed and numbered and were stacked against the far wall, ready to be swathed in bubble-wrap and transported to the Arthouse. Elliot walked across to them. 'I'm trying to be objective but it's difficult when it's your own work.'

'Because?'

'I'm trying to imagine what the viewer's experience will be without access to the references and the context of the moment when the original image was captured.'

Bishop sipped his drink. 'I see.'

'I mean the main—'

Bishop interrupted him: 'The main thing to remember is...'

'What?'

'That you don't really want to be so far up your own arse to actually speak that phrase out loud in public. I mean, *I'm trying to imagine what the viewer's experience will be without access to the references and the context of the moment when the original image was captured.* For fuck's sake, Matt.'

'Sorry.'

'It's not like you're Picasso.'

'He was a painter.'

'Fucking semantics.'

'Really?'

'Well, that photographer guy then, what's his name?'

Elliot waited.

'Famous photographer.'

'You might want to give me a clue. Maybe narrow it down a bit.'

'Guy who did the outdoor shots. Black-and-white, like yours.'

'In Glasgow?' asked Elliot. 'Oscar Marzaroli?'

Bishop shook his head. 'He wasn't Scottish.'

'American? Ansel Adams? Garry Winogrand?'

'No, I don't think he was American.'

Elliot sipped his whisky. 'Josef Koudelka?'

'Doisneau, I think that's it.'

'Robert Doisneau was French.'

'He was fabulous, wasn't he? Rosie got me a book of his photography for Christmas. Fantastic stuff.' He grinned. 'You think Rosie's hot?'

'No, but you do. Doisneau did *The Kiss*, which is pretty famous. My work isn't like that but I understand why Rosie would like it. It's very romantic. '

'He also did the one of an old carousel. Brilliant. When I was a teenager I ripped the photo out of a book, had it framed. I reckon your stuff's on a par with his even if you talk bollocks.'

'Thanks for the confidence vote, but it's just a hobby.'

'A hobby that sells, and if you ever wanted to give up working with stiffs...'

'I'll bear it in mind.'

'Why do you always shoot in black-and-white?'

'Chiaroscuro. The light and the shadow and how one needs the other to create harmony. To me it represents the contrast of life.'

'I've asked Rosie to arrange the hanging of this lot at the Arthouse. That okay with you?'

'Fine.' Elliot crossed to the CD player, pressed the play button. Turned the volume up. Loud.

'You're lucky this place is detached. No need to care about the neighbours.' Bishop's voice held bitterness.

'The old guy next door still playing up?'

'Old bastard, I wish he'd die. I'd happily kill him myself.'

'Charming.' Elliot changed the subject, walked Bishop through the exhibition, speaking above the music. 'I reckon first up will be the Cadillac. What do you think?'

'Good call.' He looked at the print. The car had been long abandoned and lay sweltering in the Detroit heat. A relic of past dreams, its paintwork was scratched and flaking. Weeds grew through its body and out through the smashed windows reaching for the sun. Other prints showed abandoned cars and trucks languishing in the snow.

Elliot moved on: 'What about the Airstream?'

'Yep. It'll dovetail nicely with our Classic.'

They studied the photographs. 'A 1963 Overlander. Twenty-six feet of decaying beauty,' said Elliot. Leaning next to it was another image. 'The Flying Cloud, again abandoned. How does this even happen?'

'Folk run out of money and maybe dreams,' said Bishop. 'Their world moves on but goes downhill and suddenly these vehicles cost more to restore than they have in the bank.'

'But to just dump them? I mean, they could sell them,' said Elliot.

'Maybe it wasn't intentional at first to let them rot. They thought they were just going through a low point and would get back on their feet. Then they would have it repaired, but they never got it together, it never happened.'

'But the Airsteam?'

'You were in Detroit, right?' said Bishop.

'Yes.'

'And the city just about went bankrupt so what do you expect? You are so bloody glass-half-full. You know that, don't you? It's not realistic.'

Elliot nodded, staring at his photographs. 'Detroit was an interesting landscape. An amazing city.'

'Yeah, I know. Original home of Motown and car manufacturing,' muttered Bishop, looking at the pictures. 'Abandoned houses, shops, retail parks...' He sipped his drink. 'Cheery it's not.'

'Am I too sympathetic?' Elliot asked. 'Too soft?'

'Tunnock's-teacake soft.'

The phone rang. Elliot crossed to the table, glanced at the number. 'I need to take this.'

Bishop nodded, lifted his glass and Elliot's. 'I'll get us a refill.'

Elliot grabbed the receiver. 'Darling,' he shut off the music, 'tell me the news. What's happening?'

She talked and he listened. It was good, all good.

Bishop returned and placed a fresh drink in front of him.

Elliot finished the call. 'Okay. Bye.'

'Everything all right?'

'Yes.'

'So, about the exhibition, then. Let's look at the rest of these pictures.'

'Fair enough.'

Chapter 8

'But it's not fair, is it?' In the front room of a first-floor squat on Tollcross Road, two young women were sprawled on a damp mattress, smoking and staring at the weather outside. Julie Kinnon was eighteen and emaciated. Her long red hair was thick with grease, pulled back from her gaunt face and secured with an elastic band. 'But it's no, Dawn, is it?'

Dawn McLeod was a year older. Her face was puffed and her young body was already bloated. 'Look, we've got this place. It'll dae meantime. You want tae take your chances back home with your da?'

Julie shuddered, touched the scar above her right eye and sucked hungrily on the cigarette. 'I'm starving, though, Dawn.'

'Well, in that case we need tae think about going back out in that weather.' Dawn puffed smoke at the ceiling. She coughed hard before she dragged on the cigarette again.

'Nae choice have we, really?' asked Julie.

'None,' agreed Dawn.

Julie scratched at her hair. 'My scalp itches.'

'I know, hen, but tomorrow we'll go intae Queen Street

station and get us a wee hot shower. Have a proper wash. How's that sound?'

'Aye, good. Sounds great.' Julie kept scratching.

'Your cousin not let you use her place? What's her name, Maggie-May?'

'Maggie-May still lives with her ma and that old alkie hates me.'

'Why?'

'Her and my ma fell out.'

'But your ma died years ago.'

'Auntie Jackie disnae forgive or forget, though. She stays in the huff. Gets worse when she's been drinking – she goes for me. Broke my arm when I was ten.'

'Why's Maggie-May still there?' asked Dawn.

'She's saving up tae get a wee flat tae rent. She's hardly ever at her ma's – she's either at work or out at rehearsals. She's the singer in a punk band.'

'Whit's it called?'

'CAC.'

'Whit's CAC?'

'It's Scots.'

'For whit?'

'Shit.'

'I could've guessed. She's not the cheeriest of folk, is she?'

Julie stared at the smoke from her cigarette. 'Anyway, her place is a no-go.'

'A no-go,' Dawn repeated. She finished her cigarette and ground the residue into the sole of her shoe. She stood, dragged a comb through her short hair and pulled her jacket tight around her. ''Mon, hen.'

Julie stood, put out her cigarette and shivered. 'Where to?'

'Thought we'd take a wee run past the Eatery. Maggie-May working the night?'

Julie shrugged, zipped up her coat and followed her friend out into the cold. She glanced back, gestured to a closed door. 'What about her?'

'Who?'

'Irena. I don't think she's too well.'

Dawn's voice was firm. 'Irena, or whatever it is she calls herself, is not our problem. She's competition, hen, remember that. We've got enough problems of our own. Okay?'

'Okay.'

They walked on into the night.

In the back room of the squat Irena, in her twenties, lay on the filthy mattress. Her eyes were closed and she was breathing deeply but erratically. Intermittently she cried in her sleep. Her language was not English and there was no one to hear. Her fair hair was tangled and her face was pale with cold. On her left cheek there was a scar in the shape of a crescent moon. Her broken nails were painted bright orange and a cheap grey coat covered her. On the floor beside the mattress, a maroon beret lay crumpled and stained.

Chapter 9

'Weather's shite,' muttered Tommy Taylor, one of two door stewards on duty at the Equestrian Eatery. He got no response from his colleague and tried again. 'Fuck me. You see this?' He stabbed his finger at the *Chronicle*, then read aloud: '"Glasgow has the lowest life expectancy of any city in the UK."'

Finally his colleague shrugged, peered out at the curtain of sleet. 'Fucking weather disnae help, but does it? What's this meant tae be? Fucking Thundersnow. Fucksake.' Her voice was low, dour, and she was extremely pissed off. Margaret Mary MacLaren, known as Maggie-May, was nothing if not congruent and she let her emotions show. Blatantly. She stood five feet eleven and a half inches in her stocking soles. Big, muscular woman, like a greyhound on steroids. She had green eyes and short dark hair, a piercing through her eyebrow and another through her lip. MacLaren could render a six-foot man unconscious with a single head butt but this wasn't her only talent. She was also lead singer with her band CAC. MacLaren certainly had her admirers. Unfortunately her colleague wasn't among them.

Taylor stretched to his full height of five feet five and ran a hand over cropped white-blond hair. His eyelashes and brows were also white. He took a sly glance at MacLaren. 'What's up with you, doll? You on the blood?' His snigger deepened to a snort. Taylor found his own brand of humour hilarious.

MacLaren peered down at him, rolled her answer around in her mouth, testing the acridity. Before she could speak, her boss appeared behind them, but stayed in the warmth of the foyer. Watching. Listening. Keith Dragon was five eleven, had the build of what he was, an ex-boxer. He was fifty-four and looked good on it, considering his past profession. Weights, running, the gym and a high-protein diet meant that he was the same weight as he had been in his twenties. And that mattered to Dragon. He wore a fitted grey suit, the cut of which emphasized his muscular build. Underneath it was a crisp white shirt and a thin blue tie. A heavy Tag Heuer watch was just visible.

MacLaren and Taylor were both silent: they knew their place. They stared straight ahead, the MO of their profession, detached, yet all-seeing. Identical. Except that MacLaren had developed a deep blush, which started at her neck and wound its way up her face until she felt as if she were glowing, like an illuminated fairy on top of a Christmas tree. She swallowed, balled her fingers into fists and dug sharp, crimson nails into the flesh of her palms until she felt blood, then silently cursed herself. The same nails had dug into Keith Dragon's back the previous night. Classic. Nightclub owner beds employee. She wondered how she could have been so stupid. She stared into the storm, listened to it wail around the building and carry the sound into the dark night. She doubted that he would even acknowledge her. She was right.

Dragon waited. Said nothing, then turned and walked back into the club.

The Equestrian Eatery wasn't a place to devour horse burgers. Necessarily. The bar-restaurant, which was located in a mansion in Mount Vernon, stood in its own grounds and was set well back from the road. Two *faux*-Grecian pillars fronted the building, giving it a grandiose façade. Many decades previously horse-riding and other equestrian pursuits had been available, but in the last year the former owners, who had run it as a pub, had been reluctantly persuaded to sell up. Dragon had refurbished it throughout and turned it into an eatery/show venue, mainly with tribute bands. It resembled the kind of joint that had flourished in the fifties in New York where dinner and a show had been the pinnacle of sophistication. Rat Pack. Elvis. The Equestrian Eatery had modelled itself on that era but had made a few simple adjustments. It had dispensed with the charm, class and talent. Tonight scampi and chips in a basket were served up as a Rat Pack tribute band played to an appreciative inebriated crowd. Dragon scanned the audience. They looked like they were having a good time.

Then he saw them. Andy Doyle and Stella Evans were at the far side of the room. Stella was twitching to the beat. Shoes too high to dance in, silver lamé dress so tight that it restricted movement. Maybe also breathing. Dragon quickly looked away. Doyle stood motionless, watching the band. His hair was cropped close to his skull; he wore a leather jacket, dark jeans and a white T-shirt. Everything accentuated his muscles.

Eventually Dragon approached them, watched the band for a few minutes before speaking. 'Doyle.'

Doyle stared at the band. 'Dragon.'

'How goes it?'

'Bit of bad news.'

'That right? Anything I can help you with?'

'Early days, but I'll give you a bell if the situation looks like it might escalate.'

Dragon opened his mouth to continue the conversation but caught the expression on Doyle's face just in time. 'Fair enough. Enjoy the evening.' But Doyle had already turned back to Stella.

Dragon left them to it.

Doyle leaned towards Stella, 'I need to let you go on home the night. I've got an unexpected business meeting with Weirdo. I'll be back soon as I can. Okay?'

'You said we'd have a night out together. You promised, Andy.'

'Just leave it, okay?'

Stella stood, hands on hips, eyes fixed on his. 'No, it's not bloody okay. It's our anniversary. Or don't you remember?'

'Something's come up.' Doyle glanced at the bar. Dragon looked across at them. 'Don't make a scene,' he hissed. 'We'll go out another night. This is important.'

'And I suppose I'm not?' Stella grabbed her coat, huffed. 'Whatever.'

Doyle followed her out of the club, watched while she climbed into her 4x4 and sped off.

It was 11.30 p.m. when the club closed and Dragon watched while the revellers streamed out into the grounds and headed towards the road. Groups congregated at taxi ranks or staggered homewards. He glanced across at MacLaren, overheard the conversation one drunk patron was having with her.

'What's a fine big lassie like you doing a job like this for? Come away on home with me.' The man winked at her. 'I tell you, you'll not regret it.'

'It's time to go on home, sir. Have a good evening.'

The bonhomie quickly disappeared and the man turned on her. 'You think you're too good for me, is that it?'

'If you'd like to go on home now,' MacLaren repeated.

'You a lezzie? Is that it? You bat for the other side?' The man leered into her face.

Dragon cleared his throat and walked in front of the CCTV camera, blocking its view. He waited. In one movement MacLaren had the man by the scruff of his neck. Then he was doubled over, nose bleeding. He did indeed leave the premises for home but he was cursing and spitting blood. Dragon turned away and saw that Andy Doyle was picked up in a grey BMW with blacked-out windows. Dragon walked across to Maggie-May, who was watching Doyle. 'Remember, whatever you've seen tonight, you've seen nothing. Okay?'

'Okay, boss.'

Dragon walked back into the club as a siren wailed in the distance.

In the shadows across the road, Dawn and Julie watched. Julie glanced quickly towards her cousin but MacLaren had turned back towards the club. Julie hurried on, making sure she matched Dawn's stride. 'Think around the park'll be the best bet?'

'If the polis and their stuff are away,' said Dawn, 'but

I'm pretty sure they'll still be there.' They walked on, eventually approaching the park. The lights on the police cars illuminated the darkness. Uniformed officers stood in attendance and the area clearly remained a crime scene. A few rubberneckers were present, unwilling to go home before finding out what had happened.

'You're right,' said Julie. 'Polis are still here. We've nae chance. Nae punter will be out and about with so much happening.'

''Mon.' Dawn crossed the road and turned into Braidfauld Street. 'It's no worth getting involved.'

Julie hurried after her. 'Where tae?'

'Nip down tae London Road. If there's nothing doing, back tae Parkhead Cross or Duke Street, mibbe Haghill.'

'But they're miles away,' said Julie, 'and it's freezing.'

Dawn's tone was resigned: 'Have we got any choice, hen?'

Julie said nothing.

Together they bent their heads into the sleet and the wind howled around them as they trudged on in silence.

Chapter 10

As she drove, Stella rehashed the argument with Doyle in her mind while she thumped the steering wheel in time to the music. She promised herself that once she got home she would pour herself a hefty vodka. She deserved it, plus it would take the edge off her mood. She glanced out of the window. 'Bloody weather,' she muttered, but she was nearly there. Nearly home. She drove to the bottom of the drive, killed the engine and the music died. Silence. 'Shit.' Stella hated silence. She'd put on another CD when she got inside. Or a DVD. 'Fuck you, Doyle,' she muttered into the darkness, 'fuck you and your business meetings.'

She made her way up the drive, heard the ping as the 4x4 locked behind her. The harsh security lights kicked in and illuminated the falling snowflakes. As she approached the door she fumbled with her key-ring, then shoved the key into the lock, turned it, leaned against the door and pushed it open. Felt a rush of warmth hit her. Home.

The blow was quick, brutal, and did the job. Stella's body crumpled, her bag landing beside her and spilling its contents. Mobile phone, lipstick, perfume, chewing gum, purse, diary and pen landed on the frozen ground. He bent over her and hauled her into position, lifted her quickly and, in the process, she dropped a shoe. He stepped over the stiletto, which lay on its side, its sole blood-red against the snow. He carried her to the car, put her into the boot and locked it.

Haedyear drove the dark green Renault Mégane and stuck to the speed limit; if anything, he stayed under it. He kept to the inside lane. Safe. Nondescript. Invisible. Stella was unconscious but it wouldn't be long before he would take her body out of the car and place her in his box. He drove on, secure in the knowledge that he was doing what was required of him. He smiled, watched the snowflakes gently fall. When he spoke, his voice was full of awe. 'I will be the disciple.' He repeated: 'I will be the disciple.' Then, growing in confidence, he asserted, 'No, I am already the disciple.' He didn't need gimmicks, like stupid cards with corny messages: he had proven himself. Twenty minutes later he saw the signs and indicated. 'Almost there, Stella,' he whispered. 'Almost there.'

Chapter 11

The desk in Andy Doyle's office was the size of a small boat. In the corner, a Gaggia machine hissed as Doyle poured two coffees. A six-foot-four man, with warrior piercings and a purple-tipped mohican, was standing on the other side of the desk. James Weir.

'Sit down, Weirdo.' Doyle placed two cups on the desk and pushed one towards his first lieutenant. 'Remember why you were first accepted into the organization?'

Weirdo nodded.

'Remind me.'

'Mark Haedyear had to...disappear.'

'Correct. And do you recall why Haedyear had to disappear?'

'He murdered a woman, name of Amanda Henderson. On your patch. Not good for business. Disrespectful. And she was a civilian, wasn't she?'

'Aye, it was very fucking disrespectful. I can't fucking abide it when folk kill civilians. And the cunt did it on my patch, so he showed no fucking respect for boundaries either. I was not pleased.' Doyle sipped his coffee, his brown eyes shrewd. Heterochromia meant that one eye was darker than the other. When he was angry, as he was

53

now, it blazed black. He spat out the name, 'Mark Haedyear.'

'He was a nutter, Mr Doyle.'

'He was indeed a grade-A nutter but now he's out.'

'Do think he's looking for a wee rammy?' said Weirdo. 'You think he wants to settle the score?'

'Could be,' said Doyle.

'He didnae know it was me that grassed on him, though, did he?'

Doyle shrugged. 'Who knows what he found out? You called the polis, didn't you?'

'I did.'

'And told them where to look and who to look at?'

'Aye. But I did it anonymously. There's nothing the polis know that could trace it to me. Or you. How would Haedyear know?'

'He's not a straightforward bastard,' said Doyle.

'Sleekit?' suggested Weirdo.

'Sleekit,' agreed Doyle, 'If he suspects anything, and I don't know if he does, he'll come at us. I want to meet him head to head.'

'Always easier that way.'

'But, as I said, he's twisted,' said Doyle.

'You want me to keep an eye out?'

'Aye, make it city-wide. Find out where he is and report back. The cunt's got a plan and I want to know what it is. If it's a head to head, and I hope it is, I'm ready for him.'

'Will do, Mr Doyle. Want me to stay here or shove off?'

Silence.

'I'll be off, then, Mr Doyle.' Weirdo waited, rotated his tongue around the roof of his mouth, flicking the metal piercing against the soft tissue. He touched his jacket, underneath which a shirt and two nipple piercings brushed up against each other. He thought of the next piercing he had booked and instinctively placed a protective hand in front of his crotch. He waited a few more seconds before he realized that his presence was not required.

'Let me know if you need me...' Weirdo's voice drifted off. Doyle sipped his coffee. Weirdo backed out of the room, his biker boots silent on the carpet as, quietly and respectfully, he closed the door behind him.

Chapter 12

Doyle rang Stella. No answer. He left a voice mail: 'I told you I'd make it up to you. For fucksake Stella, this was business.' He waited a few minutes for her to return the call. Nothing. 'Sulk all you like,' he muttered, and reached forward to switch on the radio.

The passion in the man's voice was evident: 'Decisions about Scotland should be made in Scotland and not by Westminster. These decisions should not be taken lightly. They affect not only ourselves and our families and communities but the future of our children and their children. Scotland will flourish under independence. We already are part of the global economy but if we were independent we'd become stronger, more vibrant and crucially more relevant to the people of this country. The vote on the eighteenth of September is your chance to have your voice heard. '

A truck overtook him, roared by and drowned out the radio. Doyle turned the volume up. The woman was equally passionate: 'We're better together, better and stronger. Scotland and the people who live here need to accept that there are risks involved with becoming independent. Remaining in the United Kingdom offers a myriad of benefits and allows us an economic stability that wouldn't be present in an independent Scotland.'

'Well, which way would you vote?' asked the presenter. 'We'll be taking your calls into the early hours of the morning. Keep them coming in. We want to hear your views. Right now it's the turn of Alan Wheatley from Barlanark. How will you be voting, Alan?'

'It's got to be yes. I mean, Scotland has its own identity and as a country...'

Doyle turned a corner, lost the signal for a second, then it was back.

'Thanks for that, Alan, representing the yes vote. Now we'll hear from the no vote. We have Donna Jones on the line. Go ahead, Donna, from Cambuslang. Tell us why you'll be voting no.'

'Aye, thanks, I will. I'll be voting no because I believe in the union. I mean, we'll all be better together, supporting each other. If we move away from the union, we'll be out on our own and vulnerable.'

Doyle reached over and switched it off, turned into his driveway and parked his midnight blue Mercedes beside Stella's 4x4 and walked up the driveway. He heard an owl call into the night and the falling snow dampen the sound. He glanced ahead, saw the back door ajar. *It was never left open. Never.* Felt his heartbeat race as he began to sprint. He saw her bag on the ground, its contents spilled over the snow. Saw the shoe. Doyle ran into the house and bawled, 'STELLA.' Nothing. The kitchen, the upstairs, the basement. 'STELLA.' The house covered in seconds. Every room scoured. All empty, as he'd known they would be. Doyle stood in the hallway, breathed heavily. Cursed himself. Cursed Haedyear. Flipped open his mobile, dialled Stella's number again. Heard it ring from the snowy ground at the back door before it went through to voicemail. Doyle killed the call, redialled, shouted instructions: 'Weirdo, get the fuck over here.' He slammed the phone down on the glass console table, heard the glass shatter. Ignored it. Heard his mobile chirp. A text. Doyle grabbed it, read the message and felt his heart begin to hammer.

GRASS. Only one thing feels better than having you Doyle. Having her. And letting you imagine it. Can you picture it? Well can you? Take a minute. Take all the time you need. Good. Have you got the image? You call the polis and she's dead fucking meat. You know it and I know it. I'll be in touch.

Doyle's hand shook as he hit the call icon. Listened to the ring tone. Knew the call would be ignored. Heard the line go dead. Hit his contact list. Issued orders. Finally, he heard the bell ring. He grabbed his keys and headed out of the door.

Weirdo and Doyle stood in the snow. Weirdo nodded as Doyle raged and spat out instructions: 'Scour the city...upmarket and downmarket...Get on to Sonny at the Smuggler's...Get the word out to all the fucking troops. Find Haedyear. '

Doyle climbed into the Mercedes and glared at Weirdo. 'Find that fucker and we find Stella.' He slammed the door and the car screeched into the night. Weirdo climbed into his grey BMW and followed Doyle. At the top of the road they turned in opposite directions. They both sped off.

It was going to be a long night.

Chapter 13

Glasgow was similar to many European cities in that it was in a constant state of flux. Architecturally there were historical gems, Charles Rennie Mackintosh, Alexander 'Greek' Thomson, John Honeyman, and many glorious old buildings. The best of Glasgow included Kelvingrove, the Burrell, the Clyde Auditorium and Scotland Street School. The grand established buildings sat cheek by jowl with the ongoing renovation and regeneration, which had its own teething problems. Also, there were the worst examples of the city, filthy half-derelict buildings, a blight on the landscape. They harked back to a time of hope when they had been constructed, but now all hope was gone and they gaped at the city, forlorn and choked of the oxygen of finance. The Smuggler's Rest nestled comfortably in this description, and even revelled in it. The old pub was a ghost that should have passed on to the other side but instead clung resolutely on. Pockets of Glasgow stoutly resisted renovation. The Smuggler's led this resistance and, like many resistance leaders, it wore camouflage. Its windows were nailed shut and boarded over and wore wire mesh like a mask. The pub sat in an area full of deprivation and desolation. If life expectancy was already poor in Glasgow, in comparison to other European cities, then the patrons of the Smuggler's took it down at least another couple of notches.

Weirdo parked at the back of the pub. Inside, the place was deserted, except for Shona and Heather, identical twins who sat at the corner table. They wore matching cropped tops, thick eyeliner and even thicker foundation, which accentuated rather than concealed their wrinkles. This was a lock-down and the pub had by rights closed for the night but Sonny occasionally allowed the regulars an overnight drinking session. Sonny ran the Smuggler's. He was five foot eight, the wrong side of eighteen stone and his face was smothered with tattoos. He was the boss, despite what Trading Standards might believe. His rules went, and anyone who opposed him was seen as the enemy. And that meant war. Anyone with any sense took the hint. If they didn't, they took the consequences.

Sonny bared his teeth in a smile. 'How goes it, Weirdo?

'Not so good, Sonny.'

'Sorry to hear that.'

'Aye.' Weirdo stood at the bar and surveyed the room.

'Get you a drink?' said Sonny. 'On the house?'

Weirdo shook his head.

'This a business trip, then?'

'Mark fucking Haedyear.'

'Aye.' Sonny slammed his fat hand on the bar. 'I heard the cunt escaped. It's not likely he'd be stupid enough to show a face round here but I can get the word out if you're after him?'

'Mr Doyle's looking for him,' said Weirdo.

'Right,' said Sonny.

'Bad,' said Weirdo.

'Bad? How bad?' asked Sonny.

'Urgent.'

Sonny took a deep breath, gave himself a minute to process the gravitas of the information, then spoke: 'Fair enough. So, send the troops out into the field? Every fucker out there. Nail the bastard?'

Weirdo nodded.

'Ye want tae tell me whit this is about?'

'Too early, Sonny. Doyle wants it kept shtum in the meantime. Suffice to say it's a big fucking deal. Mibbe the biggest ever for him.'

Sonny digested the news. 'That right? That big? Fuck.'

'Aye, but he disnae want the whole world tae know. If you get my drift?'

'Of course, that's understandable. It's his business.' Sonny called over to the twins. 'Here Shona, Heather, a wee job for you and yer pals. Get the fuck out there onto the streets and track this cunt down. 'Mon over and I'll give you the details.'

Weirdo stood back and smiled. The hunt was gathering pace. Mark Haedyear had no chance. Weirdo licked his lips. He could almost taste the blood.

The area beneath the bridge was inhospitable at the best of times. The stones were covered with moss, and the sound of dripping water echoed into the night air. At this time of the night, even the homeless men and women who occasionally sheltered there had dispersed, and Mark Haedyear had the place to himself. He wrapped the newspapers around his torso, looked out at the River Clyde and felt the wind hit off the water, carrying the cold back to him, depositing minute particles on his face, his lips and his hair. He watched while the sleet continued to fall and melt into the river, swelling its banks as if trying to find a release from the constraints and flood the city. Haedyear breathed in the damp, traced his tongue around his lips and listened to the movement of the freezing water. It was an hour before his eyes began to close and he allowed himself to rest, to submit to sleep and let the dreams lead him to his destiny. He dreamed that he could see a ghost boat float along the Clyde, its occupants fishing for the bodies that would lie buried for eternity. But Mark Haedyear did not need to lie beside the Clyde. He had other options yet he had chosen to inhale the stench of the city beside the river.

Chapter 14

Saturday, 1 February, 5 a.m.

Doyle was in his office, sitting behind his desk. He had spent the night making calls and had come up with nothing. Now he sipped his fifth coffee, rubbed his hand over the fresh stubble on his chin and stared at the six men lined up in front of him. Doyle didn't bother to hide the anger in his voice. 'This recent development is a personal fucking insult to me, do you understand?' He let the message sink in. 'And the details do not get out. Get it?'

'The exact detail isn't out there at all, Mr Doyle,' said Weirdo, 'just that you're requesting, as a matter of urgency, information about Haedyear's whereabouts. I hope that's okay?'

Doyle said nothing.

A thick-set man in a long leather coat spoke: 'But, Mr Doyle, I'm just saying, if we can't find Haedyear then...' The man faltered and began again. 'All I'm saying, with respect, Mr Doyle, is that if we can't find him, then would it be best to—'

Doyle's eyes blazed black as he turned on the man. 'You don't get it, Snake, do you?'

Snake flushed.

'That's a disappointment.' Doyle stared at him.

Snake studied the floor and swallowed rapidly. Sweat formed on his top lip. 'I do get it. Honest. I was just saying that...Sorry, Mr Doyle, sorry. Forget it, forget I said anything. I was just trying to be helpful—'

Doyle spoke over him: 'I know this city. I own a fucking swathe of it. Get yourselves out there. It's not that big a place. This is by far and away the most important and sensitive job I've asked you to do. Succeed, and you're in my organization for life.' He glanced at Snake. 'Fuck it up and you're gone.'

They filed out quietly. Closed the door behind them.

'Nae pressure there, then, Weirdo.' There was a tremor in Snake's voice.

Weirdo turned to him. 'You really don't get it, Snake.'

'I get it, Weirdo. Honest.'

'Explain it to me, then.'

'Doyle's pissed 'cause Haedyear's snatched his girlfriend. Right?'

'Wrong.'

Snake waited.

'See, right there, that's where you're wrong,' continued Weirdo. 'Stella's not just Mr Doyle's girlfriend.' He walked towards his car.

Snake followed him. 'Go on.'

'Stella is Mr Doyle's property. She belongs to him. This is an insult to Doyle. It's a big fuck-off public slap in the face and it means war.' Weirdo slammed the door and sped off. This was something he needed to do. He had to be the one to find Stella. He went through a mental checklist. He'd already started at the top, then seen Sonny at the Smuggler's. Later he'd go and see Julie and Dawn. But just now Weirdo had to reach a long way into his past, call in owes and favours, make promises and threats. He reached for his phone, dialled, then started to issue orders and give commands. As he drove, he kept calling and talking until the net was spread out across Glasgow. Weirdo wanted the net to be as wide as the city itself.

Chapter 15

By 6 a.m. Wheeler had returned from her run and was already in the shower. The lemon-scented gel that foamed across her body momentarily obliterated the Gothic script tattoo written between her shoulder blades, *Vita non est vivere sed valere vita est* – Life is more than merely staying alive. She'd had it done before joining the army. Later, when she'd left after yet another exhausting tour, she'd added another tattoo, *Omnia causa fiunt* – Everything happens for a reason. She switched off the water, towelled herself dry and dressed quickly, pulling on dark trousers, a heavy sweater and boots. She locked the door behind her and headed out into the grey Glasgow morning.

He was parked just outside the wrought-iron gates. She crossed to the car. 'Morning, Smiler.'

Ross grunted, started the engine. 'I hardly got any sleep at all and I didn't have time for breakfast.'

'Tough call. Why don't we pick up some coffee on the way? My treat. I know of a wee place that might be open.'

'Okay – it might bring me round.' Ross drove through the Merchant City, past the upmarket wine and tapas bars, past the scaffolding that shrouded a crumbling wreck. 'I could take the long way to the station – I quite fancy another very quick look at the crime scene without the tent and all the SOCOs. What do you think?'

'Yep. We're early for the briefing. Let's go.'

'Let's start at the beginning. The body was dumped close to the park.'

'Meaningful?'

'I was just wondering. If I was sleeping rough in the Tollcross area, wouldn't the park be a good bet? I'd feel pretty safe.'

Wheeler stared out of the window as they drove. 'I suppose. The gates are locked at night but they could be easily climbed. I'm not sure I agree with you there. I wouldn't feel at all safe.'

'But if he wanted somewhere out of the way?'

'Okay, let's take a walk around the park later,' said Wheeler. 'You ever spent any time there?'

'No. You?'

'No. At least, not socially. Professionally I've had to make the odd visit in the past. It's a good resource, though, for the community – it's got the big leisure centre, the swimming pool, the gym…There's a lot going on.'

'The pool's going to be used in the Commonwealth Games, isn't it?' asked Ross.

'Yep, inspiring Glaswegians to stay fit. The place is well used and well loved.'

'Trying to keep Glaswegians healthy is a big ask. On the plus side, though, it's also got a café.'

'True.'

'Only the café's not open twenty-four/seven, when I need it to be.'

'Trust you to think of your stomach. There's a load of CCTV cameras covering the park, so maybe…'

'Maybe we'll find something on them.' He finished the sentence for her. 'You really think so?'

'It's hard to say. We've had sleet and snow, and it being pitch dark last night would have hampered the images. Also, I don't know if the cameras include any of the road. We'll get all the CCTV in the area and we might get lucky with a car numberplate from around the time of the murder.' She paused. 'Take a left here.'

He pulled the car into the layby. Ahead was a battered caravan, the window open, the smell of rancid fat in the air. 'Christ, Wheeler, tell me this isn't it. Tell me it's not your wee place. '

'In the absence of a lovely bistro being open in the East End at this hour, or the café at Tollcross Park Leisure Centre, a coffee from Benny's Burgers will have to do.'

'Benny Robbins is not long out of Barlinnie,' said Ross. 'A year, tops.'

'He did his time, Ross, and now he's trying to make a living.'

'You trust the food? I think he'll spit in the coffee. He knows we're CID.'

'Stop being so sensitive, Ross.'

'My body's a temple and all that.'

'We ate at the Belter Bar last night, remember?'

'OK,' said Ross. 'If you trust him, throw in a roll with fried egg and potato scone.'

'My treat.' She climbed out of the car and walked to the mobile burger van. 'Hey, Benny, how are things?'

'DI Wheeler. Things are going well. My wife's pregnant again. Another girl.'

'Congratulations. When is she due?'

'Three months.'

'Three girls now, Benny. You need to start saving.'

'You're telling me. At Christmas there was shiny pink stuff everywhere. Don't care if I never see another doll. What about you? How are things with you?'

'Fine, Benny, except for last night's murder.'

'So I heard. Any leads?'

'Not so far.' Wheeler ordered two fried egg and potato-scone rolls, two coffees. Watched the potato scones being fried and soaking up the grease, saw Benny spoon the coffee granules into Styrofoam cups. 'Milk and sugars are on the table.'

'Thanks, Benny. You take care.'

He bent towards her. 'You want me to keep an ear out, see if there's any rumours floating about?'

'I'd appreciate it, Benny.'

She paid and took the paper bag with the two rolls in it, balanced the two coffees and headed back to Ross.

'I'm starving,' said Ross, as he started to devour his roll.

'You always are,' said Wheeler, taking her time, chewing through the doughy bread, the burned edges of the egg, the density of the potato scone. 'Me, on the other hand, I'm just looking to avoid indigestion.'

'You getting any tickets for the Commonwealth Games?' Ross asked, between mouthfuls.

'Maybe. I'll see. I'm not sure what's happening yet.'

'There are a few events I quite fancy. You want me to get a couple of tickets and we'll take a look? My treat.'

'Okay.' Wheeler chewed the potato scone for longer than she thought should've been necessary. 'The Games will be brilliant for the city.'

'I suppose, and at least they haven't flattened Tollcross like they have Dalmarnock.'

'The Athletes' Village?'

'The very one.'

'You're not impressed?'

'We'll see how it turns out when they finish building it. Laura's originally from Dalmarnock and she's not so sure about what they're doing there.'

'Either way, we'd better get a result on this case before the city gets its old reputation back in the world's press.'

'I know. I read an article that called Glasgow "Stab City". That won't work so well as a sound bite for the Games.'

After they had finished their rolls, Ross started the car, edged it back into the traffic and carried on towards Tollcross. He killed the engine across from the park. The alleyway was empty, other than the police tape. Wheeler climbed out and stood listening, trying to visualize what had happened to Cameron Craig, trying to get a feel for the case. Ross stood beside her. A lorry rumbled past, heading out of the city. 'It's very different now the whole road show has gone,' said Ross.

'Kind of bleaker, somehow.'

'This is what it would have been like when he was killed.'

'You think uniform got any more information last night?'

'At this stage, anything would be a gift.'

They walked the length of the alleyway, saw a lone rat scurry into the darkness. Made their way back to the warmth of the car. They drove in silence. Eventually Ross pulled into the car park at the station. Carmyle police station was in Glasgow's East End and sat at the centre of a triangle between Mount Vernon, what had been the old

Auchenshuggle bus terminus and the South Lanarkshire border. It was stranded in no man's land. Bandit country, she'd heard it called. Ross climbed out of the car, scrunched up the empty bags from the rolls and binned them. The coffee was just about the right temperature. They'd carried their cups a few yards when he began complaining. 'At least Pitt Street has some kind of civilization surrounding it.'

'Indeed it has.'

'It's right in the centre, with shops, delis, bars and cafés.'

Wheeler strode beside him. 'And your point, caller?'

'Other stations at least have a café or a chip shop nearby. A burger van parked in a layby's all we have and even then it's miles from the station.'

'We've got the shops and cafés on Tollcross Road.'

'But they're not even close to opening yet.'

'You know the trouble with you, Ross?'

'What?'

'You have delusions of grandeur.'

'You mean I've got standards.'

Wheeler opened the door of the station, 'Either way, let's get to work.' She nodded to the desk sergeant, Tommy Cunningham. 'Hi, TC.'

'Hello, DI Wheeler.' TC smirked at Ross. 'I see that Rovers are struggling. I reckon they're still looking back to their heyday.'

'That right?' said Ross.

'Let me think, when was it?'

'I'm sure it'll come to you,' muttered Ross.

'Oh, yes! Was it 1922 when they finished third in the first division?'

'You tell me, old timer. Were you at that match?'

'Going back a bit, though, isn't it? I mean for a real result.'

'Tenacity and teamwork will get us through. Not that your lot would know about that since they depend on the size of their salaries to inspire them. Not that they're doing that well even with the big bucks they're earning.'

'Oh, I don't know. I reckon we're doing okay but Rovers need to take it up a gear. Even you've got to pull yourself out of denial and admit it.'

'Really? You think? See, TC, that's where you're wrong. Let me tell you something...'

Wheeler left them to it and sprinted up the stairs to the CID suite. She was the first to arrive and sat at the front of the sparse room, nursing the dregs of her coffee, watching the whorls of steam dance into the cold air and evaporate. As usual at this time of the morning the room was freezing and the single ancient halogen heater was not even close to doing the job, but by midday the station would be a sauna. Wheeler glanced around the room: the parquet flooring was chipped, sludge-coloured paint covered the walls, and the fluorescent light flickered intermittently, just often enough to entice a migraine. At the front of the room, a picture of Cameron Craig had already been affixed to the board, along with details of the locus.

The team began to arrive and she heard mutterings about the weather, the traffic and a smattering of coughs and sneezes. No one mentioned that they had been stocious the night before or that they were suffering from hangovers. They were, despite appearances, professionals. She saw Ross come in and, behind him, Detective Chief Inspector Stewart. Stewart marched to the front of the room. As usual, his hair was shorn to a peak but his slate-grey eyes had lost some of their alertness. Even his usually pristine suit looked slightly crumpled against his tanned face and pink-gold Rolex. Wheeler wondered about the call regarding his wife, Adrianne, the previous night. She hoped it was nothing too serious. The start of a new case would normally have energized the boss but he looked jaded. When Stewart spoke, though, his voice held the same authority and the familiar measured tone, which left no doubt as to who was in charge. He stared at the assembled team. 'So, let's get updated. I came in for a bit last night and interviewed Mr Lou O'Keeffe who runs the takeaway. The victim was found beside a skip belonging to Mr O'Keeffe.'

'Anything, boss?' asked Ross.

'Nothing, his alibi checks out.'

'Watertight?'

'Yep. After he shut up shop, he went straight home to his wife.'

A few officers sighed.

'I know it sounds cosy,' Stewart continued, 'but since his wife's Sergeant Hannah O'Keeffe from the Southside station, I think we can take it as read that his alibi's watertight.' Stewart turned to Wheeler. 'Would you like to fill everyone in on the details?'

'Sure, boss.' She glanced at her notes. 'A body was found around eight p.m. by a road gritter, Clive Hill. The victim's name was Cameron Craig. He was twenty-two and homeless, living rough in the Tollcross area.'

'And we know this because?'

'Clive Hill had seen him around, chatted to him occasionally. Only got to know bits and pieces.'

'Was the victim a *Big Issue* seller?'

'Not as far as we know – at least, he had no official ID on him.'

'Get on to their headquarters.'

'Will do, boss.'

'Estimated time of death?'

'Somewhere around six p.m. It looks like he was strangled but there should be a post-mortem later on today. Dr Matt Elliot was on site and says he'll contact us when he has a definite time for the PM.'

Stewart spoke: 'You talked to Clive Hill last night?'

'I interviewed him, boss, and he seemed very shaken,' said Wheeler.

'What do we know about him?'

'He lives alone in a flat on Shettleston Road. He's aged forty-seven and has worked for the council since he left school. He works permanent nights by request as he doesn't get on with people.'

'Doesn't get on?' asked Stewart.

'He's just a bit of an introvert,' said Wheeler. 'He reports that he likes animals. He knows that he's a bit of a loner.'

'Married?' said Stewart.

'No. No partner or kids.'

'Hobbies?'

'It seems he just likes to work. And...'

'And?' Stewart prompted.

'And in his spare time he likes to walk around the city.' Wheeler knew how it sounded.

'Is he a suspect?'

Wheeler shook her head. 'I don't think so. He was just on duty that night and—'

'And he was at the scene of the crime because he had a

legitimate reason to be there.' Robertson spoke from the front row.

'Does he have any previous?' asked Stewart.

'Nothing on him at all,' said Wheeler.

'Okay,' said Stewart. 'Maybe the guy was just unlucky. And maybe he's a loner, an introvert or whatever. It's not a crime, but let's just be aware of him. He wouldn't be the first loner to kill. Go on.'

'There was a card found beside the body. Don't know if it was dropped before the body was dumped or was placed beside it. It's one of those wee positive-thinking inspirational quotes.' Wheeler held it up. 'Says, "What will you create today that will make your tomorrow better?" It's from a group that call themselves the Letum Institute.'

'The what?'

'Letum. It's Latin for death, ruin and annihilation.'

'Christ, and a card from that lot was found next to a dead body. What do we know about them?'

Boyd spoke: 'Aren't they based over in the West End? Hyndland? Their headquarters is there. They give out soup and bread to anyone who fancies a wee bite to eat. Every Saturday night, it's called *prasa* or something.'

'*Prasadam*,' said Wheeler. 'It's common practice among spiritually minded folk. Breaking bread with the poor or homeless. They have a van that they drive around the city, free food every Saturday night. They have a shelter in Duke Street, too, a sort of halfway house.'

'So they're a religious organization?'

'No. It's an organization to meet up and talk about esoteric matters,' said Wheeler.

'Meaning what?' asked a uniformed officer at the back of the room. 'A cult?'

'Hippie shit,' suggested Boyd.

'Enlightening,' muttered Wheeler. 'The Letum was founded in 1985 by Mark Davidson and Tabitha Bailey, who decided that Glasgow needed an esoteric society. They've since retired to India. The place is run by Benjamin Ramsey.'

'What do we know about Ramsey?' asked Stewart.

Wheeler read from her notes: 'Aged thirty-five, he's a writer and has published seven books, all on esoteric studies.'

A snort from the back of the room.

'He also has a degree from Oxford, so he's pretty well educated.'

'And you know all this because?' asked Stewart.

'I had a trawl through their online site last night. A lot of folk are involved in the place with all kinds of interests.'

'But they name the place Letum? Death and annihilation?' asked Boyd.

'Who knows with the esoteric crew?' said Wheeler. 'I certainly don't.'

'So maybe Cameron Craig was involved with them,' said Stewart, 'or the killer was a member.' He paused. 'Anyone here ever been involved in the alternative spiritual community and can shed any light on it?'

Silence.

'Anything at all?' He waited a heartbeat. 'Thought as much. Okay, anything else?'

Robertson raised a hand. 'I spoke to a volunteer on the soup run in George Square last night. Paul Moore reckons that Cameron sometimes stayed at a shelter. Didn't know which one, though he thought it might be Street Safe. That's all he knew about him.'

'Okay. Get on to them right away. Talk to the staff and the clientele. How many shelters are there in the city?'

'We're still updating the list, boss. Some have closed recently due to the funding cutbacks. Others are no longer offering accommodation, just a cup of hot soup or tea and sandwiches. Street Safe is still going in some capacity, and the bigger ones, like the Rayner Association, seem to manage to keep finding the funding.'

'Update me on Rayner.'

Again, Wheeler read from her notes: 'Established ten years ago, they pretty much operate city wide, have three centres and a soup van. All the centres operate part-time, sometimes just a day a week. Here in the East End they have a house near Springfield Road and another behind Parkhead Psychiatric Hospital that offer some overnight accommodation.'

'Salamanca Street,' said Ross.

'In the Southside they have a small place off Shawlands Cross, and north of the city they run a mobile soup van, driving round the schemes, chatting to the homeless, offering them soup and a roll,' said Wheeler. 'It's run on a skeleton staff. A couple are paid, but it's mostly volunteers and, from what I've seen, the buildings they work from are wrecks. I don't know how much longer they can keep going.'

'Okay. Cameron Craig lived on the streets, so get the word back out there. Speak to the homeless community and find out what they can tell us about our victim. You all know what to do. But just to add to the mix,' Stewart pinched his nose between his thumb and forefinger, then spat out, 'Mark fucking Haedyear.' Heard the grunts and mutterings around the room.

'You reckon he was involved with Cameron Craig's murder?'

'It's a possibility,' said Stewart.

'I saw Grim's report on the escape,' said Ross.

'Christ, who is informing the wee shit so quickly?' Boyd asked. 'It's not the first time he's had the heads-up before us – or at least simultaneously. He's got to have half of Glasgow on his books.'

'Grim's contacts are the least of our problems,' said Stewart. 'Someone sprang Haedyear, one of the most odious murderers I've ever encountered. Completely without conscience or regret. Despite DNA evidence, which completely nailed him for Amanda Henderson's murder, he steadfastly denied any involvement. After he was sentenced he went to his cell laughing. And now we have a dead body. Perhaps it's unconnected and certainly it's not his MO as we understand it but...'

'He's a psycho,' muttered Boyd.

'I assume everyone remembers the case?' Stewart looked around the room. 'And that the only reason he got brought in for a second interview was because of an anonymous tip-off?'

'So someone out there's feeling nervous,' said Wheeler.

'Exactly. Haedyear's bound to have some idea of who he thinks squealed on him and he's going to go after them.'

'Do you think it was Cameron Craig?' asked Wheeler.

'Let's keep an open mind,' said Stewart.

'They thought Haedyear had killed more women, didn't they?' said Boyd. 'But Amanda Henderson's murder was all they could pin on him.'

'Certainly that was the theory but, despite intense pressure before and during his trial, Haedyear gave nothing away and was convicted only of the Henderson murder,' Stewart said. 'If it's true that he hadn't killed before, then what made him begin when he did?'

'Someone like Haedyear doesn't just begin to kill at his age,' said Boyd, 'I reckon he'd done it before and got away with it. I'm convinced of it.'

'Does the Henderson family know he's out?' said Ross.

'The West End police have already contacted the husband, Richard Henderson,' said Stewart.

'Would he go after Haedyear?' asked Boyd. 'Looking for revenge?'

'Not as far as our colleagues in the West End are concerned,' said Stewart. 'I spoke with DI Barclay, who worked the original case. Barclay reckons Henderson's a troubled man and very fragile. Seems Fiona, Henderson's elder daughter, is also very troubled. She stopped talking when her mother was murdered, then began running away from home.'

'How awful for the man.' A young female officer spoke up from the second row. 'First his wife's murdered, then his daughter runs away.'

'Fiona's nineteen now and runs away on a regular basis – she has been missing for up to ten days at a time. The other daughter, Annabel, or Belle, is seventeen and studying in Stirling.'

'Do you think Haedyear will target Fiona Henderson, if he's looking for another homeless victim?' asked Robertson. 'Should we be looking for her?'

Stewart sighed. 'Let's not get carried away. We don't know if this was a one-off. And apparently Mr Henderson and his daughter have a very fractious relationship. She'd made it abundantly clear that she does not want the police to approach her or contact her in any way. If we do, she will permanently sever all ties with her family.'

'Talk about emotional blackmail,' said Ross. 'But with Haedyear out there?'

'Certainly it makes for a bloody sensitive situation. However, Fiona is an adult and has rights, which can't be ignored,' said Stewart. 'Being homeless isn't a crime. And Mr Henderson specifically instructed DI Barclay and the rest of his team to bow out. So, we need to respect that.'

'Where does that leave us?' asked Wheeler.

'As harsh as it sounds, Fiona Henderson's not our priority. And we've no reason to expect that she's even here in the East End. Finding the killer of Cameron Craig and getting that bastard Haedyear locked up again are top of our list,' said Stewart.

'Haedyear worked at Southside College, didn't he?' asked Boyd.

'Yes,' said Stewart. 'Amanda Henderson was an art historian who was asked to give a lecture at the college. Haedyear denied meeting her, but the tip-off placed him giving her a lift. Police searched the area around his home and finally discovered her but it was too late. They found DNA from the boot of his car, which linked him directly to Henderson.'

'And we have no idea who it was that called in?' asked Boyd.

'None. No trace of the number,' said Stewart. 'It was a mobile phone, pay-as-you-go, which was probably dumped.'

'Unless it was Cameron Craig who grassed on Haedyear? In which case we could be looking at revenge,' said Ross.

'We can't rule it out, but Amanda Henderson was kept underground. Haedyear's MO is a prolonged death,' said Stewart, 'but Cameron Craig's was over in seconds.'

'Maybe Haedyear was about to abduct Craig and was disturbed by someone,' suggested a uniformed officer at the back of the room.

'Then why hasn't that someone come forward?' said Wheeler.

'What's your take, Wheeler?' asked Stewart.

'Every place formerly associated with Haedyear has been checked. He's not gone near his old haunts. I think someone sprang him and that they have a plan. Right now I'm not sure what it is but I don't have Haedyear down for this murder. It's not his style. So, number one, I think we're looking for whoever killed Cameron Craig. Number two, we need to get to Haedyear before he does whatever it is he's planning to do. And, if he reverts to type, that will potentially involve a female victim held in an underground chamber.'

'I agree,' said Stewart. 'So we need to get out there. First off get to the Letum Institute, the Rayner Association, Street Safe and the other homeless units. I want everything on Cameron Craig by the end of the day. At the same time be aware of Haedyear, where he might go, what he might be up to. All reported sightings, regardless of however dubious, should be followed up.' He stared at the team. 'You're all professionals. You know what to do.' By the time Stewart had left the room, they were on their feet, Wheeler was issuing orders and the mood was one of energy and purpose.

Chapter 16

Richard Henderson walked through Rottenrow and passed a twenty-one-foot-high stainless-steel safety pin, which commemorated the old maternity hospital. Fiona had been born at Rottenrow. He crossed the road, trying to avoid the dirty slush thrown up by the cars, trucks and buses that were making their way slowly towards the city centre. He walked carefully, navigating his path through the snow. He was five foot eight and of slim build, with sandy hair, a receding hairline and a long goatee beard. He wore chinos and a light grey overcoat. The café he was looking for was just off Cathedral Street. Finally he saw it. The window at A Murder of Crows was steamed with condensation. Henderson opened the door and was immediately hit by the smell of fried bacon. He winced. The café was almost full and he scanned the place quickly in search of a seat. It had been Fiona who had suggested they meet there. She had sent a text in reply to his message and had promised him she would show.

Henderson eventually found a table at the back of the café and tried to avoid eye contact with a malevolent-looking raven. Instead he locked eyes with a mange-ridden fox, the animal's lips curled back in spite, a useless claw hung mid-air. On a raised platform a pair of stoats stared down eternity through glass eyes, while a hare shadow-boxed for the final time. Stuffed Staffy and Chihuahua pups and a half-dozen tiny fawns stood frozen in perpetuity. To Henderson, it seemed that taxidermy screamed around him. On a shelf was a row of yellowing skulls, their eye sockets gaping blind, their teeth aching in an eternal grimace.

The speakers thundered heavy metal. Loud. Insistent. The coffee machine spat and hissed, and Henderson felt a migraine stab behind his eyes. He forced himself to breathe deeply. He thought of that morning's yoga practice and let the memory calm him, willing himself to become centred. He clutched the rose crystal in his pocket. Stroked the stone. Waited for the tension to dissipate. Finally he picked up the menu and scanned the Gothic script for a vegan option. There wasn't one. Not even an offer of soya milk. A young waiter with a shaved head and extended holes in his earlobes meandered across the room, looked somewhere above Henderson's head and asked, 'Yup, what can I get you?'

'An espresso please.'

'Double shot?'

'Just a single.'

'I could throw in a bacon roll for an extra two quid – today's special?'

Henderson shuddered. 'No, thanks. Just the coffee.'

The waiter shrugged. 'Whatever, dude.'

Henderson checked his watch. She was late. As usual. He glanced at the couple sitting at the next table. They were eating the full fried breakfast. Fat dribbled from the man's lips to his chin. Henderson watched while a thick, purple tongue lolled out of the mouth and retrieved what it could before retreating to its lair. Henderson could smell the blood from the black pudding. His stomach turned. His coffee arrived in a small black cup. A jagged gold-leaf-painted trim wound its way around the rim and the saucer. Henderson let the slick, oily liquid cool for a few seconds before he tasted it. He grimaced, swallowed quickly and replaced the cup in its saucer. He waited. The clock on the wall opposite mocked him. She was now ten minutes late. When his hands shook, he placed them, palms down, on the table.

Behind the counter a television was muted, the captions rolling out information beneath the changing images. A photograph of Mark Haedyear filled the screen. Then it came, as Henderson had known it would, but it was always a shock. Always. The photograph of his wife, Amanda, had been taken when they were on holiday. She was smiling directly into the camera. 'Not a care,' Henderson announced loudly to the busy café. 'She didn't have a care in the world.' The camera cut to another news story and Amanda's face disappeared.

He finished his coffee. Took out his mobile, punched in the letters and sent the text to Fiona. If he was being honest, he didn't expect a response.

He was right.

Twenty minutes passed and he'd finished another bitter coffee before he picked up his mobile again. Sent another text, this time to Belle: *I was supposed to meet Fiona for coffee, doesn't look like she's going to show. Have you heard from her?*

A few seconds later, a reply: *No, haven't heard anything for ages. Is she home or…?*

She's gone again.

Since when?

A week.

Does she know Haedyear's escaped?

I don't know. I was going to tell her today.

You want me to try to contact her?

You could. She's blanking me.

*So what's new, Dad? She's been doing that since Mum died.
Let me try. Will get back to you.*

OK. He ended their conversation *XXX*.

Henderson watched the couple opposite heave themselves out of their chairs and head out into the snow. He had batted the waiter off a few times before he heard his mobile chirp. He scrolled through the message: *I've tried to contact her, no response. I guess it's the usual routine of keeping an eye out on the street. She knows what she's doing. There's not much point visiting the shelters. I don't think she ever uses them, don't you agree?*

He typed his reply: *Don't worry, I'll get on with it. I'm going to ask the folk at the Letum for help. You get back to studying. xxx*

And he would get on with it. He would start the familiar trawl around the city, the empty doorways she favoured, the deserted spaces under bridges. Fiona used different names and different background stories depending on her mood. He knew from the tone of the text that Belle was tired. Tired of trying to have her own life while looking out for her elder sister.

Henderson scrolled down the list of shelters, knew that even if she didn't use them he still had to check. Fiona had been disappearing on and off for years and she made sure that she wasn't found. She lived on the streets, in squats or maybe under an assumed name in shelters. It was her thing. Her independence. And they were all having to observe it. Finally, after trying her mobile again and getting no response, Henderson paid for the coffees and headed out into the snow.

Chapter 17

The Rayner hostel was situated in Salamanca Street, close to the Forge Shopping Centre and Parkhead Psychiatric Hospital, but tucked away behind a housing scheme and hidden among pubs, cafés, charity shops and a bingo hall. The building itself was worn out, pleading to be demolished. To be laid to rest. To sleep. The windows were bound with wire mesh and the old door had been recently reinforced. The sign read *Welcome to the Rayner Association*. Inside the front door there was an unmanned reception desk, a small assessment area and a larger communal space. A series of locked doors led into the sleeping quarters.

Fiona Henderson was lounging in the seating area, the brittle light from the overhead fluorescent strip accentuating the sharp contours of her face. Her blue eyes were clear and untroubled. She stared out of the window. Outside a grey sky hung over Parkhead and a group of homeless men huddled together. Fiona watched a skinny youth approach the group and say something. A man turned to him and slammed the heel of his hand into his face. The youth buckled and staggered off. The group re-formed into a circle. Fiona turned away. She held a cheap ballpoint pen in her right hand and there was an open notebook on the table in front of her. Lynne Allen, a volunteer at the centre, was trying and failing to fill in a registration form. The door opened and the manager strode into the room. Malcolm Reek's tie was knotted tightly and his shirt sleeves buttoned securely. Fiona closed her eyes.

'Open your eyes, please. Now.' Reek struggled to keep the impatience from his voice. He sighed loudly. 'Look at me. Look at me now, please.' He drummed his fingers on the table. Watched her and pursed his lips. Repeated his request: 'I'm asking you to open your eyes.'

Fiona opened her eyes momentarily, wrote in the notebook, 'What was here before? What did this area used to be?' dropped the pen and closed her eyes again.

Lynne spoke to Fiona, her voice hesitant: 'Before? Well, years ago before this area was built up, it was the old forge. Do you know what a forge is?'

Fiona, her eyes still tightly shut, nodded.

Lynne continued, 'They made steel in the forge – this whole area was for steel-making.'

Reek sighed.

Fiona relaxed, let herself drift, imagined the searing heat from a roaring furnace, the sound of men shouting to each other, the smell of molten steel and the glitter from the sparks. She heard the thunder of the furnace, felt herself warm to its heat. Felt the claustrophobia of the forge, a world turned in on itself. She reached back in time to when it had all started. The sight of her mother's body. The screams from her sister, Belle. Richard beginning to unravel. Her mother's funeral. How afterwards everything had made sense. Everything had fallen into place. Fiona had found peace because she had seen her future.

'Open your eyes, please,' Reek repeated.

Lynne looked on, concern shadowing her face. 'Just write your name, then, pet. What's your name?'

Fiona opened her eyes, reached out her hand and let her fingers trace the pages of the notebook before taking the pen up again and writing, *My name?*

Reek nodded.

Fiona took her time writing, making sure it was neat and legible, then slid the notebook across to him. *My name is Jessica fucking Rabbit.*

Reek scowled. Tight lines deepened around his mouth. His eyes flashed anger. He scrawled *The client refuses to give us her name and is being deliberately unresponsive and hostile* at the bottom of the form and underlined it twice before slamming the folder onto the desk. He stalked out, leaving the smell of stale tobacco and a stalled career behind him.

Lynne leaned towards Fiona and whispered, 'Reek's gone.'

Fiona nodded.

'You want to stay in here for a bit? You can do whatever you want – there's no rush.'

Fiona waited.

Lynne sighed and leaned forward to pat Fiona's arm, then said quietly, 'Well, you stay here and get a wee heat before going back out in that weather.' She glanced at Fiona before she left but Fiona was in a world of her own.

The light from the furnace was red-gold, the heat from it scorching the air. Fiona could feel it warm her body. She stretched out her arms, felt the tips of her fingers bathed in its warmth. She watched the men working, beads of sweat on their creased foreheads. She heard the noise of metal and the roar of the furnace. Fiona opened her eyes and smiled, reached over and drew a symbol in the notebook, looping the pen over and over until it scored the paper and finally ripped through the page. Fiona had copied the symbol out years before, when she had first come to the shelters. *Is that your favourite pattern?* they had asked her, trying to prompt her to communicate with them. *I don't recognize it. What does it mean?* But she had never explained it to them. It was her secret and Fiona hoarded her secrets like gold.

Chapter 18

Belle Henderson took off her glasses and rubbed her tired eyes. She stood at the window of her student room and watched the snow settle on the Wallace Monument, turning the grey Gothic tower white. On the road below, two students, each carrying rucksacks, were walking towards the bus stop, their heads down into the sleet and snow. Then she saw him, a lone figure hurrying through the wet. He glanced up and saw her at the window. Belle took a step back, but too late: he had raised a hand in acknowledgement. James Arnold, the class creep. Belle shivered and pulled her cardigan around her.

She checked her phone – nothing new from her father. She turned away from the window, picked up her iPad and scrolled down to the news page, found BBC Glasgow just as the segment changed. A reporter stood in front of a police cordon, in the background Tollcross Park. 'Around eight p.m. last night police were called to Tollcross Road, where they discovered the body of Cameron Craig, a twenty-two-year-old man, who had been brutally murdered. The victim was thought to have been sleeping rough in the area and police are appealing for witnesses. Earlier today DCI Stewart of Carmyle police station released a statement asking for anyone who heard or saw anything unusual to contact the station immediately. DCI Stewart confirmed that there will be a press conference later today.' The camera cut to earlier footage. 'Angry Tollcross residents have called for more police to patrol the area. A spokeswoman for the Tollcross Neighbourhood Watch, Isabel McMasters, said, "The polis are just not on the streets often enough. There should be more police presence around here. I should know. I've lived here for near on sixty year and in that time ..."'

The story changed to Mark Haedyear's escape and the reporter told Belle what she already knew, that he was still on the run. A photograph of Haedyear appeared on the screen, then one of her mother. Belle barely heard the rest of the report.

'Police are still hunting for convicted killer Mark Haedyear who escaped ... Haedyear, thirty-eight ... has served only three years of a life sentence for the murder of ... Amanda Henderson ... A spokesperson for Police Scotland earlier today issued this statement. "We ask that the public do not approach this extremely dangerous man" ... Meanwhile local MP Norman McKeller has called for a crackdown on allowing prisoners to have compassionate leave. "These people are in prison for a reason. To allow them to freely roam the streets for their own gain is horrendous. I speak for my constituency when I say that ..."'

Belle switched off the computer, studied the dregs of her coffee and decided against finishing it. She needed to get down to studying, but the text from her father had upset her. She selected one of her course books from the floor, flicked through the pages until she found the section she was looking for and settled herself into her chair to read. A second later she picked up her mobile and rang her father. He answered on the second ring. 'Yep?'

'Dad?'

'Who else would it be?' His usual retort, trying and failing to sound upbeat.

'Where are you?'

'I'm just coming up to our house. I've had a walk around Rottenrow and Cathedral Street. I checked around the Merchant City too.'

'Any sighting of her?'

'Nothing.'

Belle heard the despair in his voice. 'I've just watched the report. They're using the same picture of Mum.'

'I know, love.'

'And a homeless man was murdered outside Tollcross Park.'

'I saw the news.'

'Would Fiona have known him?' Belle asked.

'I don't know. She might have, I suppose.'

'Do you think she goes as far as Tollcross?'

'Who knows where she goes and who she's with? I know that she likes the café off Cathedral Street, A Murder of Crows. I know that she used to walk around Rottenrow. Other than that I've no idea where to look. She leads such a secret life. We're no longer part of it.'

'I think we should ask the police to get involved. We should contact Inspector Barclay.' She waited for the response. Heard the tone of his voice change.

'We promised her we'd never involve the police. You know what she threatened to do.'

Belle remembered the ultimatum that Fiona had written

in her notebook, her face contorted in anger. Fiona had used capital letters and had underlined each word of the threat. 'Dad, she's letting us sit and worry about her every time she runs off. And now Haedyear's back out there and we're supposed to do nothing?'

'I couldn't bear to lose her, Belle.'

She listened to the pain in his voice, pictured him standing on the freezing street, his Adam's apple bobbing, swallowing repeatedly and trying not to cry. She could envisage the tremor in his hands, imagined him clutching a piece of crystal or talisman from the Letum or some other esoteric group. Her poor father was unravelling – she could hear it in his voice. She tried again: 'You need to stand up to her, Dad, start setting some boundaries. She can't manipulate us for ever.'

She heard him sniff, knew what would come next. And it did. 'If only your mother was here.'

Belle said nothing.

'I know she's difficult and that it's hard for you. It's just that maybe if Amanda was here now Fiona would stop excluding us.'

'I doubt it.'

'Belle…' His voice was pleading.

'Do you want me to come home?' She glanced at her watch. 'I could make the next train to Glasgow.'

'No, you're right in the middle of studying. Plus, there's nothing you can do here. If she turns up, I'll call.' His voice sounded strained.

'Are you sure, Dad?'

'Yes.'

Belle sighed. 'I'm going to pack. I'll be home soon.'

'You don't have to come. Perhaps she'll get back to me.'

'Don't hold your breath. I doubt she'll get in touch with either of us.'

'She listens to you.'

'Dad, please don't lie. Fiona stopped listening to me years ago. She stopped listening to anyone. It was her decision and she made it.'

'One day she'll come round and go back to the Fiona we once knew.'

Classic denial, Belle thought. 'I'll be home as quickly as I can. See you soon.' She ended the call and threw the mobile onto the table. She knew that her father was struggling and that he sought solace in alternative spirituality. After her mother's death, he'd tried to contact her through various mediums. He'd even tried tarot and rune readings. But nothing had helped and now he was a brittle shell. And Fiona didn't seem to notice. Belle grabbed her phone again and texted her sister: *Just spoken to Dad. You know how this torments him. At least text him. Just to say you're okay. Haedyear's out and a man has been murdered. SO FOR FUCKSAKE GET IN TOUCH.* She pressed send and put the phone into her pocket. Then she gathered her notes and packed them into her rucksack. She went into the bedroom, grabbed a change of clothes and bundled them in too. As she packed, her expression changed from frustration to resentment.

In Glasgow's West End Richard Henderson crossed into Observatory Road and let himself into his flat. He stood in the hallway and called, 'Fiona, darling, are you home?' Silence. He went to the bedroom and changed out of his wet clothes. Inside the wardrobe, his dead wife's things hung in neat rows next to her carefully folded colourful scarves. Henderson reached out and touched one, held it to his face and tried to breathe in Amanda's scent, but it was gone: it had dissipated over the years. He closed the wardrobe door. In the kitchen he put on the kettle and stood at the bay window while it boiled. Outside, a soft film of snow had settled over the city. Below him shoppers and workers hurried through the streets, sheltering under umbrellas or swathed in coats and scarves. He watched them, wishing his daughter was among them and that she was making her way home.

He heard the click of the kettle and poured boiling water over miso soup, watching while the cubes of tofu expanded and floated to the top of the mug. Finally, he crossed to the kitchen table and picked up the *Chronicle*. Front page was the murder of Cameron Craig. On the second page was the familiar picture of his wife next to one of Haedyear. Henderson's mind flooded with images of Amanda and of their time together before evil had entered their lives. He put his head in his hands and let the tears fall.

Chapter 19

The disembodied voice trilled with excitement: 'So, a big year for Glasgow, with the Commonwealth Games coming up in the summer. This is Glasgow's time to shine, show the world that our little city is a world-class destination. And then in September the Indie debate. Where do you stand? Give us a call on...'

Ross leaned forward and turned off the radio. 'So, we're headed to the Letum places. Do you want to start at their homeless unit in Duke Street or their headquarters in Hyndland?'

'Let's start at Duke Street, then head over to the West End,' said Wheeler.

'And after that we could break for a coffee?' said Ross.

'Maybe, if you're lucky.'

'How many shelters do you reckon there are in the city?'

'Why?' asked Wheeler. 'You wondering how many of those little containers of hand-sanitizer you'll need?'

'I'm just asking.'

'You buying them in bulk now?'

'Seriously,' said Ross, 'how many shelters?'

'Altogether there are about a dozen, but they all offer

very different levels of support. A couple are just drop-in centres that open for a few hours a week. They give out information about benefits and advice on temporary housing.'

'Weren't two centres closed last year?'

'Yes – two of the bigger residential centres did, but a number of independent hostels have opened. And both the Letum and Rayner are still going but they, too, are independently run.'

'You reckon the smaller hostels are a step in the right direction?'

'If they're properly resourced,' said Wheeler. 'And also we need to look at the soup runs and the folk who give out sandwiches at night.'

'But we can't cover them all.'

'Because?'

Ross looked at her. 'Every bloody unit? You're kidding me, right?'

'I am. We're only covering a few. Boyd and Robertson will get the rest and uniform can catch anything they've missed. You're such a wuss, though. You worried you'll catch a wee germ?'

Ross ignored her, stayed silent. Drove. Eventually he spoke: 'You know the Templeton building?'

'Yeah, the old factory. Based on the Doge's Palace in Venice? What about it?'

'You been to the bar-restaurant in that place?'

'No. Is it nice?'

'Very trendy – Laura's a fan.' He glanced at her. 'You'd like it.'

'You reckon?'

'When this case is over, we could go and celebrate.'

'And forgo Boyd's choice of the Belter Bar?'

'Yeah.'

'Fine.'

'Just fine? Is there someplace you'd like better?'

'Whatever. It's a date. But for now just keep driving.'

So he did. Eventually they turned into Duke Street. 'This is meant to be the longest street in Britain,' said Ross, 'so where are we headed?'

'The unit's about halfway down. You can pull in here.'

Ross parked the car in the almost deserted street, 'Weather's keeping everybody in.' He looked out at the building. 'Place looks derelict.' But Wheeler was already out of the car. He caught up with her as she reached the door. Above it a sign read *Letum Institute*. Wheeler pressed the buzzer and waited. Eventually the door was opened by an obese man in his mid-fifties. He sported week-old stubble and silver bruises across the knuckles of his right hand. He was also a smoker – Wheeler could smell it on him. She noticed that his hand shook, and his bloodshot, rheumy eyes looked like they were crying for a pint. Not a great advertisement for healthy living, she thought, not by a long shot.

'Can I help ye?' He placed a meaty hand on the door.

They flashed their ID. He waved it away. 'Nae need for that. I can tell a mile off you're the polis.'

'We'd like a quick word, if it's convenient.'

The man pulled open the door. 'Nae bother, hen. Come on intae the heat. My name's Pat Dunbar.'

They followed Dunbar along a narrow corridor – the odour of cheap bleach stung Wheeler's nostrils and the floor tiles were so cracked in places that they shifted underfoot. It had been painted blue at one time, but now the colour had faded and damp patches spread unevenly over the walls. Dunbar led them into a bare hall, a little like a small gymnasium. Wooden floorboards, grey walls, a faint echo when they spoke.

'We'd like to ask you a few questions,' said Wheeler.

'Oh, aye?'

'If you don't mind?'

'About what?' asked Dunbar.

'A recent death in the community.'

'Oh, aye. That's all it is, then? Take your pick, hen. In this line of work we see the lot. Don't know what the stats are across the city for the homeless but our punters don't tend to last too long. This here's the Last Chance Saloon.'

'A man named Cameron Craig was murdered,' said Wheeler.

'Aye, right. I heard about it on the news.'

'Did you know him?' asked Ross.

Dunbar gave a curt nod. 'Aye, he's been in a few times, not often but he's been around.'

'Did he come in recently?'

'Haven't seen him in weeks, mibbe a month.'

'What can you tell us about him?' asked Wheeler.

'Not much. Only thing I remember about him was that he didnae have much to say for himself.'

'Anything else you can remember?' she prompted. 'Anything at all?' She waited.

Eventually Dunbar spoke: 'If I'm being honest, I didnae care for him.'

'That right?' said Ross. 'Because?'

'Couldnae put my finger on it, just the way he was with the others, sort of watching them. Seeing what he could thieve, see if there was a wee angle he could use for his own benefit. Looked like he was always after a scam.'

'You don't seem very sympathetic.'

'I reckon he was on the take.'

'And?'

'I don't like to see that. I know he had a hard life and that but, still, he wis a selfish git.'

'Go on.'

'I wis told that he was hanging about with some lassie. Mind you, it's only hearsay.'

'She have a name?' asked Wheeler.

'I'm sure she has, hen, but not one that I know of, no. She didnae use the hostels, preferred to sleep rough, but I heard that he was hanging around with her. Sounded like she wis a poor soul. And he wis gay and on the game, so it's not like he was interested in her like that.'

'He was working as a prostitute?'

'That's what the word on the street says.'

'And who told you that Cameron was taking advantage of this girl?'

'Ye just hear stuff. Might have been the wee moron.'

'And who is the wee moron?'

'Eddie Moran, cannae remember now. Mibbe Eddie made it up. Hard tae tell with Eddie. His grasp on reality isn't what you would call firm.'

'Is Eddie still using this place? Can we arrange to speak to him?'

'Haven't seen him for a fortnight – somebody said he'd died. Wouldnae surprise me. The man was on his last legs.'

'Anything else you can tell me about Cameron or the girl?'

Dunbar gave himself a minute to recollect. 'I heard she disnae talk.'

'She's mute?' Wheeler and Ross exchanged a look.

'It sounded like that. Just overheard a few guys talking. You hear things in this job. Bits and pieces.'

'The name Fiona Henderson mean anything to you?' asked Wheeler.

'Doesn't ring a bell.'

'Any idea what the girl looked like?'

'Never saw her.'

Ross glanced at Dunbar's bruised knuckles. 'Did Cameron Craig do anything to you, personally?'

Dunbar snorted. 'No, son. I know how tae look after myself. I have to be able to handle myself in this place. Couldn't dae this job otherwise.'

'Is there anyone else who might have disliked him?' asked Wheeler.

'Hard tae say, hen. By the time our punters get here they're more or less just interested in the booze. Social etiquette, making pals or whatever goes out the windae. Folk mibbe have one or two drinking buddies. Other than that they don't have a need for too much conversation, if you understand whit I'm saying. It's a bit of a solitary life and it's only heading in one direction.'

'Do many of your clients come here directly from the Bar-L?' asked Ross.

'A fair few. It's a kind of halfway house before they go back into the world or back inside. But, then, you probably know that already.'

'Any fights or disagreements among your clients?' asked Ross.

'Nothing big, a few minor spats. As I said, this here's

the Last Chance Saloon. Piss about and you're turfed out on your ear. No questions asked. The guys know that before they walk through the door. We run a tight ship. We need to.'

'So Cameron Craig wasn't friends with anyone in particular?'

'Nope, not as far as I know.'

'But he had no real enemies, no one who would want to harm him or see him harmed?' asked Wheeler.

'Well, obviously somebody didnae like him but it wouldnae be one of our lot.'

'How can you be so sure?'

'They wouldnae waste their energy.'

'When do you open in the evening?' asked Wheeler.

'Six or thereabouts.'

'Do you mind if a couple of our uniform officers come back then and visit the clients for a quick word?'

'Nae skin off my nose, hen.'

'And the girl you mentioned, if she isn't using the shelters or the drop-in centres, where else might she go?'

Dunbar thought for a moment. 'It depends. They all come and go in the city. Some sell the *Big Issue*, some use the soup run, others scavenge in bins and keep themselves to themselves. Quite a few folk beg. Others find a nice shop doorway to kip in for the night. A few of the lassies are on the game as well – some punter might take them back to his flat for an hour or so, then after that they're tossed out. Some let them stay the night. A fair few of the lassies have telt me that they feel safer on the street than they dae in the hostels.'

'Why is that?' said Wheeler.

'No sure. I'd have thought it would be better inside,

especially in weather like this. Guess it's just whatever they've experienced in their past makes them want tae stay away from folk altogether. Mibbe it's less claustro-phobic out there. Sometimes there are groups that form, kind of like an extended family. They look out for each other – that might appeal tae the lassies. Tae be honest, I'm not sure how the female mind works.' He winked at Wheeler. 'You'd be the expert on that.'

'This place is affiliated to the Letum Institute. Do you have much to do with them?' asked Ross.

'I don't get involved in that side of things. I'm not a religious man myself. If it pays the bills on this place, keeps it open for the punters and keeps it warm, then that's fair enough, I reckon. Job done. The headquarters over in Hyndland seems tae raise a fair bit of cash from all their wee gatherings. Mind you, their customer base must be the opposite end of the spectrum from ours. The two types of client don't really go together, if ye get my drift. Over there, the posh folk and over here the pish-poor.'

'And your take on the Letum HQ?' asked Ross.

'Off the record, I think it's okay in theory for them tae help out but they never actually want tae volunteer tae mop up the vomit and shit and stuff.'

Ross blanched.

Wheeler spoke: 'So if they don't have much to do with this place on a day-to-day basis, they wouldn't really know who uses it?'

'Not as far as I can see. But they dae a lot behind the scenes. See here, though.' He gestured around the room. 'We kind of run independently. We've not got anything tae dae with that side. Or HQ. Though I met an old girl once, Ms Dodds. She dropped Ramsey off.'

'Benjamin Ramsey?' said Wheeler.

'Aye, the high-heid yin. He came for a walk round, which he never usually does, and she dropped in for a nosy. Whit a piece of work that Dodds woman wis, a complete fucking pain.'

'Go on,' said Ross.

'Aye, well, I'm getting to that. She came in for a nosy, gave me a good look up and down and then announced that I had messy karma. Apparently I had issues I needed tae work through. She says she could read people.'

'I'm sure that was very helpful,' said Wheeler. 'Did you get a chance to thank her?'

Dunbar smiled. 'That I did, hen. Then I told her that I wis quite *au fait* with the idea that I had fucking crap karma, seeing how I wis on my third divorce and the wife had had the foresight tae clear out the house before she ran off with my oldest pal. At that point I wis practically homeless myself. And I can't say, looking at the state of me, that the Dodds woman had much guessing tae dae. Anyhow, stuff like that gives me the heebie-jeebies.'

'How did you get the job here, Mr Dunbar?' asked Wheeler. 'Did you go via HQ?'

'I saw the advert in the *Chronicle* a couple of years back. I fired off an application and was interviewed right here by Ramsey himself and another guy from the organization. I forget his name, heard he left a while back. Anyway, I got the job and I've been here ever since. I've never set foot in the HQ over in Hyndland. As I said, different worlds.'

'And the other staff and volunteers who work here, are they all vetted?' asked Ross.

'I'm not getting you, son,' said Dunbar. 'In whit way vetted?'

'CRB-checked for past convictions,' said Ross.

'CRB?'

'Criminal Record Bureau,' said Ross.

Dunbar looked blank.

'Think it's been updated, it's now the DBS,' said Wheeler. 'The Disclosure and Barring Service?'

Dunbar snorted. 'You're kidding me, right? See, this kind of a job's not exactly a career choice. Folk more or less fall intae it when there's nothing else on the horizon and they're in arrears with their rent.'

'The other staff?' asked Ross. 'Can you tell us about them?'

'Paid staff are me, the Monk, and wee Mary helps with the cleaning and makes the sandwiches. Volunteers are few and far between – they float in and out when it suits them. Bit like the clients themselves. The faces and names all merge after a while. I jist concentrate on providing the service. They can take it or leave it, it's their call. I can get you a list of names, if you like? There'll be one in the office.'

'Who's the Monk?' asked Ross.

'Answers to Vincent but his nickname's the Monk.'

'Because?'

'Somebody said he used tae be a monk or a priest or something. Left or got kicked out. Naebody asks him tae his face, mind you. He's not the chatty sort.'

'Full name?'

'Vincent Steele. At least, that's on the printout in the office but he'll no talk tae you.' Dunbar looked at the floor. 'He hates the polis.'

'He thinks it's his choice whether or not he talks to us?' asked Ross.

Dunbar addressed Wheeler: 'We about finished here?'

'We'll let you get on, Mr Dunbar.' Wheeler kept her tone solicitous.

'I've still to muck out the beds, mop the place over and chop the veg for tonight's soup.' Dunbar walked into the office and returned a few minutes later, holding a yellowing sheet of paper with the names he had already mentioned.

The trio made their way to the door. 'Thanks for your help, Mr Dunbar,' said Wheeler.

'Nae bother, hen.' Dunbar opened it and the welcome cold hit her. 'I hope ye catch the cunt that did Cameron.'

Once outside, Ross inhaled deeply. 'The stink in there made me want to gag.'

'Ever the drama queen, Ross, although, granted, it was pretty strong.'

'But, really, there's no need for that overdose.'

'You think maybe they were having to clean something up?' said Wheeler. 'Maybe a client was sick or worse. What if...' She let the image hang in the air.

'Yuk.' Ross reached into his pocket, pulled out a small hand-sanitizing container, squirted the liquid into a palm, then rubbed both together.

'That put you off going for a coffee later?'

'No chance.'

'Thought not.' They walked back to the car. 'So Cameron Craig was on the game and the girl who doesn't talk's got to be Fiona Henderson.'

'And Cameron Craig knew her and Dunbar suggested that he was on the make.'

'It's something,' said Wheeler.

'And also this Monk guy doesn't like the police,' said Ross.

'A lot of folk don't like us,' said Wheeler. 'There's no need to be so sensitive.'

'You think we should come back and interview him?' Ross unlocked the car for her.

'Boyd and Robertson can pick it up later,' said Wheeler, climbing in. 'Next up for us is the Letum Institute head-quarters. Hyndland.'

'Hyndland,' agreed Ross. 'Posh. Then coffee?'

'You're on,' said Wheeler.

Ross indicated, then pulled out into the road and turned the windscreen wipers on. The snow fell relentlessly.

Chapter 20

Communication Two

We are all lost souls.

Cameron Craig was small and bony. A child's mind encased in a young man's body. A cheap denim jacket stretched across narrow shoulders. Thin arms protruding from a grubby T-shirt. Too-tight jeans suggested stick-thin legs. He was a Twiglet. I wonder what he needed to feed on. It was easy to stop and chat with Cameron, tip a pound coin into his outstretched hand. I spoke to him often, always when he was alone. I am a neighbour, a friend, an easy conversationalist. I learned why he was on the street. He had been going to a homeless unit in Duke Street, but it was dry and he was addicted to alcohol. And, among other things, he didn't like the manager of the place, a man called Dunbar. It seemed natural that Cameron and I would meet. I thought it fortuitous when our universes collided.

In the short time we spoke, I uncovered Cameron's wretched history. I won't bore you with the tedious details. In essence, Cameron had been given up for adoption at age four and had grown into stunted manhood in a series of children's homes and foster places. From there, he'd graduated to a young-offenders' institution and then to a homeless refuge. Finally he ended up on the street, which became a home of sorts. As he spoke, I listened compassion-ately. I do compassion well. But, despite his exterior of bravado, Cameron exuded hopelessness. He alluded to the fact that he'd had a difficult time in the institution, that he'd been targeted. Oh, don't let the authorities or do-gooders fool you: rape is routine in young offenders' institutions, homes and prisons. And it's not only the inmates who indulge their passions.

I despised Cameron. A tirelessly weak boy, he showed no remorse for being so. I knew that he was hiding something. I could tell: I spend my life observ-ing the debris of the human condition. I encouraged him to trust me, and once he did, the chase was on.

'My life has been a mess,' Cameron complained, his face twisted with pain.

'Is that right?'

'My father never loved me.'

Well, *boo-hoo.* 'Really? I'm sure that's not true.'

'No.' He stared at the pavement. 'To him I was a freak.'

'Why would he think that?'

'I was born... I am intersex.'

Oh, my, what fun those boys must have had at the institution. I nodded sympathetically. 'I understand.'

Cameron raised his tear-filled eyes and spoke as if his soul was breaking: 'Boys,' his voice faltered, 'unusual boys, have the opportunity to make more money.'

Oh dear. Cameron was a prostitute. A common whore. Or not so common, as it transpired. When he began to cry, his head hung on his chest, while great gulps of air and tears escaped noisily. I patted his back. It was all I could be seen to do in public. A caring stranger. Cameron's descent into his personal hell would be swift. One word came to me as Cameron cried.

Disposable.

Chapter 21

'Take a left here, number thirty-eight,' said Wheeler. Ross turned the car and drove down a street lined with BMWs, Alfa Romeos and Range Rovers, found the single remaining parking place and killed the engine. The red sandstone townhouse was impressive, double-fronted with stained-glass windows and a heavy oak door. The gardens to the front of the property were impeccably manicured. 'So this is the esoteric side of the Letum,' said Wheeler, 'the one that brings in the money.'

'Doesn't look too shabby.' Ross stepped out of the car and into the sleet.

They walked up the gravel path to the door. A polished brass plaque read, *The Letum Institute. We Welcome All Faiths and None.* Above the door, a symbol had been carved into the sandstone. Wheeler reached up and traced her finger around it. 'The lemniscate.'

Ross glanced at it. 'Figure of eight asleep on its side? Significance?'

'The lemniscate's the symbol for eternity.'

'Right.' Ross rang the bell.

The door was opened by a tall, sinewy man in his mid-thirties. He wore skinny black jeans, a blue T-shirt and a fitted black jacket. Day-old stubble was carefully shaped. A gold earring twinkled from each earlobe. He smiled. 'Can I help you?'

Wheeler spoke: 'DIs Wheeler and Ross.' They flashed their ID. 'I called earlier.'

The man stood back, ushering them inside. 'The police, of course. I'm Ben Ramsey.' He offered a hand. Nails manicured, neat. Wheeler shook it, then she and Ross stomped their boots on the step, dislodging the slush before moving into the large hallway. Wheeler caught her breath – the place was freezing cold.

'I'm afraid the boiler's broken but an engineer's on his way. For now, though, let's go into the library. It'll be more comfortable – at least there's a log fire. Fitting, really, since today's Imbolc.' Ramsey opened the door to a cavernous room. Shelves ran the full length of each wall and were filled with books. At the far side an open fire blazed.

Wheeler felt the heat hit her cheeks. 'Isn't Imbolc the celebration of fire in the pagan calendar?'

'It is, and it's good to celebrate the light and heat midway between the Winter Solstice and the Spring Equinox. And we need it now, especially since the bloody boiler's gone.'

Wheeler saw them immediately and crossed the room. The glass bowl resting on the coffee table was filled with cards. She lifted one and read aloud, '"Follow your own path, for only that way will you find peace."' There was a picture of a sunset. The card was the same type as the one found beside Cameron's body.

Ramsey stood beside her and she caught a hit of aftershave. Fresh, crisp. 'Can I get you something to drink? Some tea or coffee, perhaps?'

'No, thanks,' said Wheeler. 'You know why we're here, Mr Ramsey?'

'Please, call me Ben.'

'A man's body was found in the Tollcross area last night.'

'You mentioned on the phone that there had been an incident. Cameron Craig, that was his name, wasn't it? Dreadful business altogether. I didn't know the young man in question and I'm unfamiliar with the Tollcross area, so I doubt that I'd have anything meaningful to add to your investigation. But you said earlier that he had been homeless, so the best person to speak to regarding this issue would be—'

Ross interrupted: 'We've just come from the unit in Duke Street – we've spoken to Pat Dunbar.'

'That's who I was going to suggest.'

Wheeler held up a card. 'One of these was found close to the body.'

Ramsey paused. 'Is that right?'

'Yes,' said Ross. 'Do you have any idea how it came to be there?'

'None at all.'

'Does it mean that Cameron Craig was here at the Institute?' asked Ross.

'No, Inspector. If your victim was homeless, it's very unlikely that he would ever have come here. Our Duke Street unit operates as a completely separate entity.'

'And the homeless folk never come here?' asked Ross. 'Why not?'

Ramsey sighed. 'Have you ever studied Maslow's Hierarchy of Needs, Inspector Ross?'

'No.'

'Basically it's a pyramid, and the homeless people who attend our Duke Street unit are at the bottom of it, if you like. They are primarily concerned with their biological and physiological needs. That is, they need a safe place to stay and somewhere warm where they can sleep. Perhaps some hot soup and a shower.' Ramsey coughed. 'Whereas at the top of the pyramid there are individuals who are working on self-actualization. This means that the people who attend our lectures here in the West End are more likely to further their self-fulfilment and realize their full potential.'

'Right,' said Ross. 'So the homeless don't want to realize their potential?'

'I didn't say that.'

'Can you tell us how many staff work here?' asked Wheeler.

'It varies. We have volunteers, mainly university students who come to the centre and work through the summer, then move on. The paid staff are myself, our secretary Ms Dodds and a part-time cleaner, who's on holiday at present. We raise funds for the less fortunate but primarily we are here to promote awareness of spirituality.' He gestured around the room. 'This centre is mainly a place to rent out to interested groups.'

'Who are?' asked Ross.

'They include tarot readers, past-life regression therapists, astrologists, shamans and those who work to align the *chakra*s. We welcome scholars of the esoteric and the merely curious. We have weekly meetings and lectures. Some experiential workshops also take place. We offer a vibrant community resource. In fact, I would say that it's world class and open to all.'

'But not to Cameron Craig?' said Ross.

'Of course our centre is open to the homeless but I'm pretty certain that he *wouldn't* rather than *couldn't* have attended our talks. I'm afraid that he just doesn't fit our demographic.'

'Then why was there a card lying next to his body?' asked Wheeler.

'Perhaps one of our volunteers gave it to him. Maybe it was handed out at the soup run. I know that they often take a few cards out with them. I believe that the cards can raise morale and aid positive thinking. Homeless isn't all these people are and, given the right conditions, they have the potential to turn their lives around. The cards may help with this process.'

'Are they left at the centres?' asked Ross.

'We did try to leave some but unfortunately they were used to facilitate rolled-up cigarettes. "Roaches" was the term I think they used.' Ramsey smiled at Wheeler. 'What did the card say? The one found beside Cameron Craig.'

'"What will you create today that will make your tomorrow better?"' said Wheeler.

'I feel great pity for the young man,' said Ramsey. 'What a waste of a life.'

'And you're absolutely sure that you'd never met him?' asked Ross.

'Yes. I'm an academic and very much based here but I appreciate that our staff are pretty overworked. There are many homeless people who find it safer to sleep in the day, maybe in an empty doorway where it's relatively safe, then stay awake at night when it's more dangerous. Some of our clients turn to prostitution as a method of making money. We are not here to judge. Others roam the city at night. Cameron Craig may have leaned towards this method of survival.'

'Method of survival?' repeated Ross. 'But he didn't, though, did he? Survive, that is. Besides, they're homeless people, they're not under siege.'

'That's just where you're wrong, Inspector Ross.' A bitter edge had crept into Ramsey's voice. 'It's about just that. Surviving. If you even wake up in the morning, when you're homeless, it's a good day, but I'd imagine you've never been in that predicament yourself.'

'And I guess you haven't either,' said Ross.

'Okay.' Wheeler kept her voice calm, neutral. 'Mr Ramsey, can you get us a list of the groups who use the Institute?'

Ramsey stood. 'Of course.'

'I would appreciate it,' said Wheeler. When Ramsey left the room she turned to Ross. 'Honestly, Ross, it's not a pissing contest.'

Ross kept his voice low. 'Sorry, but he's a condescending bugger.'

'And you, on the other hand, are perfect?'

Ross shrugged. 'Pretty much.'

'And here's the list,' said Ramsey, coming back into the room.

Wheeler took it. 'Thank you. Do you keep a record of the people who attend the talks? Are they part of a specific group or just interested folk who wander in off the street?'

'People just come along and pay on the door. It's a pretty diverse crowd.' Ramsey gestured to the list. 'I think most of the phone numbers are up to date, but if not, give me a call and I can sort out alternative contacts. But, really, our lecturers are very spiritual people and not the sort of person you're looking for. I can vouch for that.' He sat down next to Wheeler, smiled at her. 'Really, Inspector Wheeler, I do want to help but I haven't anything much to offer.'

Wheeler glanced at the printout. 'Tarot reading, séances to communicate with those who have passed over. And death midwifery? I mean, what's that exactly?'

'When people are ready to cross over to the other side.'

'You mean when they're dying?' asked Ross.

'If you insist on using that phrase, then, yes, when their soul is ready to leave this realm, we help to facilitate this, to rebirth them, if you like. It's about support and spiritual friendship.'

'Is it not all a bit heavy on death?' asked Ross.

'It depends on how you view death, Inspector. If you see it as an end, that's one thing. However, if you view it as part of an ongoing journey, as is symbolized by the lemniscate on the outside of our building, then other worlds open up for us.'

'But "Letum" means death and annihilation,' Wheeler interjected, 'so there's a bit of an ending in it, surely.'

'A continuation, DI Wheeler. The Letum attracts every kind of believer and those who have no beliefs. Those who are searching and those who are merely curious.'

'Like the folk who ask questions of the ouija board,' muttered Ross.

'We no longer use ouija boards. That practice was popular until the seventies, but today we favour direct contact through either mediumship or channelling.'

'You've lost me,' said Wheeler.

'In essence, channelling is when a spirit speaks through a practitioner. Trance is when a spirit enters into them and they speak the words of the spirit guide.'

'Really? And do a lot of people attend these classes?' Ross couldn't hide the sarcasm.

'You'd be surprised. We have ten regular weekly meetings and hundreds of attendees over the year. I myself debate on an academic level, often with academics holding opposing beliefs. The spirituality versus science debate is often very well attended. It's a topical subject and emotions can run high.'

'I'll bet they can,' said Ross.

'I resent your tone, DI Ross, but I'm used to similar. We are often misunderstood. Ignorant people tend to make up their own stories.'

Ross cleared his throat.

Ramsey closed his eyes. 'You have a dog, Inspector Ross, do you not?'

Wheeler answered, 'Yes, he has a pet.' She looked at Ross. 'You have dog hair all over you.'

'A dog that...' Ramsey continued '...give me a moment...there it is, the image, the setting.' He opened his eyes. 'I have it. An old car. What happened? Did someone throw a dog from a car? And then you arrived and took the dog?'

Ross looked at the floor.

'Oh, and one more thing, Inspector Ross, let me see. There something unusual about her – yes, that's it. She has three legs.'

Wheeler looked around the room. 'Tourists, Mr Ramsey?'

'Ben.'

'Ben, I imagine you have lots of tourists?'

'Yes. Our leaflets are available at a few select shops across the city and we also have an online presence. We have quite a large international following who support our work.'

119

Wheeler sighed. 'So this place is wide open?'

'We pride ourselves on it, DI Wheeler, but it doesn't help you with this case. This was such a tragic way to pass over to the other side. Although...' Ramsey paused.

'Although?' prompted Ross.

'Well, it's to do with the belief in reincarnation. I take it you're familiar with the concept?'

Wheeler nodded. Ross listened.

'There's an argument to say that before we reincarnate we agree on a spiritual contract and also how we will die.'

'So if you were to link this to Cameron Craig's death, you could argue that he agreed to be killed?' said Ross.

'In a previous life, perhaps,' said Ramsey.

'To be murdered?' Wheeler asked. 'Just so that we're straight about this.'

'It's an incredibly complex subject, Inspectors, but some of our members believe that, with every birth, we reincarnate as good or evil and that eventually all souls get a chance to experience both the light and the shadow side of ourselves as human beings. Have you any idea what kind of a person you're looking for?'

'Someone who believed that Cameron needed to fulfil his contract?' said Ross.

'That's not what I implied,' said Ramsey. 'It's merely a personal belief that certain individuals hold.'

'Do you have contact details for these particular types of believers?' asked Wheeler.

'No, but there is someone who offered past-life regression and she may be able to help you.' He disappeared into the next room. They heard drawers being opened and closed.

Wheeler turned to Ross. 'What do you think? He was right about the mutt.'

'I think he could read me about the dog, which any decent theatre act could do. But the rest of it gives me the creeps.'

'But if you believed in it, Ross?'

'Do you think Cameron Craig believed in this stuff?'

'No, but whoever killed him might have. What if the killer believed he was put on earth to fulfil Cameron Craig's destiny?'

'Like an avenging angel?'

'Exactly, but a very superior one,' said Wheeler.

'So do you reckon our killer is here at the Letum, hiding behind all this psycho-spiritual malarkey?'

Wheeler held out the list. 'Do you want to have a look at this and maybe broaden your horizons?'

Ross took it, scanned it. Shook his head.

Ramsey returned with a sheet of paper. 'Here we are. Lotus Flower. Will there be anything else?'

Wheeler and Ross rose to leave. 'Thank you, Ben,' said Wheeler. 'You've been very helpful.' They walked into the hall. The door to a smaller room was ajar and a woman sat behind a desk studying cards set out before her. She was in her mid-sixties and her cropped hair was mauve. She wore cherry-red lipstick, and thick blusher coloured her cheeks. Her eyebrows were inked black.

'This is our secretary, Ms Dodds,' said Ramsey.

Dodds looked up. 'I'm doing a spread for the dead boy. If I overheard correctly, there was a card from our organization found close to the deceased.'

'Yes.' Wheeler crossed to the desk and glanced at the cards. 'May I?'

Dodds sat back in her seat. 'You may.'

'I'm DI Wheeler and this is—'

'DI Ross, yes, I overheard you in the next room. I have excellent hearing. I sense that DI Ross is a sceptic.'

Wheeler asked, 'Can you talk me through this reading?'

'It's a spread to ask the spirit guides what happened to Cameron Craig.'

Wheeler leaned forward, pointed to the last card. 'What about this one?'

'That's the Magician, a very important card in the tarot deck. Occultists look at the supernatural as the old ways, an ancient tradition. The cards themselves originated around the thirteenth or fourteenth century. Many people use tarot today as a simple form of divination. It can offer guidance in an otherwise confusing world.'

'To confused people?' said Ross.

'Detective Inspector Ross,' her mouth twisted and curled around his name, 'the people who use the tarot are as sane as you or I and the information from the cards must be deciphered. It is much like a murder inquiry, I'd imagine, when evidence and facts are amassed and you must try to piece events together.'

Ross kept his voice even. 'The cards? In layman's terms, Ms Dodds?'

'In this instance the Magician signifies a person of skill, or perhaps cunning would be more accurate. The killer certainly believes that they are linked to the divine and that they are of a higher intelligence. The position of the card here,' she gestured to the layout, 'indicates their belief that they can and will outwit you.'

'Anything else?' asked Wheeler.

Dodds pointed to three cards grouped together, all

images of swords. 'These suggest a struggle, at first moral but later it will be physical...Yes, rest assured that there will be physical combat. You are in the spread, DI Wheeler. You must be very careful.' Dodds stood and offered her hand. Wheeler shook and felt the damp sweat from the older woman's skin spread like a noxious oil to her own. Ross had pointedly moved to the door, was through it and waiting in the hall. Ramsey held open the door, and on her way out, Wheeler glanced again at the symbol of infinity. She heard the heavy door slam behind her as she headed out into the street.

The weather had changed: the wind had stalled and the sleet had softened to an occasional flurry. Suddenly it was as if the city had relaxed. Wheeler wiped her hand on her coat. 'I thought Ramsey was trying his best and gave us nothing much, but Dodds was a peach. What did you think?'

'She gave me the boak.' Ross reached into his pocket, took out the small container of hand sanitizer, squirted some on both hands before rubbing them together. 'You want some?'

'You're a wuss, Ross – you wouldn't even shake her hand.'

'She was a creepy, crêpy old thing. The whole place made me queasy.'

'You're going to need to channel your inner hippie, Ross, to be any good on this case.'

'Channel my inner chip addiction instead. I'm starved. We could break for lunch?'

'You ever stop thinking about food?'

'Nope. Where suits?'

'Byres Road is close enough. Let's find a café that's not

too busy.' They reached the car just as the wind picked up again. 'I need to make a call.' As Ross drove she opened her mobile, called the number for Lotus Flower, heard it go through to a machine. Wheeler left a message. As they approached a junction they stopped at a red light. She watched the people on the streets battle the weather and saw an old woman trudge through the slush. She was wrapped in a long, filthy greatcoat and her trousers were torn. A frayed woollen scarf was tied tightly around her head. Wheeler watched her shuffle into an alleyway, pick up a discarded bottle and stare at it as if it were gold, before carefully placing it in the shopping trolley beside her and patting it into place. When the light changed, they passed the woman, and Wheeler saw that she wasn't that old, maybe late forties. Behind her was a poster for the referendum: 'We're Better Together.' Wheeler knew that the uniformed police were combing the city, speaking to the homeless and trying to find information about Cameron Craig, but she also knew that they couldn't solve the homeless problem.

Ross pulled into a parking space. 'You okay? You seem quiet?'

Wheeler thought of the homeless woman they had just passed. 'I'm fine.'

'You buying?' asked Ross, locking the car.

'You kidding?' Wheeler strode towards the café, opened the door and felt the warmth of the air envelop her. She made a silent pledge to donate to one of the homeless charities.

Chapter 22

In the East End of the city Boyd drove carefully through the sleet along a deserted Downfield Street. The street had a mixture of housing, some flats, some semi-detached, and four-in-a-block houses. A sheltered complex for the elderly sat on one side of the street. They drove past a small grass area surrounded by iron railings.

'The D,' said Boyd.

'Come again?' said Robertson.

'The bit of greenery, it's in the shape of a D.'

'That right?' Robertson sounded bored and didn't bother to hide it.

'Well, a bit of local information might help. If you knew the area and the people a bit better, it might make a difference.'

'Right, and you know this place?'

'I grew up close to this area,' said Boyd.

'That must be going back a bit,' muttered Robertson.

Boyd took a left into Rattray Street, drove on past the McVitie's factory and pulled up outside a crumbling single-storey building. He killed the engine and glanced up at the structure. The faded sign above the centre read *Street Safe*. 'Well, fuck me, this was up for demolition years back, when it was a methadone clinic. Pretty sure it was on the council's list for the bulldozers.'

The centre was open and they walked into the foyer. 'A right wee fusion of smells going on here,' said Boyd. 'I'd guess stewed coffee, stale sweat and a hit of cleaning fluid. Could be worse, I suppose, given what can go on in these kind of places.'

'Certainly your olfactory sense is in evidence, unlike your manners,' Robertson hissed, 'and, for fucksake, keep your voice down.'

'Christ almighty, Robertson, there's no one in earshot,' said Boyd. 'And that's the first time I've heard you swear. Ever.'

'Get used to it,' said Robertson.

They followed the corridor to a large open-plan room. Long trestle tables had been set up and plates of ham sandwiches put out. Margarine had been scraped over thin slices of white bread before the cheap meat had been added. A group of men sat drinking from chipped mugs and eating the food. A couple were ravenous and crammed the sandwiches into their mouths with filthy fingers, their nails thick with grease. A worker was pouring coffee from a battered metal kettle. He was about six feet six tall and his head, hands and feet were all exceptionally large. His size meant that the kettle he was holding looked like a toy. He put it down and turned to them. 'I heard you lot might be around. ' He wiped a hand on a grimy tea towel before offering it. 'I'm Francis Wright. I volunteer here at Street Safe.'

Robertson and Boyd flashed their ID. Robertson spoke: 'We just wanted to ask you and then maybe some of the clients a few questions about Cameron Craig.'

'Yeah, I heard about it. Awful. Let's take it over here.' Wright walked towards the kitchen, far enough to keep their conversation private but close enough to keep an eye on the men.

Robertson followed him. 'Did you know Cameron Craig, Mr Wright?'

'Not at all, really. He came in now and again for a mug of tea. Some of the guys, they tell you their life stories. Others you see every day for weeks and you don't even know if the name they're using is the real one. But it's their choice.'

'How long have you volunteered here?' asked Robertson.

'I dropped out of university six years ago. Thought I'd take a year off. Never did go back.'

Boyd had wandered over. He nodded to Wright. 'Volunteering with a homeless charity? A good cause and all that?'

'Yeah,' said Wright. 'Just trying to give something back to the community.'

'What were you studying at uni?' asked Boyd.

'Religious studies and philosophy. Why?'

Boyd glanced at Robertson, who ignored him. 'You ever hear of the Letum Institute?'

'Yeah, over in the West End. I've been to a few lectures. It's a very interesting place. I've heard a couple of good debates there.'

'Like what?' asked Boyd.

'Science versus religion, that kind of thing. Scientific fact versus spiritual belief. It's an ongoing debate. A few months back, the guy at the Letum took on a scientist. It was a good night.'

'You know the little cards they give out?' said Robertson.

'Yeah, the wee positive-thinking cards. What about them?'

'How would someone like Cameron come across one?'

'Your guess is as good as mine. I suppose he might have picked it up somewhere or it was given to him. I doubt he'd ever have gone to the Letum. It's pretty academic.

'But it's affiliated with the homeless unit in Duke Street?' said Boyd.

'Yeah, but my understanding is that the Letum headquarters in Hyndland just raise financial support for the homeless unit, kind of like creating good karma.'

'Do you know if Cameron Craig was religious?' asked Robertson.

'Not as far as I knew. He certainly never mentioned anything like that when he was here.'

'You mind if I circulate, maybe ask the clients a few questions about him?' asked Boyd.

'Go right ahead,' said Wright.

Boyd crossed to the men.

'Is there anything you can tell me about Cameron Craig, Mr Wright? Take a moment and think back. Is there anything at all?' asked Robertson.

Wright shook his head. 'Sorry. The guy came and went and kept his head down. He was like most of the others. He didn't say much.'

'Was he popular?' said Robertson.

'With the staff or the other clients?'

'Both.'

'I'm not sure anyone is popular. It's not like these folk are at the top of their game and are even remotely interesting or entertaining. If you're outside and you share your drink then, bloody hell, you're popular but that tends never to happen. Mainly we look after them as a charitable exercise – it's not like we'd ever be best friends. I think the Letum's the same. Charity pure and simple.' Wright paused. 'Wait. I did hear something about Cameron Craig – that he'd been through the system, fostered or something. But so many of our clients, their story becomes fractured. Some of it gets told straight, some of it gets repeated with omissions, while at other times it gets embellished. It's difficult to know where the truth begins and ends. Anyway, I need to get back to work. We finished here?'

Robertson ignored the question. 'You know anyone who would have a grudge against Cameron Craig?'

'Against a homeless guy? I can't think who would – I mean, he's already kind of down on his luck, isn't he? Not much to get jealous of or resentful about, is there?'

'Maybe he had a fall-out with another client?' said Robertson.

'Maybe. But not that I know of,' said Wright. 'Now can I get on?'

This time Robertson nodded.

Outside, they walked to the car.

Across the road, a figure hid in the shadow of a doorway. Fiona Henderson watched Boyd and Robertson climb into the vehicle. When they slammed the doors she put her hands together and clapped in a silent farewell.

Inside the car, Robertson turned to Boyd. 'What was your take on Wright?'

'He gave us nothing. Supercilious git, if you ask me. All that giving something back. I doubt it.'

'What about the men? Did they say anything?'

'Fuck-all,' said Boyd. 'Reckon they can't be arsed helping "the filth", as they referred to us.' He started the engine.

'Great,' said Robertson. 'The staff are dismissive of us and the punters hate us.'

'Happy days,' said Boyd, pulling out into the traffic.

Perched on the hill, the flight of angels was frozen in motion as the weather raged around them. They stood patiently gazing heavenward, keeping eternity in sight. There were more than three thousand monuments in the Victorian cemetery, Celtic crosses, ornate mausoleums and tombs, but they all stood in silence. No tourists came in this weather so they were alone with their God. Almost. Only one man trudged onwards. The collar of Haedyear's filthy coat was pulled up around his face, his woollen hat low over his forehead but his green eyes sparkled with joy. He carried a takeaway coffee and a sandwich. He found a sheltered perch on one of the larger mausoleums, settled himself and ate. Smiled. Haedyear didn't bother to read the name on the tomb. What did it matter? He was already at home with the dead.

Chapter 23

The café was warm, they had finished their soup and the bread basket was empty. Ross continued his tirade: 'I mean, come on, Wheeler, all that stuff about tarot cards and Ramsey saying that folk make contracts before they're born. I mean, he can't really believe it, surely.'

'I think he does,' said Wheeler, 'and I also think there are centres world-wide just like the Letum. My sister lives in Glastonbury and I'm pretty certain the Letum wouldn't be out of place there. As far as reincarnation and the belief in other lives, it's pretty commonplace in certain communities, Ross.'

'Well, I reckon it's a pretty sinister belief to suggest that someone would contract to be murdered. Ramsey believes some weird shit – and don't get me going again on Dodds.'

'But why was a card left beside Cameron Craig?'

'Could be our killer is a member of the Letum group of weirdos,' said Ross.

'True, or it could be someone who hates the Letum and what it stands for or who has a grudge against Ramsey. In which case, planting the card directs us to the Letum and potentially away from our killer.'

'Fair point.'

'We just need to make sure we keep an open mind and not let personal beliefs shape our thinking. Let that happen and we're liable to miss something crucial.'

'Lecture over?'

'I'm not just thinking about you, Ross. What about the rest of the station? They're hardly known for their esoteric inclinations. I just don't want us to make assumptions.'

'You ready for coffee?'

'Have we time before the press conference?' Wheeler glanced at her watch, 'Okay, if we're quick.'

Ross went to the counter and ordered two coffees and two Danish pastries. When he returned he asked, 'Did you believe Ramsey when he said the homeless folk don't go to the HQ?'

'I don't think he was lying. The HQ is primarily to promote esoteric beliefs and engage in spiritual debate. Ramsey said he was part of the whole science versus spirituality argument.'

The coffee and pastries arrived and the waitress unloaded the tray. When she had gone, Ross spoke: 'I think Ramsey's a sanctimonious git who pretends he's one of the good guys.'

'But isn't?'

'No.'

'You reckon he's our killer?' Wheeler sipped her coffee, bit into the pastry. 'You have him down for Cameron Craig's murder?'

'I just didn't believe him.'

'What was his motive?'

Ross sighed. 'None as yet.'

'Okay, let's hold that gut instinct while we find out more. In the meantime, what about the assertion that we're going to have a physical struggle with the killer?' asked Wheeler.

'I think she meant that you would be targeted. I found that odd – that she kind of singled you out.'

'If she was in any way believable,' said Wheeler.

'Which she wasn't,' said Ross.

'Okay, so I'm safe, then. That's a relief.' Wheeler laughed. 'Let's get back to the station. Are you about ready to go?'

Ross pulled on his jacket, went to the counter to pay.

Her mobile rang and she recognized the number: DCI Stewart. She stepped out of the café to answer it. 'Boss?'

'Where are you?'

'Just on our way back to the station.'

'Good. You and Ross will be delivering the press conference, so get yourself up to speed.'

'Is everything okay?'

'Adrianne's condition has deteriorated.' The phone went dead.

Ross caught up with her. 'You all set?'

'We'll need to be. I just took a call from Stewart. His wife's ill so we're talking to the press.'

'Shit. I hope she's okay.'

'Me too,' said Wheeler. 'I think the boss has enough trouble at the station without a personal crisis at home.'

Ross edged the car into the traffic as Wheeler switched on the radio: 'Police are still searching for the killer of nurse Karen Cooper who was murdered outside her home on Monday evening in the Langside area of the city. Police spokesperson Detective Sergeant Mike Barr said earlier today that they are continuing their inquiries and pursuing a number of leads.

'In other news, local MP Andrew Jardine said he was outraged that a killer like Mark Haedyear could have absconded with such apparent ease. Mr Jardine said, "This is a disaster for the community, and to think that the system is so flawed and so unstable that someone like Mark Haedyear could simply walk out of a building unheeded is disgraceful. I will make it a priority to have this incident investigated thoroughly. The public must feel safe in their homes and the police and prison officials have to be seen to be doing their job."

'A leading charity has warned of dire consequences for the homeless community as funding is slashed. Sheila Munroe who works for City Streets UK had this to say: "We are deeply concerned about the dramatic increase in the number of adults and children being registered as homeless. Many centres have been forced to close and this has meant that those who are already vulnerable have been forced to live rough on the streets of Glasgow."

'Another report criticizes the police for their slow response in investigating those reported as missing. A spokesperson for Police Scotland said, "We can confirm that all persons reported missing are entered onto the Police National Computer. However, we are aware that we often receive conflicting information whereby someone is reported missing when in fact they have simply left the area. There is a need for clear communication which we—"'

Ross reached forward and switched it off. 'Christ, it's all good news.'

'I know,' said Wheeler, taking out her mobile. 'Let me just get the update from Boyd and Robertson, see if they got anything about Cameron Craig at Street Safe.'

The phone was answered immediately. 'Boyd, it's me. What did you get at Street Safe?' Wheeler listened for a few minutes, 'Not much, then. Listen, I want you and Robertson to go to the Letum homeless place in Duke Street later on this afternoon. Apparently there's a guy there name of Vincent Steele, nicknamed the Monk. Have a word with him, see what he knows about Cameron Craig. In the meantime, pay a visit to the Rayner place in Salamanca Street – the manager's a guy called Malcolm Reek. See if you can get hold of him and call me if there are any concrete leads.'

Chapter 24

'Cadaver in a crate,' whispered Daniel Jones, a skinny young reporter with fierce acne.

'Body in a bin,' said Toby Smith, who had visible sweat stains around each armpit.

'Corpse in a coffin,' said Jones.

'Stiff in a sarcophagus,' retorted Smith.

'Carcass in a casket,' sniggered Jones, his voice low. 'I'm on a roll. I win this round.'

The room was full of press but the two rookie reporters sat in the front row, killing time by discussing headlines that they would like to have written, if they'd ever had a headline they could have called their own. In an attempt to cover his acne, Jones had tried for the popular heavy-bearded look, but his follicles had let him down badly and stray wisps of hair clung in an abject fashion to his spotty chin. Smith, on the other hand, was flaccid of body and mind and favoured such a low-maintenance approach to personal hygiene that no female had ever troubled to accept his suggestion of a date.

Graham Reaper sat behind them and ignored them. Instead, he thought about his next pint of heavy and drew his tongue over parched lips. He tapped his pen on his notebook and watched while cameras were set up and microphones placed on the table at the front of the stage. He had expected to see DCI Stewart stride into the room but instead saw DIs Wheeler and Ross walk onto the stage and settle themselves behind the table. Saw them take a moment before they began the conference.

DI Wheeler spoke: 'Thank you for attending today. We are appealing for information about a murder that occurred yesterday evening in the Tollcross area of the city. The body of a young man, Cameron Craig, aged twenty-two, was discovered in an alleyway off Tollcross Road around eight p.m. This was a particularly brutal murder and we are appealing for any witnesses who were in the vicinity of the junction of Tollcross Road, Wellshot Road and Braidfauld Street between six and eight p.m. to come forward if they saw or heard anyone acting suspiciously. I would emphasize again that this was a cold-blooded murder and the victim was a vulnerable member of society.'

Wheeler stared at the audience. 'Any questions?'

Jones asked: 'Is this murder linked to Mark Haedyear's escape? I mean, now we have a known killer on the loose.'

'At this point in the investigation we are keeping an open mind,' said Wheeler.

'Was there anything from CCTV coverage?' Reaper was pretty sure there hadn't been or he would have heard about it. Still, it did no harm to ask.

'At present we're still collating CCTV footage from a number of establishments,' said Wheeler.

'Is quality an issue, DI Wheeler, due to weather conditions?' asked Reaper. 'The weather last night was abysmal.'

'Aye. Thundersnow. I could hardly see my hand in front of me, never mind trying to pick anything up on CCTV,' another reporter muttered.

'As I said, we're still collating CCTV,' said Wheeler. 'Anything else?'

'Was Cameron Craig going towards the city centre or coming away from it?' asked Smith.

'At present we don't know which way the victim was travelling,' said Wheeler, 'If he was indeed travelling.'

'And he was sleeping rough?' asked Jones.

'Yes, we believe the victim was homeless and was sleeping rough in the area,' said Wheeler.

'Apart from Cameron Craig being homeless, what else do you know about him?' asked a reporter from the back of the room.

'At this stage very little, which is why we are appealing to the public for information.' Wheeler faced the cameras. 'If you know anything at all, regardless of how unimportant you might feel it to be, call the station immediately. All calls are completely confidential.'

'Do you have any idea who you are looking for?' asked Smith.

'This was a heinous crime. This callous killer murdered a vulnerable member of society in cold blood,' said Wheeler, 'so we know that he or she is an extremely dangerous individual and we appeal to the community to contact us if they have any information at all.'

Reaper watched while Wheeler fielded a few stupid questions from the rookie reporters, then ended the press conference. He watched her and Ross leave the room and knew not only from what Wheeler had said but by her tone that the police had nothing and that the conference had been called solely to appeal for information. Reaper's contact had already pretty much told him that. Well, if the police had nothing to share, he knew of someone who had. Reaper stood and made his way to the door. He checked his watch. There was time for a pint. Just the one, he promised himself. Aye, mibbe.

Chapter 25

Despite Christmas and New Year being over, a number of venues around Glasgow's city centre had strung bands of fairy lights above walkways to create glittering corridors of light in contrast to the grey January weather. Outside the Gallery of Modern Art the statue of the Duke of Wellington wore a jaunty orange traffic cone on his head, as did his horse. Shoppers surged around it and walked beneath the corridors of light towards Royal Exchange Square, Buchanan Street, Argyle and Sauchiehall Streets and into the warmth provided by the many shops, cafés, restaurants and bars.

Six miles east of the corridors of light, the forest was silent as sleet fell over the naked trees, their bare branches reaching heavenward. Five woodlands spread out to make up the forest and the forest floor was frozen, hard and silent. But underground there was movement and life. The badger sett had tunnels, which wove their way to secret chambers. It was a safe place for the badgers to live and no one disturbed them. It was too remote. Too inhospitable.

Stella inhaled deeply and absorbed the scent of earth, vegetation and animal shit. There wasn't much oxygen, but there was enough for her to breathe. Then the nausea kicked in and flashes of light behind her eyes exploded like little bombs. Her skull felt as if it was cracked. The pain made her want to vomit. Instead she used her tongue to dislodge the soil that had wormed its way into her mouth. She pushed the particles out little by little until she could breathe with less pain. She gave herself time to get accustomed to the semi-darkness. She made herself focus on the one tiny pillar of light, the air-hole. She told herself that she needed to think clearly. She reached a hand in front of her and tentatively felt around the box. There was a plastic water bottle, but it was small. She wondered if that meant he would be returning for her soon or . . .? She stopped there, wouldn't let her mind go to that place. She closed her eyes, breathed deeply, calmed herself. She had never prayed before in her life and she sure as fuck wasn't going to start now. She listened and heard the muffled sounds of birdsong. Stella opened her mouth and tried to scream but her bruised throat contracted and instead she made a weak hacking noise. She reached up and pressed on the ceiling of the box, felt the roughness of the wood. A film of soil drifted into her eyes, her nostrils and her mouth. She coughed for a few seconds before she began again to heave and batter against the wood until her fingers bled. She rested for a few minutes, then began again.

Above her the forest was silent and a film of sleet shrouded the ground. There was nothing to let anyone know that Stella was there. Nothing at all.

Chapter 26

Boyd turned the car into Salamanca Street and pulled into the last remaining parking space. Looked up at the building. 'Christ, is that it?'

Robertson ignored him.

They parked and walked to the hostel. Boyd glanced at the front door and the wire mesh around the windows. 'Both reinforced,' he said. 'Not very inviting, but never mind. The wee plaque says *Welcome to the Rayner Association*, so it's a welcome of sorts.' He rang the bell. Nothing. 'Probably busted,' he said. He hammered on the door, rattling it in its frame. Still nothing. 'Christ, you wouldn't want to be desperate.' He hammered again. Eventually they heard a bolt being slid back, then another, and the door creaked open.

A solid-built woman in a checked shirt and jeans stared at them. 'We're not open. Did you not read the sign?' She nodded to an A4 sheet, which gave the opening hours.

'We're not clients, we're CID,' said Boyd, flashing his card.

'Aye, very good, and I told you. Read the sign. We're not open yet.'

She made to close the door. Boyd stepped forward, put

his foot in the doorway. 'I understand that you're busy but we need to have a chat. Now, if you don't mind. Right now.'

The woman sighed but dragged the door open and stood aside to let them in. 'Please yourself but you'll have to talk while I'm working – the beds aren't going to make themselves.' She turned away, walked past an unmanned reception desk and through into an empty assessment area. Boyd and Robertson followed her.

'And you are?' asked Boyd.

'Vicky Clark.'

'You work here full-time?'

'Part-time, for my sins.' The woman already sounded bored.

'We'd like to speak with the manager, Malcolm Reek,' said Robertson.

'Reek's finished for the day, but I've got his mobile number here, if you like?'

'Please,' said Robertson.

'Here.' Clark reached into the pocket of her jeans, retrieved a crumpled business card and handed it to Robertson. 'His mobile's on that. If he's not answering, leave a message and he'll get back to you.'

'We're investigating a death, the murder of Cameron Craig,' said Boyd.

'I heard about that,' said Clark. 'Go on.'

'Did you know him?' asked Boyd.

'Not really. I met him a few times. He came and went but it's been months since I saw him. Sorry, I can't really help you. Maybe try Reek. He's got a better memory for faces than I have. '

'Is there anything you can tell us?' Boyd tried but failed to keep the frustration out of his voice.

143

Clark picked up on it. Frowned at him. Didn't trouble to keep the sarcasm out of her tone: 'See, son, as far as I'm concerned, there are three different levels of homeless. One, two and three. Cameron Craig was number three. Number one, there's your accidental or unintentional, the folk who've been evicted or kicked out of their house.' Her eyes flashed anger. 'You understand me?'

Boyd got the tone, studied the floor. 'Go on,' he said.

'These are the folk waiting to be rehoused in temporary or supported accommodation. You get it?'

'We do,' said Robertson.

'Number two, there are folk who can't hold down a flat, can't fathom how to budget for rent, electricity or gas. Having to sort out their council-tax bill would send them into fucking free fall. They need a load of support if they're ever going to survive in a flat. And they don't even know if they want to be there. They feel claustrophobic and are paranoid because of the neighbours. A lot of them have mental-health issues so they feel they stick out like a sore thumb. They think the neighbours talk about them and, to be honest, they're right. They're talked about, pointed at, muttered or shouted at, and it's a nightmare for them.'

'And?' asked Boyd.

'Number three are the rest, the ones who sleep rough. They don't want to be in a hostel or in a flat. They're the folk we might want to reach out to but we can't get through to them. The folk we pass by when they're curled up in a shop doorway, in a scummy blanket, freezing cold but who insist on taking their chances out on the street. They want to live outside. If you ask me, Cameron Craig was like that. So, no, I can't tell you much about him or any of them because it's their business and I respect that.

Then you come in here and want me to tell you his life story. Well, like most of the folk who come and go here, I just don't know the story. Okay?'

'Any idea why he would want to live on the street?' asked Robertson.

'None. I never asked him and he never said. It's a free country, son. It was his choice.'

'If you had to guess?' Robertson persisted.

'If I had to guess, I'd think that he didn't trust people and, to be honest, given what happened to him, he was right not to. And before you ask, I've no idea who might have done this.' Clark shook her head. 'But whoever it was needs shot. Now is that it?'

'Can you tell us who else works here?' asked Boyd.

'Me, Malcolm Reek, and a lassie called Lynne Allen volunteers. There's a few other volunteers. I don't know them but Reek will have all their details. Now, you mind if I get on? You boys let yourselves out. You know the way.'

Chapter 27

'We're already running late.' Wheeler shut down her computer and grabbed her bag and coat. 'Right. Let's get off to the post-mortem. See if Matt Elliot can tell us any more than we already know.'

Five minutes later they were heading to the Southside, to the new mortuary at the Southern General Hospital complex. Wheeler recognized it the moment it began: the familiar sound of Ross whining.

'I'm just saying that it used to be a lot easier when it was more central.'

'I take it, Ross, that you're complaining about the city mortuary being moved across to the Southern General?'

'When it was central it was easier to access,' said Ross. 'Now it's bloody miles from anywhere.'

'Anywhere being the city centre or the West End?' said Wheeler.

'I'm just saying, it's miles away,' said Ross, as he drove along the M8 towards the Clyde tunnel.

'And getting back to the case in hand, uniform finally located Cameron Craig's parents,' said Wheeler.

'And how did they take it?'

'They didn't want to know. Told uniform that they put

their son up for adoption when he was four years old. They said they made a detailed statement at the time, instructing social services that they wanted no further contact with Cameron.'

'And now he's dead they still don't want to know?'

'Apparently the father became irate and demanded that his wishes be respected. He was adamant that Cameron Craig had nothing to do with them.'

'Charming,' said Ross. 'What a pair to have as parents.'

'Their son got murdered and they don't want to be bothered with the inconvenience,' said Wheeler. 'Apparently the father finished the conversation by saying that his son was better off dead.'

'What a fucking awful attitude. How can they even live with themselves?' said Ross.

'Agreed,' said Wheeler.

'Please tell me they don't have other kids.'

'They have two girls, both much younger than Cameron. Whatever the litmus test was, the girls passed it. Only Cameron failed.'

'I'm guessing the girls don't know about Cameron's existence?'

'You're dead right,' said Wheeler. 'Mr and Mrs Craig were adamant that their daughters would not find out about their brother. They said that the matter was now closed.'

'End of,' said Ross. 'As far as Mr and Mrs Craig are concerned.'

'End of,' repeated Wheeler.

'Nightmare.' Ross drove on and followed the signs for the Southern General. He turned into Govan Road, then into the hospital complex.

'We're late,' said Wheeler.

'You said already,' said Ross. 'I don't mind if we miss a bit. It's not my favourite aspect of police work.'

They sprinted towards the door.

'You're not going to complain about the sound of the wee saw, are you?' said Wheeler.

'The Stryker saw? It makes that shitty noise.' He opened the door for her. 'I can't stand the vicious wee thing.'

'Ah, diddums,' she cooed, walking into the cool corridor. 'You need me to hold your hand?'

Ross paused to contemplate the offer. 'Well, if you could, Wheeler? I mean, I'd definitely find it reassuring. Shall we just see how it goes?'

Wheeler wasn't sure if he found the hard slap to his arm comforting since 'Ouch, bloody hell, that hurt,' was all the feedback she had to go on.

Inside the mortuary, Matt Elliot was waiting for them. The lab technicians stood behind him and the place had an air of solemnity, which was perfectly fitting, except that when Callum Fraser had performed the post-mortems, the atmosphere, despite the work involved, had been more cheerful. More workaday, thought Wheeler, if there was such a way to describe what happened in a mortuary. She took her place beside Ross. She knew that, as with every suspicious death or murder, the investigation would be far more detailed and therefore take longer than usual. Everything would need to be photographed, recorded and measured. Blood and organ samples would be collected for testing. Every tiny detail would be set down, and by the end of the process they might have some real insight into what had happened to Cameron Craig. And, if they were very lucky, some trace of DNA, which would eventually lead them to the killer.

While Elliot continued his preparations, Wheeler noted the gleam of the pristine tiles, the shine on the stainless-steel table on which Cameron Craig's body rested. It had been specially designed to accommodate the drainage of blood. She glanced at Ross and saw that he was concentrating on the floor.

Finally they were ready to begin.

Matt Elliot cleared his throat, spoke loudly and enunciated clearly enough for the microphone to pick up his exact words. He recorded both the time and the date before he went on to name those present. Then he moved towards the body and named the victim. He recorded Cameron Craig's age, his height and weight.

Wheeler listened while Elliot described the victim's clothing. She recognized the cheap T-shirt, jeans and denim jacket from the crime scene. Elliot recorded that the victim wore no jewellery before he carefully removed Cameron Craig's clothing and passed it to the technicians to be bagged and labelled. Finally the naked corpse was exposed under the harsh lights. Elliot noted in detail the pattern of bruises around the victim's neck and stood back to allow the photographer to record them. When he had finished, Elliot lifted the victim's right hand and Wheeler stepped forward. 'Are those the defence wounds you mentioned at the crime scene?'

'Yes, DI Wheeler, they are. See here? The two fingernails on his right hand are broken and his hand is bruised. The killer overpowered him but the victim may yet provide some helpful details for us.' Elliot carefully scraped the particles from underneath each of Cameron Craig's fingernails. The particles were bagged and labelled. Then

Elliot clipped all of the fingernails and deposited the result, with the disposable nail clipper, in another bag and sealed it. He waited while it was labelled before he continued with the examination. Carefully and methodically he worked his way around the body and continued his assessment of the victim. Finally he turned to Wheeler and asked, 'Did you know that Cameron Craig was intersex?'

'No,' said Wheeler. 'I did not.'

Ross cleared his throat. 'Intersex? Dr Elliot, can you update me?'

'Individuals whose biological sex cannot be categorized as explicitly female or male,' said Elliot. 'Biologically, an intersex person may also have aspects of both sexes, which is what we see here…but in some cases the individual may lack certain attributes with which to be clearly defined.'

'How common is this?' asked Ross.

'At a very rough guess, around one in every two thousand of us is born intersex.'

'Quite a significant number,' said Ross.

'It's not that unusual,' said Elliot.

'Significance in Cameron's death?' asked Ross.

'Too early to call,' said Wheeler. She heard a siren wail as an ambulance shrieked its way towards the hospital before abruptly dying. She looked at Elliot. 'Anything else?'

'There are ruptures, tears and abrasions around the anus,' said Elliot.

'Can you tell if it was consensual or…otherwise?' asked Ross.

'If you are asking if he was raped on the night of his

death, then I can tell you that he wasn't. These tears are maybe two or three weeks old.'

'It's been suggested that the victim had been working as a prostitute,' said Ross.

Elliot continued his inspection. 'It's certainly a possibility.'

With the help of the lab technicians, Elliot continued to work. Eventually he stood back and gestured to Wheeler and Ross. 'This area at the back of the neck has been shaved.'

Wheeler and Ross leaned in and saw that a line of hair had been taken from the back of Cameron Craig's neck.

'Some kind of a sign or a trophy?' said Ross.

'Could be,' agreed Wheeler, 'but why shave his neck?'

'A way of marking his victim?' suggested Ross.

'Either way, let's keep this detail out of the press.' She turned to Elliot. 'We'll leave it here.'

'Sure,' said Elliot. 'If anything else turns up, I'll call.'

They left the building and walked through the sleet to the car.

'You think the victim being intersex was connected to his death?' asked Ross.

'Too early to call. It's another piece of the jigsaw,' said Wheeler. 'Let's keep digging.'

Chapter 28

At the Letum headquarters in Hyndland, bright security lights illuminated the manicured gardens and lit up the red sandstone townhouse. Inside, a blue chandelier twinkled and reflected the light from the myriad candles dotted around the room. In the centre of the room was a heavy oak table. A large ceramic oil burner had been filled with vetivert oil and the powerful musky scent infused the air. Ms Dodds sat opposite Richard Henderson. Dodds had her eyes closed, her lipsticked mouth set in a thin slash of concentration. Her mauve hair was black in the candlelight. As usual her cheeks were rouged and her eyebrows inked black. She looked like a sleeping antique doll until her mouth began to twitch. Finally she spoke: 'Mr Henderson, you are a valued member of the Letum family. Please begin.'

Henderson's words were rushed and ran together. 'You see, I'm desperate – and I'm fearful that my daughter Belle will go to the police. I don't know what to do – Fiona's still missing and...' he swallowed hard, then began again, his voice thin with fear '...the man who murdered her mother has escaped – and I'm scared that he'll...'

'And a boy, Cameron Craig, was murdered,' said Dodds. 'The police have already been here.'

'Have they?' asked Henderson. 'Why?'

'One of our cards was found close to his body,' said Dodds.

'Did you know him?' asked Henderson.

'No. At least, not on the physical realm, but we are all interconnected on the spiritual realm and I asked the spirits about him.'

'And what did they tell you?'

'They gave me information pertaining to the boy and his death but it is not for this reading. If we communicate with the spirits about Cameron Craig in this reading it will contaminate the questions you are asking. You need to hold clear boundaries with the spirits.' Dodds opened her eyes and peered at Henderson. 'You must choose. Do you require information about your daughter? Or Cameron Craig? Decide what it is you want, Mr Henderson.'

'I need to know about my daughter, Fiona, where she is,' said Henderson, 'and what has happened to her.'

Dodds reached forward, picked up the tarot deck, expertly shuffled the cards and then began to lay them out in a five-card spread. Henderson began to speak but she shushed him. 'You have said enough. You must let the spirits speak.' Slowly she turned over the first card. 'The Tower, which means change and upheaval. Old players are now leaving the stage and new players are arriving. There will be upset and violence.'

Henderson shuddered.

'But I also see that there is deceit here.'

'Deceit?' asked Henderson. 'What kind of deceit?'

Dodds turned over the second card. 'Again it is a card from the major arcadia, the Devil. He commands loyalty and servitude. This is a symbol of a forceful connection.' Dodds sighed. 'But yet again I see deceit. Mr Henderson, you are asking the spirits for clarity, but someone in this tale is lying. May I ask you, who might that be?'

Henderson studied his hands. 'Fiona lies. She uses false names and makes up stories to cover her tracks. It's part of who she became after her mother was killed.'

'Very well.' Dodds turned over the third card. 'The Hanged Man. Someone has had a change of heart and this is life-changing for them. Someone in this spread has changed allegiance. Does this have meaning for you, Mr Henderson?'

Henderson shook his head. 'No.'

'Then I will proceed,' said Dodds. She turned over the fourth card. 'It is the eight of swords, which means that a crisis is rapidly approaching.'

'Oh, my, please don't let—'

'Ssh.' Dodds pressed a forefinger to her cherry lips. 'You have had your chance and now the cards will speak . Ask them one question and one question only. In your mind, focus on that question. Then wait and the cards will answer.'

Henderson closed his eyes. 'Where is Fiona?'

Dodds paused before she turned over the final card. 'The Magician,' she said.

Henderson shifted in his chair.

'So, Mr Henderson, we now have deceit and violence and crisis.' Dodds closed her eyes, recited a short incantation and waited, as if listening for direction. A minute passed. She opened her eyes again. She shuffled the cards for a few seconds, then carefully, reverentially, set out a three-card spread. She turned them over and studied them. They were all swords.

Henderson looked at the spread, blinked.

'The cards are not ready to offer up Fiona's location,' said Dodds.

'Can you ask them again?' Henderson pleaded.

'There's no point, Mr Henderson. They have spoken.'

'Can you tell me if she's safe?'

Dodds stared at the cards and reached out to touch each one in turn.

'What are they saying?' whispered Henderson.

Dodds spoke: 'Fiona is surrounded by blood.'

'Where?' asked Henderson.

'The cards will not give up her location because she does not want to be found.'

'I don't believe you,' said Henderson.

'But there is something that the cards will reveal, Mr Henderson,' said Dodds.

'What?'

'They ask a question.'

'Go on.'

'You have asked me to interpret the cards and you have allowed me to invoke the spirits to help you find your daughter. Is this not true?'

'Yes,' said Henderson.

'And as a member of the Letum Institute, Mr Henderson, you have asked me to do this in good faith?'

'Yes,' said Henderson.

The candle on the table flickered, the wick almost extinguished. A pool of wax melted into a crescent. Finally the light died. Dodds stared at Henderson. 'Then something is not quite right, Mr Henderson.'

'I don't understand,' said Henderson.

'Fiona Henderson is not your daughter.'

Chapter 29

In the CID suite at Carmyle police station, Wheeler and Ross were preparing to leave. They had shut down their computers and were sorting through piles of paperwork. Boyd was typing up his reports.

'So, discovering that Cameron Craig was intersex,' said Wheeler, neatly filing papers in her in, out and pending trays, 'has been our biggest development in the case today.'

'Agreed,' said Ross, stuffing everything into his pending tray.

'You think it's linked to his death?'

'I don't know. Do you reckon he was targeted because of it?'

'Could be a punter discovered he was intersex and wasn't pleased,' said Boyd. 'There are all sorts of nutters out there, just looking for a reason. Any reason, no matter how random, and they snap.'

'Then you think it was random, not premeditated?' asked Ross.

'Could be. We're not picking up any signals from the homeless community to say that Cameron was in any danger,' said Boyd.

'Pat Dunbar at the Letum in Duke Street didn't have a good word to say about Cameron,' said Ross.

'I think that was just a personality clash. He sounded protective of the girl Cameron mentioned, who's got to be Fiona Henderson. Dunbar thought Cameron was looking for an angle to manipulate her. I don't have Dunbar down for a killer but he linked Cameron with Fiona. We need to have a word with her.'

'Except that she's given specific instructions that she won't communicate with the police,' said Ross.

'Then we'll need to be careful, but we still need to speak to her. She may have been one of the last people to see Cameron Craig alive. She could have vital information.'

'You think the killer will go after her?' asked Boyd.

'We need to find her first,' said Wheeler. 'Despite orders from the boss, I want you to keep an eye out for her. Make discreet but thorough enquiries.'

'And if it backfires with her family?' said Ross.

'I'll deal with that when and if it happens,' said Wheeler, pulling on her coat. 'It's been a long day. Let's take some time off and regroup in the morning. Ross, you need to recover from your ordeal at the post-mortem. Take it easy tonight.'

'Very funny, Wheeler. I coped with it fine, and despite what I think of Matt Elliot, I reckon he's pretty good at his job.'

'You don't care for our stand-in pathologist?' asked Wheeler.

'As a human being, not so much. He's a bit up his own arse for my liking.'

'Is that because you're perfect?' said Wheeler. 'Is it really difficult to deal with us mere mortals?'

'Being perfect is an affliction, Wheeler, what with having such high standards and all that.'

'If you ask me, it's only one of your many afflictions,' said Wheeler. They walked through the door, heard it bang behind them.

Downstairs, Tommy Cunningham was dunking a digestive biscuit in his tea and stated the obvious: 'Weather's filthy out.'

'Night, TC,' said Wheeler.

'Night, Wheeler.'

Ross walked on.

Outside in the sleet Wheeler's hair began to dampen. She flicked it back and strode to her car.

Ross was at her side. 'Fancy a drink?'

'You're out of luck there, Ross. I'm on my way to the GFT.' She mimicked an American drawl: 'And tonight at the renowned Glasgow Film Theatre, there will be a special showing of *The Jazz Baroness* featuring the musical genius Thelonious Monk. You want to come with me, there's a bar and we could get a drink there after the film. My treat.'

He shook his head. 'You're all right.'

She glanced at him. 'You okay?'

He was silent for a few seconds before he spoke. 'Sarah miscarried.'

'Christ, Ross, when did you find out?'

'She called just after the press conference.'

'Shouldn't you be with her?'

'I offered, but she doesn't want to see me just yet. Her mother and sisters are with her. '

'I'm sorry.'

'It's okay.'

'It's not okay.'

'I'm fine.'

She squinted at him through the sleet. 'Where's best for that drink?'

'What about your arty-farty thing? *The Jazz Baroness*?'

'It's on all week,' she lied. 'So where are we headed?'

He stood, staring at the ground again, letting the sleet soak his hair. Wheeler thought he looked as if he was about to cry. She reached out to him and punched him hard on the arm. 'Christ, pull yourself together, Ross. Now, what about that drink? Would the Kelvin Bistro suit you? You hungry? Stupid question. You're a bloody gannet.' She peered at him, six two and gym-honed muscle. There was a trace of a smile. He was coming round a bit. 'Sometimes I could kill you with my bare hands.'

'With your bare hands, Wheeler? That's quite intimate, really. In fact, that may be the most romantic thing you've said to me yet. And the Kelvin sounds good. You go home and dump your car and I'll meet you there.'

She slammed the car door and started the engine.

Forty-five minutes later Ross was at the bar and had ordered a bottle of Chardonnay.

'Are you having food?' asked the barman.

'Yeah, said Ross, 'but in the meantime we'll have a bowl of nuts.'

A few minutes later, Wheeler had poured two large glasses from the chilled bottle and sat back, sipping her wine and watching him. 'So, go on then, talk. How's Sarah?'

'She's resigned. The pregnancy wasn't planned, but you knew that anyway.'

'How about you?'

'Relieved, to be honest.' He picked up a peanut and chewed it thoughtfully. Reached for another, took two.

'You two going to give it another go?' Wheeler started on the nuts, taking a handful and chomping them while waiting for him to answer. She knew better than to get involved. She'd only met Sarah once and they hadn't bonded.

'Not on my part but she wants us to try again.'

'Because?'

'I don't know why. Maybe she feels that if we were okay to have a child together there's a chance we can work it out.'

'What do you want, Ross?'

'For me it was over before she even got pregnant. We were never suited. We'd split up before she found out about the baby, remember?'

'Yep.'

'The thing is – I mean, it sounds odd but I was kind of getting used to the thought of being a dad, and now all that's gone, it feels weird. I got a bit emotionally hooked into being a father.'

'Not so much. Contrary to popular belief at the station, Ross, I know that you have emotions.'

'Anyway, it's over and I just want to move on. There's no point in getting back with Sarah.'

'You sure?'

'Positive.'

'And you and Laura Mearns are just good friends?'

'Yes.'

'Does that mean you're footloose?'

'Incredible to believe, I know, but it certainly looks that way.'

A waitress approached and unloaded a tray: small plates containing roasted garlic and cheese baguettes, thick tortilla, potatoes in a fragrant tomato sauce and bowls of green and black olives glistening with oil.

Ross reached over and started on the potatoes. After a couple of mouthfuls he spoke: 'So, enough of my love life or lack of it. What about you?'

'What about me?'

'You dating?'

'Is it any of your business?'

'What about Matt Elliot?'

'He seems like a nice guy.'

'So what is it about him that you like so much? asked Ross.

'I didn't say I liked him.'

'But you do. I can tell. Is it his unusual eye colour? What was it – violet?' said Ross. 'Or the tall, rangy good looks? Maybe it's the whole arty-farty stuff.'

'This wine's gone to your head, Ross, and you're making even less sense than usual, which I've got to say is quite an achievement.'

'Laura was pretty impressed with his work in the mortuary and the fact that he's a photographer.'

'He's a good pathologist, you said so yourself, and as for the photography, well, it's wise to keep a balance. '

'Did you hear the jazz from his car as he drove off?'

'I didn't notice,' she lied.

'I think he was trying to impress you.'

Wheeler poured two more glasses and looked at the empty bottle. Shook her head. Tutted. 'This place is roasting hot. I think maybe the wine's evaporated.'

Ross got the hint. 'I'll order another. You want more food?'

She looked at the almost empty plates. 'They're awfully small portions. Maybe a couple more. Just to keep you company. The waitress has disappeared, though.'

'Aye, right,' he muttered, making his way to the bar. 'So I'll go and queue again.'

Wheeler sipped her wine and thought about the film. It would have started at the GFT. Thelonious Monk was one of her favourites and to sit in the dark in the cinema and inhabit his world was to have been a gift to herself, to balance the violence she saw in her job. She wondered fleetingly if Matt Elliot would be there – he was certainly trying to balance his scientific work with the creativity of his photography. And he had been playing Thelonious Monk's 'Bolivar Blues' when he'd driven away from the crime scene. She watched Ross chat to a girl at the bar, saw the colour rise in her cheeks as she held eye contact. Ross looked like he was flirting. Wheeler decided that it had been worth missing the film if it had helped him to pull himself together.

She looked around. The bistro had a photography exhibition entitled Rain. It was mainly black-and-white photographs on the theme. An abandoned carousel, the gaudy horses stationery in the rain; a willow tree dipping its branches into a rising stream, the banks bursting; tents at a flooded music festival, caked with mud. An information sheet told her that all the prints were available to buy.

Ross returned to their table, put down the bottle of wine. 'I've ordered a couple of pizza slices and a bowl of fritters. Okay?'

'I saw you flirting.'

'You were watching?'

163

'The whole place was watching,' she lied. 'You're a tart, Ross, you do know that, don't you?'

'You jealous?'

She choked on her wine. 'In your dreams, sunshine.' She saw the girl at the bar glance over at Ross and saw him pretend not to notice. She was glad he was okay.

When the food arrived, they ate.

'What's your take on Cameron Craig's neck being shaved?' asked Wheeler.

'Some kind of weird remembrance token or a trophy?'

'But trophies are usually more specific,' said Wheeler.

'Not always. They can be fragments of the victim.'

'To prolong the death,' said Wheeler.

'To remind the killer of his success,' said Ross.

'Shaved hair is very intimate,' said Wheeler.

'But so is killing someone,' said Ross.

It was almost midnight when Ross flagged down a taxi and insisted that he dropped her home, despite it being out of his way. 'I don't want you marauding around accosting single men.' Wheeler ignored him and settled herself into the warmth of the taxi. Ten minutes later he dropped her at Brunswick Street in the Merchant City and Wheeler pressed the remote control that opened the heavy wrought-iron gates which led to the courtyard garden. The worn copper tubs shone in the moonlight, hugging their contents of evergreens and ivy. She stood for a second and looked at her neighbourhood. Like much of Glasgow, it was halfway towards gentrification. Designer shops sat beside derelict buildings, and the well-heeled citizens of the Merchant City shared the same pavements as the hooligans and delinquents. Across the road the

Italian restaurant was closing and the staff were clearing up after the evening's service. Damiano Abate, the manager, peered out through the large window and waved across to her. Wheeler waved back before the gates closed behind her.

Inside her flat, she crossed to the CD player and pulled out Sonny Rollins's *Saxophone Colossus*. Her favourite, 'St Thomas', was the first track. She lowered the volume, went through to the kitchen and made coffee. She sat on her sofa, listened to the music and stared at the framed prints she loved. Fergusson's *Torse de Femme*, *Pink Parasol*, *The Orange Blind*, *Reflections*. Wheeler loved living alone in her Spartan flat. She'd left the army with everything she'd owned in one rucksack, and that was her philosophy. Live lightly. She felt the same about relationships: nothing too heavy suited her; she had no need for complications. Besides, that way it was easier to move on. Outside her window, sleet fell over the city, the moon shone weakly and the street-lights threaded through Glasgow like fairy garlands, glittering bright in the cold, dark night.

In the West End, Ross paid the taxi driver and walked to his flat. He felt the sleet on his face. He wanted to go to bed. He wanted to curl up in the warmth and dream of anything except the loss of a child he'd never wanted in the first place. He'd forced himself to flirt tonight, had known Wheeler was watching. Didn't want her to think he had gone soft. Now all he needed was sleep. But he knew there was no chance. And he was right. Once he opened the door, she was there, hurtling across the hallway, the lead already in her mouth. She whimpered softly as her three legs carried her towards him, like a small, robust bull. She hit him like a tornado. He felt the beat of her tail against his leg, her sturdy body wriggling against him. Ross bent down, fixed the lead to her collar and closed the door softly behind them. It would be an hour before he was in bed. And by then he would be freezing cold, battered by the wind and wet from the sleet. She on the other hand would be delighted that he was home and would curl her damp torso into his back as he slept, her three feet twitching, snoring quietly and dreaming her dog dreams.

Chapter 30

Fiona trudged through the sleet. Ahead of her was a row of shops. The pawnbroker's window was heavily shuttered but visible behind the metal latticework. The electronic clock leered into the night: 00:45. As the sleet fell around her, Fiona stood motionless, letting it course down her back and crawl under her coat, leaving her sweatshirt a sodden, useless mess. Water pooled in her shoes and gathered in the hemline of her jeans, binding the denim fabric to her legs. Mummifying her. Fiona smiled. She studied the scene before her and made for the pawnbroker's. She squelched into the doorway, crouched against the door and curled up, her shoulders hard against the metal grille. She wrapped her coat tight around her and sat very still. Then quietly, insistently, she began to rock backwards and forwards.

Across from Fiona a man paused in the shadows. He watched her for a second, then stepped into the deserted road, his long legs covering the distance quickly. He towered over her, his bulk obliterating the street-lights. He saw her hands twitch. He bent down, tapped her roughly on the shoulder. Watched her flinch. He smiled, baring a row of perfect teeth, except for the oversized incisors. 'It's Vincent Steele, Fiona.'

Silence.

He tried again. 'Remember me from the Letum hostel?'

She blinked up at him.

'The homeless unit on Duke Street?' he prompted. 'I'll take you back there. It's warm...and safe.'

Fiona said nothing. Looked away.

'Hey, Fiona! Did you hear me?'

Silence.

Steele struggled to keep his tone the right side of solicitous. 'Come on back with me. You don't need to be out here alone.'

She shook her head.

He glanced around, saw the outline of two figures approaching through the sleet. 'Look, it's not safe here,' he hissed. 'Didn't you hear what happened to Cameron Craig?'

She ignored him. Breathed in the cold night air. Watched the figures approach.

Steele growled his frustration.

Fiona continued to watch.

The figures came closer.

Steele crouched in the doorway, his breath a stream of grey in the cold night air. 'Why won't you come with me?' He held out his hand.

Silence.

'Well?' He shoved Fiona's shoulder.

She kept her eyes on the two figures.

'Did you hear me?'

Silence.

Dawn and Julie, their hoods up around their faces, stood on the pavement opposite and watched. Waited.

Steele straightened and glanced across at them. He

balled a phrase in his mouth and let it wash around his gums. He wanted to spit the words onto the snow but swallowed them instead.

'Hiya, Vincent,' called Dawn, but there was a tremor in her voice. 'It's freezing out the night.'

Steele nodded to her, then began to back away. He left Fiona in the filthy doorway and walked on, his head bent into the sleet. He saw the flash of light in the sky, heard the thunder rumble. He walked into the dark night. Above him the sky raged. Finally he found the words to fit, glanced back and spat them into the gutter: 'Ungrateful bitch.' He kept walking while sleet settled on his face and eyes, temporarily obscuring his sight. But his anger fed him and made him oblivious to the cold.

Steele walked on, past the pubs and chip shops, the kebab shop and the takeaway. They were all closed and lay in darkness. On he walked towards the alleyway where he knew the women congregated. One was at the entrance, leaning against a wall. Sleet dusted her shoulders, like icing sugar on a lumpy cake. She smiled, licked her lips and thrust her hips forward. He paused and considered the offer, but she was worn out. Exhausted. Finished. He glanced around. They were alone. 'You want some company, handsome?' Her voice was slurred.

He shook his head, walked on, until he reached the area close to Blythswood Square. He found her at the mouth of the alleyway. The foreign girl looked frozen, her dark hair plastered to her skull, her short grey coat open to expose a gold lamé top and dark shorts. Steele felt his excitement rise. He let his anger wrap itself around him and flow, like adrenalin, into his fists. He had started towards her when a car came from behind and overtook him. Steele watched as it slowed and she got in. But it was too quick. There had been no discussion or negotiation about the price. He was a regular punter. Steele watched as the car took off and disappeared into the night.

Steele was alone again but his anger must out. He turned and walked back to the other woman. The old, worn-out one. He gave her full rein. Once it was over he cleaned the blood from his knuckles with snow. There was no chance that she would report him to the police. They never did. He walked on, his anger sated. Finally he arrived at a desolate spot. He stood out in the open and let the snow settle on him. He listened to the far-off thunder. He heard his breathing slow and his heartbeat steady. There was no need to worry. Stay calm. Breathe. Just breathe.

In the shadows, keeping a safe distance, Julie and Dawn watched Steele cleanse himself.

The man continued his journey. He kept to the backstreets and alleyways, shuffling along in too-large shoes, the laces missing, the soles stuffed with old newspaper. His coat was torn and filthy. His hands were bunched into his pockets for heat. A woollen hat, like a misshapen tea cosy, was pulled tight over his head. He smelt of stale urine. He turned a corner and saw a stout woman walking a black greyhound on a leash. The dog wore a quilted tartan coat. The woman gave the man a wide berth and pulled the leash sharply, ensuring that the dog did not go near him. She quickened her pace and was soon gone. He was the only person in the street. He shuffled on through the sleet, aware that it had soaked his coat and seeped into his shoes. He felt the newspaper absorb the wet and start to rot.

Finally the man reached the small park. There was a deserted children's playground at the far side: Mark Haedyear shuffled over to it and settled himself on the bench. He had a clear view of the open space before him, ensuring that no one could approach him without being seen. He pulled a cold sausage roll from a bag in his pocket and began to rip pieces from it, stuffing the cold pastry and congealed sausagemeat into his mouth. As he devoured it, crumbs fell onto the concrete slab beneath the bench. When he'd finished, he screwed up the greasy paper bag and shoved it into his pocket. He left the park and walked, head down, into the sleet. As he walked, his footsteps faded in the slush, ensuring that he left no trace.

It was as if they had known to keep away and had recognized the danger. Mark Haedyear was more than half a mile away before the bravest of the rats ventured out of its nest to pick at the pastry crumbs. Once finished, the animal scampered back to its nest, ensuring that every last trace of Haedyear's visit had been removed.

Chapter 31

Weirdo nudged the 4x4 into the outside lane and headed for Tollcross Road. He was working his way through his check-list. Haedyear wasn't going to be out and about, mixing openly. He'd slink around in the shadows of the city or hole up in some deserted wasteground. Either way they'd hunt him down. After leaving Doyle, Weirdo had visited all the main players, the big guns. Now he needed to get the word out to the bottom feeders. And why not start right at the very bottom? Weirdo pulled up outside the squat, took a second to go inside. Saw the two girls lying on the mattress.

'Dawn. Julie.'

They spoke in unison: 'Weirdo.'

'How goes it with you two?'

'No so great, Weirdo. We're skint. Nae punters out and about 'cause of the weather. We're just back. We're soaked,' said Dawn.

'That young guy being murdered disnae help neither,' said Julie, and took a sly glance at Weirdo. 'Name of Cameron Craig. You know anything about it?'

'Nothing at all. He a friend of yours?'

'Didnae know him. Seen him about but he wisnae the chatty type. Kept himself tae himself.'

'You know the guy who escaped from the jail?'

Both women stared back at him, spoke in unison. 'Naw.'

'You've not heard there's a dangerous fucker about?'

'Same as most nights, then,' said Dawn. 'Even the folk in the hostels can be creepy.'

'Aye, that Francis Wright gives me the boak,' said Julie.

'But he's no nearly as bad as Vincent Steele, is he, hen?' said Dawn. 'The Monk.'

'Naw, right enough. Vincent is the pits,' agreed Julie. 'Vicious.'

Weirdo spoke over her: 'Well, this fucker is one serious bastard. Name of Haedyear. Mark Haedyear.'

Julie scowled. 'Disnae ring any bells.'

'Think back. A woman name of Amanda Henderson got abducted, few years ago now, mind you. On the telly, in the papers, everything.'

Julie thought about it. 'That the bastard who locked the poor wummin in a box. Buried her alive?'

'The very one, Julie,' said Weirdo. 'Left her there to starve to death.'

'Christ. What a sicko.'

'Shit,' said Dawn, drawing her jacket around her. Hugged herself.

Weirdo let them remember the detail, visualize it. He gave them time to picture how they would feel if Haedyear ever got to them. It would place Haedyear firmly in their minds.

Dawn shivered. 'Is he likely tae be a punter, Weirdo? Is that why you're here? Tae warn us?'

'Could be he might be a punter but I doubt it. I think he'll keep the head down and a low profile. He'll live rough if he's got any sense.'

'Any ideas where?' asked Julie.

'Fuck knows,' said Weirdo.

'Where's he fae, originally? I mean where's hame?' asked Dawn. 'Would he go back there?'

'Southside, Clarkston way.'

'Posh.'

'Aye, he's a posh git. Went tae uni and everything.'

'So, if you're not here just tae warn us tae be careful, whit is it you want?'

'Mr Doyle wants him.'

'Right,' said Dawn.

'Bad,' said Weirdo.

'How bad?'

Weirdo weighted his words for emphasis: 'Very fucking bad indeed.'

'How come Mr Doyle wants him?' asked Dawn.

Weirdo tapped the side of his nose with a forefinger. 'You girls work on a need-to-know basis.'

Dawn spoke: 'And I guess we don't need tae know all the details. Except you want us tae track the bastard and mibbe risk our lives in the process. And for that we're just in,' she curled her index fingers into quotation marks, 'a need-tae-know situation.'

'Sounds dangerous,' said Julie.

'Very dangerous,' repeated Dawn. She stared at Weirdo. 'What's in it for us?'

He moved into the centre of the room, careful to keep his biker boots away from the filthy mattress. He stretched to his full height of six four. Gave it a minute to let his presence fill the room. The two women went quiet and shrank into themselves, their brief moment of confidence over. Weirdo let them consider their options. Knew that they had none. He kept his voice low, measured. 'Mr Doyle wants to find out where the sleekit bastard's holed up. Glasgow is not such a big fucking place. Talk to your pals. Listen to your punters. The man in the chippy when you're getting your tea, the guy in the offy when you're buying your cans. Think about it as a big net being thrown over the city. Get everybody you know to look out for the fucker.' Weirdo's voice rose as he got carried away with his own enthusiasm for motivational speaking. 'Let's do it! Let's get the bastard! Okay?'

Silence.

Dawn and Julie stared at the floor. Dawn chewed at her lip. Finally she said, 'Aye, that's all great and that, Weirdo, but we kind of need to know what he looks like.'

Weirdo blinked. 'Oh, aye. Good call. He's five foot nine, skinny, crew-cut dirty-blond hair, green eyes. Shifty-looking bastard.'

Dawn risked a sly glance. 'You sure you cannae tell us how come Mr Doyle's looking for him?'

'You don't need to know that. It would put you in a dangerous situation to have that information. All you need to know is that Mr Doyle is looking for him, okay?'

'Okay.'

'How will we get in touch?' asked Julie. 'You know, if we see this Haedyear guy? You got a number we could call?'

He had, but Weirdo wasn't about to give it out to the two dossers. 'You get any information you take it to Sonny down at the Smuggler's. He knows how to contact me.'

At the door Weirdo turned, tossed a tenner back into the room. 'That's for a couple of bags of chips and some cans, but mind you don't get pissed. I want you on the job. You find Haedyear and you'll be quids in, I promise you that.' He left, the sound of biker boots on the concrete steps.

Dawn and Julie looked at each other. Dawn spoke: 'Quids in, you hear that, hen?'

'Aye, but he's a nasty-sounding fucker, that Haedyear.' Julie reached for the tenner.

'But if we did find him, Julie, hen, it would be a wee bit of money for us.'

'Aye, well, I suppose so, and Mr Doyle would be pleased. And Weirdo,' said Julie.

'We going for it, then?' asked Dawn.

Julie raised an imaginary glass in toast. 'What dae you think, hen? Let's get a few wee cans down us first, calm our nerves.'

Dawn swallowed. 'Think I'm going tae need it.'

Chapter 32

Wheeler walked through the door to the CID suite and heard the hum of solid hard work. The place was full of officers. Some were on the phone following up leads, some were calling people who had been out when door-to-door enquiries had been conducted, while others were researching online and digging for clues to the case. She glanced across at Ross. His head was down and he was scrolling through a list on his computer screen. A uni-formed officer at the back of the room put down the phone. 'Just got the update from the *Big Issue* office about Cameron Craig.'

'Go on,' said Wheeler.

'They've no trace of him selling the magazine or being involved anyway. In fact, they hadn't heard of him at all other than through Grim's report in the *Chronicle*.'

'Great. Another closed door.' Wheeler dumped her coat over the back of her chair and her bag on the floor. 'Boyd, you get a chance to check out Vincent Steele?'

'Yep. A big bruiser of a guy. I wouldn't trust him to water my plants, never mind work with vulnerable people, but his alibi checks out time-wise. He was nowhere near Tollcross Road when Cameron Craig was murdered.'

'Okay, keep digging,' said Wheeler. 'We'll get something eventually.'

The envelope was on her desk. Wheeler opened it and took out a sheet of paper.

'That an early Valentine's card?' said Ross.

Wheeler ignored him, scanned the neatly typed letter.

Hello Katherine,

I watched you on television suggesting that I am cold-blooded and callous. Really, Katherine, in our world where language is used to accurately reflect us, do you really believe these archaic terms?

Oh, please! Mischievous I may own up to but cold-blooded? I refute that. What gives you the right to stand up at your little press conference and pretend that we live in a moral society and that somehow I exist on the perimeter? And whose morals? Surely not the morals of a civilization constantly at war? *Hell bent* on the destruction of each other and their habitat while inflicting once-in-a-lifetime, never-before-seen cruelty? A civilization where money is worshipped over life? Are these the morals I should choose? Do you think so?

Do you *really* think so?

I doubt that you do. You are an intelligent woman. If you weren't, if you were a small-minded, insignificant, brainless wonder, then I wouldn't be interested in you. Instead, you and I will have an adventure together.

Am I in chaos? Have I been cast into chaotic mode? Look at our world, look at our language – genocide, murder, matricide, patricide, assassination, ethnic cleansing, massacre, execution. Need I go on? We have invented more names for death than for life. Why? Because we feed on trauma and brutality. Tell me, is our world civilized?

But wait, I haven't introduced myself.

Ross put a mug of coffee beside her. 'Anything interesting?'

'A tirade about the use of language and the definition of words.'

'And this was sent to you because?'

'The nut saw me on telly and has decided that we're now best pals.'

'Besties. BFF.'

'Yep, that's it. Thanks for the coffee.'

Ross put his coffee mug on her desk, peered over her shoulder and read aloud. '"But wait, I haven't introduced myself. I am an angel of mercy. A messenger from God. And we are soul-mates."' Ross paused. 'Told you it was an early Valentine.'

'"We vibrate at the same frequency." Someone with a messiah complex. Not quite the usual approach,' said Wheeler. 'You got any biscuits to go with the coffee?'

Ross stared across at Boyd.

Boyd looked up. 'What? Am I the resident pig?'

'If the sty fits...' said Ross.

Boyd took a packet of digestives from the top drawer of his desk, brought them across and dumped them in front of Wheeler.

Ross continued to read: '"Katherine, Kat. You would like to get to know me, wouldn't you? Why, even the thought thrills me and maybe one day we will be together.

Until then, let's get to know each other. I will watch you, and you will think and dream and become obsessed with me. Let me raise a glass. To us."'

The phone rang and Ross went back to his desk. 'Tell me if it gets any more interesting.'

'Loony fan-mail stuff.' Wheeler dunked a biscuit in her coffee, flicked to the second page, continued reading, then froze.

It was during one of those intense dark nights that I first chanced upon Cameron. A lost soul is one who is beyond redemption. Well, he has his redemption now. Don't you agree, Kat? The boy was pathetic. He was miserable, but I knew that I could help him escape from his misery. I befriended him and twisted him until I saw fear in his eyes. His father's prophecy, 'That thing would be better off dead', did indeed unfold as Cameron moved towards death at a steady pace. As my orgy of bitter exchanges continued, he began to vanish inside himself, as if somewhere deep within his soul a light was being extinguished.

In the end I didn't have to do much. He had no self-esteem, no push, only pity. Our society had erased his life before I did. As intersex in the care and penal system, he had suffered abuse. He had become a victim.

I remember his fragile voice pleading. For what? A compassionate world? I told him not to hold his breath.

His death was no loss: he was a parasite on society. His life, like so many others who exist on the periphery of our society, was disposable.

'Fuck.' Wheeler sat back in her chair. 'That information wasn't out there.'

'What info?' asked Ross, putting down the phone.

'That Cameron Craig was intersex.'

'No, it wasn't, but this guy knows?' asked Ross.

'Yes.' Wheeler read aloud: '"As intersex...he had suffered abuse. He had become a victim...His death was no loss: he was a parasite on society. His life...was disposable."'

'So now we have a confession?' asked Ross.

'We have what appears to be a confession, but others might know that Cameron was intersex. He was on the game, so his punters would know. Let's keep an open mind...but if this is from the killer, he's starting a dialogue with us.'

'He's starting a dialogue with you,' said Ross.

'He wants to boast about what he's done. And from the tone of the letter, this is only the beginning of the dialogue, which means—'

'Which means that he's going to kill again.' Ross grabbed an evidence bag and crossed to her desk. 'This is going to Forensics for fingerprints.' He dropped it into the bag.

'When was it delivered?' asked Wheeler.

'When TC brought it up, he said it had been propped outside the door,' said Boyd.

'He may be caught on CCTV.'

'Ours?' asked Ross.

Wheeler shook her head. 'Christ, what am I thinking? Our CCTV's crap. Let me go see TC, see if he remembers anything unusual.'

Ross held up the bag. 'I'll get this sent off.'

But she was through the door and gone before he had finished the sentence.

Chapter 33

The Arthouse was situated just off Great Western Road in the West End, overlooking the Botanic Gardens. The building had started life in 1928 as a church. By the mid-seventies it had become a nightclub, which closed a decade later when an arson attack had left it badly damaged. Despite the damage, its location had been enough to inspire Philip Bishop to buy it and create the Arthouse, a bijou space that incorporated a bar, bistro and an exhibition area. Bishop had instructed his architect to create an industrial-chic effect in the old church, so some of the brickwork had been left exposed and grey steel pillars stood like sentinels in the corners of the building. The bistro served fusion food in minuscule portions and the staff who glided around the building wore black. A covered walkway, lit by a ceiling of fairy lights, led to the cocktail bar, which was housed in an old Airstream Classic. Tables and chairs had been placed around the Classic, which was at least thirty feet long and completely restored. Her rounded silver aluminium body gleamed in the electric light. Each night the resident mixologist, Marc Dalgleish, shook and strained and served cocktails with a flair honed at Parisian bars for well over a decade. And if Dalgleish had to start his day with a pick-me-up of a double shot of tequila, well, no one mentioned this quirk and the music of the night was whatever inspired him.

On the other side of the room a huge steel pendulum was suspended from the ceiling, its point dipping into the circle of sand beneath, creating endless intricate Celtic patterns.

Matt Elliot stood opposite a short woman with spiked black hair. She wore black Comme des Garçons, flat, thick-soled shoes and a slash of scarlet lipstick. While he waited for her to finish talking, he sipped his double espresso. He was in round two of the debate with the manager of the art gallery, Rosie Hume, and if Elliot read her body language correctly, she was seriously underwhelmed by his work and also by him.

'So, yeah, Matt, I got your emails with the hanging instructions and layout for your photographs. I'd already spoken to Phil and he's completely hands-off about it, so it's down to us to thrash it out.'

'Thrash it out?'

'Well, as I told Phil, your suggestions, TBH, don't really work for this space.'

'In what way?'

'Let me try to simplify it for you.' Hume walked ahead and gestured for him to follow. Her hands moved quickly, scarlet nails flashing as she spoke: 'I mean just here, in the alcove. The only light is electric. There's no natural light. In your email you said you wanted to hang the triptych here but I think a single photograph would be best, or the viewer wouldn't get to see the work properly. What says you?'

'I don't agree,' said Elliot. 'This is definitely where the triptych should hang.' He forced a tight smile. 'I wasn't expecting much sunlight in Glasgow in February.'

'Stay with me,' said Hume. 'Think of how much room they need to breathe. I mean, one picture would work in this space, but three all squashed together? Really?'

'The triptych has to hang here.'

Hume stared at some space above his head. 'IMO, they need to be hung separately.'

Elliot stated the obvious: 'Then it wouldn't form a triptych.'

'It doesn't need to, does it? I mean, really? Come on?'

'That's how it was conceived.'

'I think you'll agree that sometimes artists can be too close to their works to be objective. Trust me, I have a lot of experience of this type of thing. I'm pretty spot on when it comes to hanging artwork.'

'I can imagine.'

'After all, this is your baby and, OMG, can that bring its own issues.'

'My baby?'

'Yeah, yeah. Way too close.'

Elliot finished his coffee. 'Can you even hear yourself speak?'

Hume put her head to the side, stared at him for a second. Blinked. Said nothing.

Elliot continued, 'Forgive me but I don't agree. I think of my photographs as just that. Pictures that tell a story. Perhaps art, but pretty distinct from an actual human being.'

Hume looked at the floor and chewed her lip. 'I guess that's it, then. Emotion rules. Whatever you want. If you really can't relax enough to let me hang a few pictures, WTF? I have to get on.' She walked ahead of him, scarlet nails flashing. He had been dismissed.

Chapter 34

Ross walked along the corridor and heard Tommy Cunningham's raised voice: 'No, I completely hear what you're saying but I also understand that DI Barclay from the West End station has already contacted your father, Richard.'

'Yes, he did.' Belle Henderson stood at the front desk, arms crossed in front of her.

'And your father specifically asked that there be no formal police intervention at this point. He's fearful that it would lead to Fiona becoming permanently estranged from her family.'

Ross made for the stairs but Belle darted in front of him and blocked his way. 'I need you to hear what I'm saying.'

'My colleague Sergeant Cunningham is dealing with you, Ms Henderson.'

Cunningham gestured towards a row of chairs. 'If you wanted a word, DI Ross, I see that we're quiet at the moment.'

Belle marched across to the chairs. Sat.

Ross sighed. 'Thanks, Sergeant. Very good of you to facilitate the meeting.' He lowered his voice. 'Any update on the letter? Or is it too early?'

'Nothing yet. They're processing it as quickly as possible,' said Cunningham.

'You speak to Wheeler about how you found it?'

'I did, and bugger-all help I was to her. The bloody thing was just left propped up outside the door.'

'CCTV any use?' asked Ross.

'Less than useless. Showed a grey shadow of a figure in a hoodie slip into view and leave the letter against the door. Hard to see if it was even a male or female. Wheeler watched the tape a few times but nothing doing. Whoever it was, they were in and out in seconds.'

'Let me know immediately when there's any development,' said Ross. 'Anything at all.'

'Will do,' said Cunningham.

Ross sat beside Belle. 'How can I help?'

'My sister Fiona Henderson is missing.'

Ross kept his voice gentle. 'We know.' He listened while she emptied a rush of emotion. The words tumbled out and ran together.

'My mum was murdered – Mark Haedyear – Fiona's not contacting Dad. How could she do this to us?'

Ross interrupted: 'Her details are already on file.'

'My father is unravelling before my eyes,' said Belle. 'That's why I'm here. I want to formally report Fiona as missing.'

'Your father has asked that we don't officially be seen to interfere, due to the sensitive nature of their relationship, but, believe me, we are keeping a look-out for her.'

'There's a homeless unit in Salamanca Street.'

'Yes, the Rayner Association. Malcolm Reek's the manager,' said Ross.

'I didn't speak to him. I spoke to Lynne Allen, a

volunteer there. She said that a young woman came in and wouldn't speak but she wrote answers in a book. It must have been Fiona. That's why I'm here. Fiona's in the East End. I just know it.'

Ross took out his notebook. 'Okay, we'll get someone out to talk to the volunteer. Tell me about Fiona. Did she ever write about Cameron Craig?'

'The guy who was murdered?'

'Yes.'

'No, why?'

'I think she knew him.'

'Do you think she's in danger?'

'I don't know, but we are looking for her. Are you sure his name never cropped up?'

'Certain.'

'We need to speak to her. If she contacts you, will you call me?' Ross handed her a card. 'Now, tell me about Fiona. Why is she living rough? Take your time. Would you like a coffee or tea? A glass of water?'

'I'm fine,' said Belle. 'Fiona began behaving erratically after Mum died. She wandered the streets. She also stopped talking. Just like that, she became an elective mute.'

'Does she stay in the homeless shelters?'

'No, the fact that she went to the Rayner place seemed unusual. Although we always call the hostels just in case. It looks like she went in, but when they asked for her name she wrote some rubbish and later walked out.'

'I'm assuming she's on some kind of medication?' asked Ross. 'Does she have it with her?'

'She refuses to see a psychiatrist or a doctor,' said Belle. 'She's adamant that it's her life, her choice. You've no idea how strong-willed she is, Inspector. Dad's terrified that if he doesn't do as she says he'll lose her.'

'And yet you're here.'

Belle's voice was clear. 'Inspector Ross, what Fiona's doing is emotional blackmail. I understand that she may be mentally ill, believe me, I get that, but Fiona is also a cruel and spiteful person. If you ask me, she enjoys watching Dad suffer. Otherwise why threaten to disown us if we involve the police?'

'She may be fearful?' said Ross.

'You don't know her,' said Belle. 'Nothing frightens my sister.'

Outside, the weather moved itself up a gear and a gale-force wind rattled the old windows of the station. Above them, the fluorescent light flickered.

Belle looked directly at Ross. 'Do you think Mark Haedyear killed Cameron Craig?'

Ross met her stare. 'I don't know.'

'Cameron Craig was homeless and so is Fiona. Haedyear escaped and now Cameron Craig is dead.'

'We don't know if these facts are connected.'

'The place where Mum was kept...' Belle swallowed.

'The place Haedyear used previously was dismantled. That whole area has been searched and is being watched.'

'If you find Fiona, will you bring her back?'

'She may not want to come.'

Belle looked at the floor. 'I just don't understand. Why does she get to dictate?'

'She has rights.'

'The right to torture Dad? He's falling apart. He's becoming almost obsessed with this esoteric nonsense and that Letum place.'

'The Letum over at Hyndland?'

'Yes. Dad loves all that kind of stuff – he says it helped him to cope after Mum died. Ben Ramsey spent a lot of time at our house. He really tried to support Dad.'

'So Fiona knew Ben Ramsey?'

Belle nodded. 'I think she had a bit of a teenage crush on him at one point. He had to let her down gently.'

'I thought she despised everything esoteric?'

'Later she came to despise it. I don't know if it was the hold that it seemed to have over Dad, or that Ben Ramsey wasn't interested in her.'

'Wasn't she a bit young for him?'

'Fiona usually got her own way with everything. If she wanted something or someone, she would make sure she was successful. But she wasn't with Ben. It was the first time she didn't get her way.' Belle bit her bottom lip. 'If you do find her, will you at least tell her to contact us?'

'We'll speak to her about her options and find out what she wants to do.'

'And then?'

'We'll do everything we can to persuade her to at least let you know she's okay.'

Belle seemed to deflate, as if all the fight had gone out of her. 'Fiona will hate me for this.'

'You did it out of concern.'

Belle stood, pulled her coat around her and made for the door 'Thank you for listening to me, Inspector Ross.'

Ross opened the door for her and watched as she walked into the freezing cold. Then he took the stairs to the CID suite.

Chapter 35

Wheeler was at her desk, a photocopy of the letter in front of her.

'I was intercepted by Belle Henderson,' said Ross.

'Has she heard anything from her sister?' said Wheeler.

'No, she wanted to register Fiona as missing.'

'Did you tell her we're already looking for her?'

'I did.'

'And?'

'I think she just wanted to talk. Her father's taking it very badly and Belle's only a young girl. It's a hell of a situation to have to deal with, especially after her mother was murdered.'

'Did she know if Fiona had any contact with Cameron?'

'Belle had no idea, but she did say she's pretty certain that Fiona was seen at the homeless unit in Salamanca Street, the Rayner Association.'

'Get uniform out to check.'

'One other thing. Belle said her father was obsessive about esoteric beliefs and that he often went to the Letum.'

'Richard Henderson is linked to the Letum?' said Wheeler.

'Yes, and Ben Ramsey spent a lot of time at the

Henderson home after the murder. Apparently he was very supportive of Richard Henderson. Belle reckons that Fiona had a bit of a crush on Ramsey.'

'And?'

'And he wasn't going to go there.'

The phone on her desk rang. 'Kat?'

She recognized the voice. 'Matt.'

'Some of the early results on Cameron Craig's post-mortem are back and I thought I'd share them with you first.'

'Great. What have you got for me?'

'Are you sitting down?'

Wheeler gestured to Ross to listen and put the phone on speaker. 'Go on, Matt.'

'We found traces of skin under Cameron Craig's fingernails.'

'And?'

'And I've identified the DNA.'

'You're kidding me? We have our killer's DNA?'

'I'm afraid not, but the DNA is still significant.'

'Go on,' said Wheeler.

'That's why I asked if you were sitting down. The DNA match points to Karen Cooper.'

'The DNA belongs to Karen Cooper, the nurse who was strangled outside her flat? Southside, over by Langside. When was it? Last Monday?' said Wheeler.

'Yes, her body was found on Monday, the twenty-seventh of January from what I read in the report.'

'And particles of her skin have been found under Cameron Craig's nails?'

'Yes.'

'Let me get this straight. Cameron Craig strangled

Karen Cooper on Monday, and by Friday he's dead?'

'It certainly looks that way,' said Elliot. 'Were you involved in the Cooper case at all?'

'No, it wasn't our jurisdiction. The Southside CID worked it. As far as I know they had no concrete leads.'

'Well, they have now.'

'But Southside were positive that an attempted rape had been taking place, when the killer was disturbed and panicked. That doesn't fit with what we know about Cameron Craig.'

'I don't know any great detail about the Karen Cooper case, but the post-mortem results are here. I'm afraid I have to go. I just wanted to share the news with you. I'll send a detailed report to the Southside police.'

'I'll make contact with them too. Thanks, Matt.'

'Anytime, Kat,' Elliot said.

Wheeler turned to Ross. 'Did you get all that?'

'Cameron Craig murdered Karen Cooper? I thought that case was attempted rape.'

'Which doesn't fit with what we know about him.' Wheeler picked up the phone again, called Southside CID and asked to be put through to DS Mike Barr.

He answered on the third ring. 'DS Barr.'

'It's me, Wheeler.'

'And what is it you need, DI Wheeler?'

She laughed. 'Christ, am I that transparent?'

'Let's just say congruent, Wheeler. And, as I recall, you were never one for social chitchat.'

'I just got a call from Matt Elliot.'

'The new pathologist over at the Southern General?'

'Yeah. It seems we both have an interest in a recent murder case,' said Wheeler. 'Karen Cooper?'

'Go on.'

'Looks like we have a link to your victim.'

'You've got the killer?'

'In a manner of speaking.'

'You've got my full attention, Wheeler.'

'Dr Elliot's sending over a detailed report but in the meantime why don't we meet up for a quick chat? Are you free for a coffee if I come to you?'

'The station's mobbed and there are no spare desks. I'll meet you halfway. I can get out for an hour or so. But shouldn't we be picking up our suspect?'

'Don't worry, he's not going anywhere,' said Wheeler. 'Where's best for coffee? Dalmarnock is halfway between us but there's nothing there.'

'Apart from the foundations for the new Athletes' Village. Maybe there'll be a chip van or something.' He paused. 'Or maybe we should meet in the city centre. Makes sense. The coffee lounge at the Terminus Hotel in half an hour?'

'Fine.'

'A hotel meet-up. Wheeler, I'm honoured.'

'In your dreams, Barr. They've got tons of parking, which means that we'll be in and out in a heartbeat.'

'You underestimate me, Wheeler.'

'See you there.' She put down the phone.

Ross was beside her. 'You off out?'

'I'm going to meet with Mike Barr from Southside CID.'

'You want company?' said Ross.

'I'm a big girl, Ross.'

'I mean, having two minds on it would double the intelligence.'

'Right. Intelligence.'

'I'm only offering. You know Mike Barr already?'

'I do.' Wheeler shut down her computer and grabbed her coat.

'You know that he has a reputation?'

Wheeler smiled. 'As a good cop?'

Ross flushed. 'Well, I heard that he...'

'I know what you meant, Ross. I'm joking. Barr and I worked together years back. I'm going to be fine.'

'He should be okay in a coffee shop, I suppose. Which one?'

'We're meeting at the Terminus Hotel,' said Wheeler.

Ross tried for a reply but she was gone.

Chapter 36

The Terminus was grade-two listed. Built in 1858, it had recently been refurbished as a 'destination' hotel and the bar was all polished wood, ornate mirrors and subdued lighting. But the coffee lounge was light and airy, filled with oversized cream sofas and soft lighting. Although tea and coffee came with tourist prices, the car parking was free and the lounge was usually empty during the day when tourists were on excursions. Although a minimalist, Wheeler loved the place, mainly because of the Colourist prints. She settled herself opposite J. D. Fergusson's *Dieppe 14 July 1905: Night* and was once again energized by the colour and the composition of the picture. To her right was Peploe's *Pink Roses, Chinese Vase* and on the left Fergusson's *Danu Mother of the Gods*. When the waitress appeared, Wheeler ordered coffee and biscuits for two.

DS Mike Barr was three minutes late and strode into the room as if he owned it. Five ten, square jaw, Marine haircut. 'Good to see you again, Wheeler. Can I say you look great or is that now viewed as sexual harassment?'

'Not if it stops there.'

Barr made to hug her. Wheeler offered her hand. They shook. The coffee arrived and she poured two cups.

He smiled at her. 'How come we never got together?'

She sipped the coffee. 'This is very good and, to answer your question, we were together. We were colleagues.'

'We could have been more, you know that. We still could.'

'Right, Barr. Just me, you and a dozen others.'

'I'm wounded.'

'You'll get over it.'

'You know that's not true.' He offered her the plate of biscuits.

She shook her head, held up her hand. 'Okay, enough of the pleasantries. Let's talk about the case.'

'Okay, Wheeler, but just so you know, I'm hurt.'

'Okay, Barr, but just so you know, you're married.'

He chuckled. 'You were always one for the petty detail.'

'It matters to some folk, you know.'

'What does?'

'The old vows malarkey.'

'Does it matter to you?' Again the smile. She nearly slapped him.

'No – frankly, I could never be arsed, but to some folk it still has meaning. I'd imagine your wife might be one of them.'

He looked into his cup, poured more for them both. 'You're so bloody principled.'

'Right. So, about the case, Barr?'

'Well, DI Wheeler,' he had taken the huff, 'you tell me.' He drank his coffee. Made sure that she knew he was Still In The Huff.

'Christ,' she said, 'it's like dealing with a baby. Let me be the adult here.' So she told him about the skin particles found under Cameron Craig's fingernails.

Barr thawed. 'Right, and he was the homeless guy found strangled, Tollcross Road?'

'Yeah.'

'Anything else you know about him?'

'He was working as a prostitute.'

Barr sat back in his seat, took a moment. 'He was on the game?'

'Looks like it,' said Wheeler.

Barr stated the obvious: 'So it doesn't make sense that he was going to rape Karen Cooper.'

'Why were you so sure it was a failed rape?'

'When we found her, her trousers were around her ankles.'

Wheeler sighed. 'Rape is about power, control, revenge. You know that.'

'But if Cameron Craig was gay?'

'We don't know that he was gay,' said Wheeler, 'only that he worked as a prostitute.'

'And I'll bet that none of his punters have come forward?'

'Of course not,' said Wheeler. 'What leads did you have for Karen Cooper's murder? Did you have anyone in the frame for it?'

'We had fuck-all in the way of leads, to be honest, although we interviewed the ex-boyfriend, Tommy Taylor.'

'Tell me about him.'

'He's got a bit of a reputation for being too quick with his hands. He's had a few verbal warnings, mainly small stuff. Keeps his nose clean now that he has a permanent job.'

'Where?'

'He's a bouncer – sorry, door steward – at the Equestrian Eatery, Mount Vernon.'

'Okay, so Karen Cooper's ex was known for using his fists. And they split up and now she's dead.'

'Taylor says he's been single since they split. Swears on his mother's grave that he never went near her, never even saw her again after they broke up.'

'Do you believe him?'

Barr shrugged. 'Doesn't matter what I believe, does it? Evidence is what we were after, Wheeler, you know that. We can have all the hunches we like, but if the evidence doesn't stack up, we're fucked. And we couldn't link Tommy Taylor to Karen Cooper's death in any way. Doesn't mean he didn't do it, though.'

'Gut instinct?'

'Gut instinct says Taylor killed her. But, as I said, we've nothing in the way of evidence and now you're telling me that it was Cameron Craig.'

'Why did Taylor and Cooper split?'

'He says she slept with a couple of other guys.'

'Did he give you any names?'

'No, he says that he just took her word for it. She said it happened on work nights out.'

'And she told him about it? Why?'

'Taylor says they had an argument and she threw it in his face. So there was our motive right there for him to be the killer – jealousy.'

'What else?' said Wheeler.

'Her friends said that Taylor was paranoid, used her as a punch-bag whenever he took the notion. They reckon he fabricated the whole she-slept-around story.'

'Tommy Taylor sounds charming.'

'Aye, he's a charmer right enough.'

'Where does he live?'

'Strathbungo.'

'Southside, and his ex-girlfriend was just across the park in Langside?'

'Yep.'

'Let's back up a second. The Equestrian Eatery's run by Keith Dragon, isn't it?'

'Yeah, Dragon owns it.'

'Is he anyone who should be on our radar?' said Wheeler. 'Uniform had a discreet word when he moved into the premises but there was nothing obvious. As far as we know he's clean.'

'Came up from London, seems okay, at least so far,' said Barr.

'Why the East End of Glasgow after the bright lights?'

'It's cheap and, besides, his wife's from the East End, originally from Prosen Street. They live in Muiryfauld Drive now.'

'The big sandstone villas?'

'Right.'

'So you have nothing to link Tommy Taylor to Karen Cooper's murder?'

'Not a shred of evidence.'

'Except your gut instinct.'

'Which means SFA.'

'And now we know Cameron Craig killed her. I can't see the link, can you?'

'We can't always see the link, Wheeler.'

Wheeler finished her coffee. 'If it adds up, fair enough. It's a result.'

'Right.'

Wheeler stood and dropped a five-pound note on the table for her coffee and uneaten biscuits.

'Evidence, Wheeler. It's what got Maurice Mason convicted in your case and it's all that will count in mine. We now have scientific proof and, thanks to Matt Elliot, the case looks watertight. Cameron Craig killed Karen Cooper.'

'Why? What was his motive?'

'Who cares? Case closed. It's a result. I reckon I'll go out for a drink later to celebrate. Care to join me?'

'No, thanks, Barr.'

'Because you're bitter you didn't solve it?'

'It was never my case to solve, it was yours. I'm right back at square one. All I have to do is find out who killed Cameron Craig.' She thought of telling Barr about the letter she'd received.

'Good luck with that,' he said.

'Thanks.' She decided to keep the information to herself.

He handed her back the money. 'My treat, Wheeler. You can owe me one.'

She shook her head, put the money back on the table. 'Best that I don't, Barr.'

Outside, Wheeler called Ross. She saw Barr watching her from the window of the hotel. She ignored him, strode to her car and drove off.

Chapter 37

As arranged, they met up in the car park at the station.

'Who's driving?' Ross glanced up just in time to catch the keys, which were sailing through the air towards him. 'Might have known. Where does the ex-boyfriend live?'

'Marywood Square.'

'Where?'

'Strathbungo.'

He opened the car door. 'And Strathbungo is in which direction exactly?'

'The Southside, muppet. Have you no geographical knowledge of the city at all?'

Ross harrumphed as he got into the car and waited until she had belted up before nosing it out onto the road. Finally he spoke: 'So, how did it go with Mike Barr?'

'He's pretty pleased that they have a result, but his gut instinct had the ex Tommy Taylor for Karen Cooper's murder.'

'Evidence?'

'None.'

'How was the hotel?'

'Gorgeous.'

'Good.' He sniffed.

Thirty minutes later they drove down Pollokshaws Road. 'I can't turn into Marywood from here,' said Ross.

'No, you have to go all the way around – it's one way. Take a right into Queens Square, left along Moray Place, then left again into Marywood.'

Ross drove down Queens Square. 'So, it's not actually a square, it's just a road?' said Ross.

'Well observed, Ross. See? This is why you're CID.'

He carried on to Marywood Square, which, again, wasn't a square. 'So how does that work then, calling them squares when they're not?' asked Ross.

'Let's unpick that mystery later, shall we?' said Wheeler.

Tommy Taylor lived in a basement flat halfway down Marywood Square. There was one parking space available and Ross manoeuvred the car into place. 'The parking's a nightmare around here.'

'You complaining again?' She strode ahead of him.

'Just commenting.' He caught up with her.

'You struggling to keep up?'

'Hardly. Gym three times a week plus the odd run,' he boasted. 'You still running?'

'Yep. Still as fit as when I left the army.'

'Yeah, right.'

'Plus you do all that dog walking with what's its name?'

'It's a her and she'll have a name soon.'

'Okay. I'm sorry. What's her name going to be?'

Ross stared ahead. 'I'm thinking of Kat. Her name might be Kat. It's a nice enough name.'

'Kat?' Wheeler attempted outrage. 'Don't you dare.'

'Because?'

'She's a bloody three-legged mini bull.'

'And your point, caller?' Ross overtook her and strode on.

'You're such a hero – you know that, don't you, Ross? First you rescue the mutt and keep it. But because you're shy, you can't bear to mention your heroics to anyone at the station. You. Are. Such. A. Hero.'

Ross ignored her.

'But if you call that mutt Kat, I will tell the team all about it. It's your call.'

'Okay. What do you suggest I call her?'

'Leave it with me. Let me get back to you.'

Ross stopped outside the flat. 'Here it is.'

Wheeler pressed the intercom. Waited. Nothing. Pressed again, harder. Finally a voice answered, 'What?'

'Mr Taylor?'

'Whatever you're selling I don't want it. Or if this is about the bloody Neighbourhood Watch letters, you can tell the nosy fuckers to—'

'DIs Wheeler and Ross, Carmyle police. We'd like to come in and have a word, please.'

'Sorry, but it's not convenient, I'm in the middle of—'

Ross cut him off. 'It's CID, Mr Taylor. You either let us in now or you can come down the station for a chat.'

There was a long pause before Taylor spoke. 'Okay, but, really, this isn't a good time. I'm downstairs.' A buzzer sounded and the door sprang its lock. They let themselves into a dark foyer. The stairway was internal; originally the building would have been a townhouse. It had been converted into three separate flats. Wheeler and Ross walked down old stone stairs to what would have been the cellar and the servants' quarters. Wheeler could smell damp. Spots of green fungus clung to the underside of the stairs.

Tommy Taylor was waiting for them at the bottom. The door to his flat was open and a strong smell of coffee hung in the air. He ushered them into a large bright living room and stood waiting. He didn't bother asking them to sit. 'Well?'

'We have some news, Mr Taylor.'

Taylor blinked white lashes over pale eyes and waited. His white-blond hair was damp.

'Perhaps you'd like to sit down.'

'I'm fine where I am. Go on.'

'It's about your ex-girlfriend, Karen Cooper.'

'Yeah? So? The Southside polis already interviewed me. I was nowhere near her when she got done in. Okay?'

Wheeler paused before she spoke. 'Yes, we liaised with our Southside colleagues and they told us that your story holds up.'

'It's not a story,' said Taylor, 'it's the fucking truth. Look, I've been over this already with Barr and his lot.' He stared at Wheeler. 'You got anything to say, then you'd better spit it out.'

Ross stepped forward. 'As I said, we can do it here or I can drag you across to the East End, to Carmyle police station.'

Taylor stepped close to Ross and stared up at him. 'Is that meant to be some sort of a threat?'

Wheeler didn't need another pissing contest. 'Mr Taylor, we have some new evidence.'

Taylor eyed her warily. 'And I told you, if you've got anything to say, spit it out.'

'Does the name Cameron Craig mean anything to you?'

'The guy that copped it? Tollcross Road area?'

'The very one.'

'I read about it in the *Chronicle*.'

Wheeler noted the flat tone. Tommy Taylor wasn't interested in the news. 'There's evidence to suggest Cameron Craig might have been connected with Karen Cooper's murder.'

'In what way connected?'

'I'm not at liberty to say at present.' Wheeler and Ross sat on the sofa. Wheeler spoke: 'Can you tell me where you were on Friday night around eight p.m.?'

'Why?'

'Just answer the question,' said Ross.

'Why should I?' snarled Taylor. 'What are you accusing me of?'

Wheeler kept her voice smooth. 'We just need the information to help eliminate you from our investigation.'

'What investigation?'

'Cameron Craig was murdered in Tollcross on Friday night.'

'So? I was at the club.'

'The Equestrian Eatery?' asked Wheeler.

'I'm a door steward there.'

'Can anyone verify this?'

'Aye, the staff who worked alongside me. Maggie-May MacLaren was on the same shift. We worked the doors together. Plus, there were loads of punters in that night. And my boss Keith Dragon will vouch for me being there.'

'Tollcross Road is fairly near your place of work,' said Ross. 'What would you say, Mr Taylor, a ten-minute drive? Maybe less?'

Taylor walked to the door. 'I see where this is going. In the absence of any evidence that I killed Karen Cooper, you now want to set me up for Cameron Craig's murder.

Well, you two are up Shit Creek.' He held the door open. 'Now, I'd appreciate it if you'd just fuck off out of here.'

'We're just looking for information, Mr Taylor,' said Wheeler.

'Out.'

Wheeler handed Taylor her card. 'You think of anything, you get in touch. Okay?'

The door slammed behind them.

Wheeler and Ross climbed the stairs.

'That went well,' said Ross.

'Not too bad at all,' agreed Wheeler. 'Your take on the lovely Mr Taylor?'

'The wee shite is both defensive and aggressive, which is a bad combination. I think he's hiding something.'

'You reckon he killed Cameron Craig?'

'He says he has a watertight alibi.'

'I'll get Boyd and Robertson to check it out. It should be easy enough to verify.'

'But he's guilty of something,' said Ross. 'I just know it.'

'Then all we have to do is find out what it was he did,' said Wheeler.

Chapter 38

They were in the East End at Street Safe. Julie and Dawn sat together on the scarred wooden bench, their arms touching. Julie breathed in the smell of bleach, felt her nostrils burn. She hated that smell.

They sat in silence and waited for the tea to come round. When it did they helped themselves to sandwiches made from cheap pan bread, a scraping of margarine and a sliver of hard cheese. The food didn't hit the spot and both Julie and Dawn finished their tea still hungry for a substance they both craved but couldn't afford.

'You in for the night, then?'

Julie looked up at the man. Francis Wright stared back at her. He licked his lips. Smiled. She blinked, thought he must be at least six foot six. It was mostly muscle. His hands were like shovels. Julie felt her body tense. Felt Dawn tense beside her. She watched Wright register their unease.

'Hold it. I'm on your side, girls.' The smile. The lick of his lips. The confidence. 'None of your wee pals want to come in with you the night? Maybe that wee foreign lassie who sometimes dosses at the squat with you?'

Julie stared at the lino, memorized the pattern. Faded blue flowers over a cream background.

'Well?'

'Don't know where she is. Goes out on her own, never tells us nothing.'

'Right.' He lowered his voice: 'So, is the wee foreign lassie competition for you and Dawn? Business not thriving at this time of the year?'

Julie said nothing.

'You okay, Julie, hen? Only you seem a bit edgy.'

She ignored him. Blue flowers spread across a cream background.

'You hear me?' His tone harsher. He bent over her. She could smell tobacco on his breath. He leaned in close and whispered, 'Or are you too good to talk to the likes of me?' He stood back, picked up the teapot and poured out two cups of tea. Behind him a woman appeared. She glanced around the room and took it all in.

Wright turned to her. 'Hey Betty,' his tone was butter soft, 'I was just asking these two wee lassies how they're doing.'

'That right, Frank?' She smiled at Julie and Dawn. 'All okay, girls?'

'But they're awful quiet,' said Wright, 'I think maybe they're... What's the name for it? Aye, I've got it now. Maybe they're mutes.' He laughed, baring his teeth. His eyes were cold.

'You not answering the man, girls?' Betty's voice was sharp.

Julie spoke: 'Aye, I heard him okay, Betty. You're all right, Francis. I'm fine. Ta.'

'Fine, ta, Francis,' repeated Dawn.

Wright stared at them, blinked hard. 'Glad to hear it. You two going back out there the night?'

Dawn and Julie nodded. 'Stuff to dae.'

'You two mind and take good care out there. Can't be too careful.' He went into the office.

The breadcrumbs dried in Julie's mouth but she forced herself to swallow them. She watched Betty laugh and follow Wright into the office. Heard the door slam behind them. Heard Betty continue to laugh. Beside her, Julie felt Dawn's body relax.

'We need tae go back out the night Dawn, hen.'

'I know.'

'If we find that fucker Haedyear, we're quids in. You heard Weirdo.'

'Yes,' said Dawn, yawning, 'but I'm knackered.'

'I know, hen,' said Julie, 'but I promise, it'll soon be over. Let's go.' They left the centre, pulled the hoods of their coats up against the sleet and walked into the freezing night.

Chapter 39

Doyle drove his Mercedes past the Equestrian Eatery and along Tollcross Road, past the turn for Fullerton, on through the junction with Braidfauld Street, and Wellshot Road. Tollcross Park was on his right as he drove, rows of tenement flats on his left. He continued until he reached the smaller cobbled entrance to the park. When he saw the address he was looking for he indicated and pulled in across from the park gates. The flat was on the ground floor. Doyle rang the bell and the door was opened immediately by a man in his mid-forties. He had thick dark stubble, deep brown eyes and black hair. His nose had been broken a number of times and he more than outdid Doyle in muscle tone.

Doyle spoke first. 'Tuck.'

The man responded, 'Doyle.'

Tuck stood back and let Doyle take all the space he needed to pass into the hall before he closed the door and followed him through to the living room. Doyle was already seated.

'Stella's gone.' Doyle let the information breathe for a few seconds before he continued. 'That fucker Haedyear has her.'

'You sure it's him?'

'Yes.'

'How?'

'Text.'

'Saying what?'

Doyle took out his mobile, scrolled down the messages, held one up for Tuck to read. *GRASS.*

'Right. You don't think she's...?' said Tuck.

Doyle looked at the floor, his mouth a thin line. 'He keeps them alive for a while. Starves them. Least, that's what he's inside for.'

'I read about it. Sick fucker.'

'Women. He goes after the vulnerable.'

'The bastard's a coward. Why not come for you?'

Doyle nodded. 'Aye, then it would've been a fair fight.'

'But first he takes that teacher Henderson and now Stella.' Tuck tutted. 'Stella's harmless, wouldn't hurt a fly.'

'He's a goner,' said Doyle. 'Dead meat.'

'Where's he likely tae be holding her?' asked Tuck.

'Fuck knows, but the Southside's his old haunt.'

'Oh, aye?'

'Aye. But he knows we're on to him and the polis are after him so he'll cast his net wide.'

'Mibbe,' said Tuck.

'What are you thinking?'

'I'll keep it city-wide. Best to cover all possibilities.'

'Well, get out there, Tuck. Somebody knows where Haedyear is, and if we get to him, we get to Stella. I've got the troops on the ground scouring the city but I need you to do the other stuff.'

'Mark Haedyear.' Tuck repeated the name quietly. He raised his right hand, curled two fingers back, pointed two ahead, held his thumb at a right angle and kept his voice steady. 'Bang,' he whispered. 'Bang, bang.'

Doyle stood. 'Keep me informed, Tuck. Anything. Anything at all, I want to know. I know you see a lot on your walks. I don't know what fucking alchemy you do out there in the woods but I know you get results.'

'There's more than a dozen woods to cover.'

'I didn't know there were so many.'

'Then there are the parks. Glasgow Green's spread over 136 acres and is open twenty-four/seven.'

'Glasgow's a fucking huge green space just when I don't need it to be.'

'We'll find her, Doyle.'

'Do you need Weirdo or Snake?'

'I work alone. You know that.'

'I'm just offering, Tuck.'

'I'll start with Auchenshuggle Wood, the field of rye.' Tuck stood. 'I'll walk the length of it, see if I hear Stella on the wind.'

'You're an old hippie, Tuck.'

'Never denied it. I've walked all of Glasgow. Tramped over her land, listened to the beat of her heart. Felt her pain and discovered the beauty of her soul.'

'Fucksake, now you're a bastard poet but take somebody with you. Anyone in the organization? Anyone at all. Haedyear's a sick bastard.'

Tuck shook his head. 'And I repeat, Doyle, I work alone. Always have done.' He let Doyle out and went into the bedroom. He pulled on a thick coat, a scarf and heavy boots. Three minutes later he locked the door and stepped into the night. He walked up Tollcross Road, along Braidfauld Street to the old Auchenshuggle terminus and turned into London Road. He watched the sleet fall gently in front of the orange street-lights, the flakes illuminated momentarily as golden drops before they cascaded onto the pavement and died. He watched cars and taxis pass on their slow, measured dance in recognition of the weather.

As he walked, the traffic thinned and he listened, for footsteps, for owls, for the rustle of hedges, for the breathing of another human being, for the sound of a heartbeat. A skinny, mange-ridden fox cub slunk out of the undergrowth and walked beside him. Tuck dug into his pocket, found the sandwich, threw it. The cub snatched it and retreated into the bushes. Tuck had often encountered foxes and badgers and had even seen deer in the wood. He understood the land. He had honed his skills in the army when stationed half a world away and had trained himself to listen for enemy attack, for ambush, for gunfire and for bombs being planted. He had left the army with an aversion to people but a love of nature. If Stella was alive he would find her. But if not, if Haedyear had killed her, he would track him down. Tuck burrowed his hands deep into his pockets, curled one hand once more into a gun. 'Bang,' he whispered, into the dark night. 'Bang. Bang.'

He walked on, covering the ground quickly until finally he reached Auchenshuggle Wood. He walked into the wood and breathed deeply. He stilled himself and closed his eyes. He had trained himself to filter out the usual noises, to listen for the infinitesimal vibration from the earth or a sound carried on the wind. It would be a long night but Tuck was where he wanted to be. He was home.

Chapter 40

The opening riff of the Diamond Church Street Choir hammered around the old church. The Arthouse was full and the cocktail lounge offered Manhattans, mint juleps and Chicagos. Americana was playing. Wilco, Lucinda Williams and the Jayhawks were in line to follow the Gaslight Anthem later in the evening.

Elliot shouted above the noise, 'Sorry I'm late. Got held up.'

'Work?' asked Philip Bishop.

'It's always work,' replied Elliot.

'What are you drinking?'

'Something soft. I'm driving.'

Bishop went to the bar, ordered himself a cocktail and Elliot a mocktail. When he returned, Elliot was looking at his photographs.

'They're fucking gorgeous, Elliot. What do you think of the triptych?' He handed Elliot his drink.

'Because of the way she hung it, it's no longer a triptych. It's not what I agreed with Rosie.'

Bishop's voice was hesitant. 'But it works?'

Elliot shrugged. 'If you say so.'

'Cheers, then?'

Elliot raised his glass, sipped his mocktail. 'Delicious,' he lied. 'How is it going with you and Rosie?'

'Pretty well, I think. We'll see.'

Springsteen's 'Easy Money' began.

Rosie Hume crossed to them. 'Can I have a word, Phil?'

Bishop looked at Elliot. 'You mind if I abandon you for a bit? Be back in a sec.'

Elliot smiled as his friend crossed the room, deep in conversation with Rosie Hume. Elliot listened to Springsteen finish, heard Bragg and Wilco's 'California Stars' begin. He sipped his mocktail and watched them. Hume was still gesticulating, red lips working around emphatic letters and words. Elliot turned away and studied the crowd while he finished his drink. He made his way to the bar, shouted his order and, when he offered to pay for the drinks, was told by the mixologist Dalgleish, 'On the house, compliments of Mr Bishop.' Elliot balanced the drinks as he wove his way through the crowd to an empty table. He listened to Dylan's 'Idiot Wind' and glanced back at his friend, decided from the body language that Bishop stood no chance against Hume. Elliot spoke out loud: 'Bishop, you're a sucker.'

He made for the exit. He was done there. He opened the glass door and almost collided with her. 'Excuse me, Laura, sorry.'

Laura Mearns righted herself. 'No worries, Matt. My fault for running to get out of this sleet. You leaving already?'

'Yeah, I've work to do.'

'Your exhibition's on inside, isn't it? I'm dying to see it.'

Elliot noticed the man behind her. 'DI Ross. We've already met.'

'Dr Elliot.'

Elliot held open the glass door, ushered them through. 'Enjoy yourselves.'

Laura looked over her shoulder. 'You're welcome to join us for a quick drink, if you like, Matt?'

Elliot glanced at Ross.

Ross stared at the the floor.

'Thanks, Laura, maybe another time.' Elliot let the door close after them. After the heat and noise of the Arthouse, he was glad of the cold air and breathed it in gulps. He pulled out his mobile and began to text: *Hi Kat, just wondered if you'd like to come to the Arthouse and have a look at my exhibition. Let me know if you have a free night. Matt.* He pressed send.

Chapter 41

Communication Three

Hello,

It's act three of our little encounters – our intimate encounters. Since we last met I've been in a somewhat reflective mood, melancholy even. A touch introspective, perhaps. But I have been thinking about you and I'm glad that you've returned to keep me company on my walk. Do you like it here beside the river?

The bridge is one of my favourite places. From the shadows I can observe people deciding whether or not they are going to continue living. It's a simple decision. Yes or no. Some jump and appear to move towards the heavens, as if trying to touch the stars, before they plummet into the river. I like to think that their spirits are soaring above us, or beside us, in between the spaces we leave. Others trudge back to their own personal hell, their footsteps getting heavier with each step. A bridge is symbolic: it links the two worlds. Life and death, sanity and madness. Are the ones who jump sane, and are the ones trudging homewards with heavy footsteps insane? Or vice versa? You decide.

219

Look up there, above us, in the middle of the bridge, the girl. Do you see her? She looks like a jumper, doesn't she? I wonder what she'll do. Shall we stay and watch? She certainly looks like she's contemplating suicide. Otherwise why would she be here?

Above us, the moon, pale and insipid, gazes down on the black, icy water as if bored with its own reflection. This is no time to be outside in such a sprawling, impersonal city, although my path here tonight was lit by strings of electric stars twinkling mutely against the blackened sky.

I've been watching her now for ten minutes, standing alone, alternating between gripping the rail of the bridge and relaxing her hands. I'd say she looks twenty-two or -three, fair hair, and the short grey coat wrapped tightly around her body was cheap. When the wind blows it opens and I catch sight of black shorts and something gold on top. She wears a maroon beret. She is surrounded by death – she needs only to reach out and touch it. I know, I can sense her thoughts. I can smell her fear. I hear the rumble of lorries in the distance and all of city life continues around her while she decides her fate.

I intervene.

My movements are feline as I silently cross the bridge and approach her. When she turns, her face is fearful, alarm fills her eyes, until she registers my apparel and the silver white of the collar nestling at my neck, as white as meringue and equally comforting.

'Father?' She has an accent. I notice a small scar on her cheek. A crescent moon.

'My dear.' My voice is soft, solicitous. My hand briefly touches her elbow. 'Can I be of help?'

Leaning towards her, I am aware of the fog in her dark eyes. I realize that she is drunk or drugged. How fortuitous.

'Father?' She repeats the question as if she can't quite believe the apparition.

I smile gently in encouragement.

It is then that she begins to sob, quietly at first, then in great bursts of rage and anguish. Apparently this was not how her life was meant to be. During this out-pouring she is holding onto my arm, her nails, which are painted a garish orange, digging into my flesh. She emits rapid, tortured sounds from bruised, fuchsia-stained lips. 'Forgive me…I was about to…' Her voice tails off.

I wait. Patience is a virtue and I am nothing if not virtuous.

Once the waterworks have subsided, I begin my well-rehearsed speech.

'My dear, this is no place to be, out all alone at this time. Come, let me take you home.'

She shakes her head as I knew she would. There would be no going home tonight or in the future. By the look of her, she has some fearful problem that she can see no way of resolving. Patting her trembling arm, I hazard a guess. A promise of a better life here in Glasgow, which did not materialize. A very long way from home. A fecund body forced into service, then discarded, and now a life on the streets. Some would call her a harlot. But who am I to judge?

'I have no home.' Her eyes are beseeching. A man of the cloth is always a safe bet. I nod.

'I...sleep in a squat. It is filthy.'

'I have a large house,' I answer softly. And so I do, an old manse, which helpfully still retains the stone carving spelling out M-a-n-s-e – it may as well read 'safe house'. It suggests both protection and shelter.

'Come back for a short while, while we get you settled.' Again, the use of 'we' works wonders. By 'we', I mean myself and my inner demons. 'Do you have a car?'

'No.'

Of course not. The tears have abated and, overhead, the clouds clear for a moment and a lush, galactic spread of stars is momentarily glimpsed. She looks up and smiles a watery smile. Perhaps she interprets this as a good omen. I do hope not.

'Well, my car is here. Not too far.' Not far at all. Just over there in the shadows.

She begins to walk towards her destiny. On the short journey, she tells me her name, Irena. I offer her the chocolate and nougat I'd purchased earlier for just such an encounter. They are sweet, thick and comforting.

Once home, I see her glance up at the inscription, which reads, *1926 The Old Manse*. It is a solid and secure house. A safe house. The familiar feeling of ownership takes over. Irena is now my property.

In between sniffles, the wretch beseeches me, 'Is this all in...What do you call it?' Her eyes seek reassurance in my collar.

'Confidential...confidentiality?' I offer. 'Oh, yes,

Irena, what happens here remains between the two of us.'

'I have a man who comes to see me. He comes often. I thought...he might...' She trails off.

'Does he have a name?'

'He wouldn't tell me but I found out.'

'Go on.'

'Mr Dragon. Keith Dragon. He runs a big place, nightclub. Big shot. Married.'

'And him being married bothered you?'

'No. No. Not bother me. I wanted it to be me. He have nice big house. I want big house.'

'Go on, Irena.'

'I told him lie.'

'What was the lie?'

'I told him I had kid back home. Needed more money.'

'So you tried to trick Mr Dragon?'

'Of course.'

'Did you want him to leave his wife?'

'What is that saying? Dog eat dog. Mr Dragon told me that.'

'Did he now?'

'Yes, and I wanted to be the dog that ate.'

'And Mrs Dragon?'

'She had a full bowl for long enough. My turn now.'

Dog eat dog indeed. Well, I already knew of Mr Keith Dragon but now I decide that I shall include him in my plan.

Chapter 42

Tracing someone who was reluctant to be found had been difficult but not impossible. Two men were, independently, looking for an ex-prisoner recently released from Barlinnie. Both men were not the type to make enquiries directly either to Barlinnie or social services: their ways were more subtle. In Glasgow, as in all cities, people talk and the men located the person of interest quickly. He resided in Possilpark. Both men requested a meeting.

The ex-prisoner, Jake Whitestone, had accepted their requests to visit him at the Devil's Waiting Room, aware that it would be two more visitors than he'd ever received while he had been inside. Whitestone knew that he had to make a choice between the two men and that his choice would have implications. Whitestone lay on his bed and stared at the ceiling. Of course he'd recognized the names immediately and now all he had to do was decide which of the men would respect his wishes. Whitestone thought about the consequences of talking to anyone at all, and his mind was flooded with violent images. He tried and failed to put them out of his mind. He lay in the dark of his room and heard the weather outside heave and rail against the night sky.

* * *

A worm slithered across her face, trailing slime. Skin touched skin. Stella stuck out her tongue and licked the worm. It tasted damp. It tasted of soil. She felt it wriggle. It was the closest she had come to a living creature since she had been abducted and she relished its presence. Both of them were alive. *'Alive,'* she whispered to the worm. *'I am alive.'* She listened, thought she heard an owl call. She knew that it was night. She also knew that he would be back for her. But when? And who was he? Stella trawled through her memory. Was it that bastard – what was his name? She searched a foggy brain trying to retrieve a name, failed. She remembered the article in the *Chronicle* about a woman who had been kept underground. Stella forced herself to concentrate. Amanda Henderson, that was it. But what was his name? Finally she had it. Haedyear. Mark Haedyear. She was pretty sure that she'd never met the guy. So why was she there? If it was random, how had he known where she lived? Had he followed her home from the Equestrian Eatery? And, if so, why? Stella allowed herself time to think and came up with the only logical answer. Doyle.

Stella closed her eyes. She knew that Doyle would have the team out looking for her. All she could do was wait. She had tried to force her way out. It was useless. She had to wait. Stella replayed the revenge fantasy over and over in her mind, each time inflicting additional pain on the man who'd put her there. Her voice was a whisper, 'You bastard, you will be so fucking sorry you did this...' She felt her heartbeat quicken, the fog in her mind clear.

She was getting stronger and when she met Haedyear again she would be ready for him. As a reward, Stella allowed herself the tiniest sip of water.

Chapter 43

Monday, 3 February

The sandstone villa overlooked Tollcross Park. At 6 a.m. the house was still in darkness but he had been tossing and turning for four hours. Keith Dragon couldn't sleep. When the alarm sounded, he let the shrill noise echo around the room until it woke her. 'Would you shut that fucking thing off?' He took his time but eventually the room was silent again. His wife, Sue, pulled a pillow close to her face and fell back to sleep. He heard the beginning of a snore.

Dragon got up, grabbed his running gear and dressed quickly. He stepped into his all-terrain running shoes and was out of the house in minutes. He ran past his car and his wife's people-carrier, and as he ran, he increased his speed. Eventually he passed the house Maggie-May shared with her alcoholic mother. He thought back to Thursday night with Maggie-May. It had been a mistake. It wouldn't happen again. Since then he'd gone back to his usual routine. Dragon ran on, turned into Downfield Street and on to London Road, past the old cemetery. He covered the frozen ground quickly and enjoyed the feel of taut muscle tone, the sound of his new running shoes as they slammed onto the frozen earth and the regular beat of his heart as he tore along.

Last night he'd gone to his usual, Irena. She was exactly where he knew she would be, standing in the alleyway just off Blythswood Square. She was in black shorts and a gold halter-neck top. Dragon understood that Maggie-May had been a balls-up: this was his preferred way to operate. Work. Sleep. Sex. And sex was best when it was a financial transaction. Once Sue had had the kid she'd given up on sex. Now the two of them were baggage. Baggage he'd once felt society had required him to obtain. He knew better now. He'd already spoken to his lawyer.

It was seven fifteen and he was almost at the end of his run. Dragon stretched his legs for the final sprint to the door but he had to brake suddenly when his foot caught on something. He tried to stop but he was mid-stride and stumbled. It was a second or two before he regained his balance. He turned back to peer at the object. Irena lay at an angle, her coat open to reveal the black shorts and gold top. Her dead eyes stared at the weak winter sky. A card lay beside her: 'Seek the future you so desire.' Despite the exertion of his run, Dragon felt as if his heart had stopped beating. He bent over and closed his eyes as he drank in the freezing air. Finally, when the dizziness had abated he pulled out his mobile and punched in the numbers. He kept his voice steady, calm. Only when he had finished the call did he allow himself to dig the heels of his hands into his eyes, grinding them closed. Somehow inflicting pain was a comfort, like the bloodletting he had done in the old days.

Chapter 44

Wheeler met Ross as he came through the door of the station. She tossed him the keys. 'You drive. I'll tell you about it on the way.' Ross caught the keys and followed her out through the doorway. 'Talk about easing your way into the day.'

The only available car stank of greasy chips and vinegar. 'I'll bet Boyd had this out last night,' muttered Ross, securing his seatbelt.

'Let's go,' said Wheeler.

'An address might help.'

'Muiryfauld Drive. Keith Dragon was out running this morning and tripped over an object. He called the police straight away.'

'Because he tripped?' said Ross.

'Over a dead body,' said Wheeler.

'You serious?'

'Deadly.'

'Keith Dragon went out for a run and tripped over a dead body?'

'Apparently.'

'What do we have on the victim?'

'Nothing much, a young woman. No identification yet. I don't have any other details.'

Ten minutes later the flashing lights of the parked police cars came into view. The road had been closed and police tape cordoned off the area. Uniformed police officers reinforced the barrier. The SOCOs were already on site and the tent had been erected. Ross parked up. Wheeler looked beyond the tent at the old stone villa, which stood back from the road. 'Georgian, I think. It's quite symmetrical. I always think Georgian architecture looks handsome and well balanced.'

'Bit like me,' muttered Ross, as they approached a uniformed officer who was keeping the log. They gave their names.

Wheeler spoke: 'What do we have?'

'Female victim, DI Wheeler. The pathologist is with the body now. And,' he held up a clear plastic evidence bag,' we have this.'

Wheeler took it. 'Another card from the Letum Institute?' She read aloud, '"Seek the future you so desire."'

Ross said, 'It's him, isn't it?'

'It looks like it.' Wheeler turned to the uniformed officer. 'Anything else?'

'Keith Dragon's already on his way to the station.'

'Good. I'll speak to him there,' said Wheeler.

'But his wife is still in the house.'

'Okay, we'll get to her in a while.'

They made their way to the tent. Inside Matt Elliot was crouched beside the body. He glanced up. 'Still busy?'

'Getting busier by the look of it,' said Wheeler. 'What do we have?'

'Female, early twenties,' said Elliot.

Wheeler looked at the body and saw that the victim had fair hair and a scar on her cheek. She took in the clothing. 'Not the weather for shorts, is it?'

Ross shook his head. 'She must have been frozen. A working girl.'

'Certainly looks like it,' said Wheeler. She glanced at Elliot. 'Same MO as Cameron Craig?'

'I can't be sure until I get her back to the lab, but I would say it seems very probable.'

'Had she been shaved?' asked Wheeler.

Elliot paused. 'I was just about to check her neck.' He leaned close to the body and carefully held the woman's hair to one side. 'Yes, a small area has been shaved.'

'It's him,' said Wheeler. 'Bastard.'

'Also, she wasn't killed here. The blood pool contradicts it,' said Elliot. 'I'll have more for you after the post-mortem but I'd say you're looking at a victim who was killed elsewhere and then moved.'

'Moved to right in front of Keith Dragon's house,' said Wheeler.

'Is he known to you?' asked Elliot.

'He is now,' said Ross.

'Let me know what time for the PM,' said Wheeler. 'And, by the way, Mike Barr thinks you're a genius.'

'Who and why?' asked Elliot.

'Southside CID. He headed up the Karen Cooper murder inquiry. Now he's in the process of closing it, thanks to you.'

'Thanks to DNA evidence from Cameron Craig's fingernails. How is that investigation going?'

'Nothing as yet on our killer. Except,' she gestured to the body, 'that he's killed again.'

They left Elliot and walked towards the house.

'Still busy?' asked Ross.

'Matt offered to take me to his exhibition. I told him I'd go when I had a couple of hours free.' Wheeler opened the door. 'Let's have a chat with Mrs Dragon.'

Inside, a uniformed officer led them through to the kitchen. Sue Dragon was sitting at a breakfast bar drinking coffee. She was in her early thirties, bleached blonde, wore thick lipstick and had squeezed herself into a fitted dress that was at least one size too small. She wore red stilettos. Wheeler and Ross flashed their ID and Wheeler did the introductions.

'Yeah, I can see that you're the polis – the place is crawling with you lot,' said Dragon. 'Bloody inconvenient to have you here.'

'I'm sorry?' said Ross.

'What are the neighbours going to think?'

'That there's been an incident, I'd imagine,' said Ross.

'Smartarse.' Dragon scowled. 'Can you get this over and done with quickly? Only my daughter Posey's got her dance exam later today and I don't want her upset.'

'Your daughter's still here?' asked Wheeler.

'Do I look stupid? My ma came and took her first thing, but still,' Dragon huffed, 'it's her house and I want her back in time to get ready for the dancing.'

'A woman's been killed, Mrs Dragon,' said Wheeler.

'So I noticed but it's nothing to dae with us. And it's poor wee Posey's big day today.'

'And we intend to find who did it,' said Wheeler.

'You need to go get the killer, then, don't you, and not hang around here? We've got nothing to do with it so…' she shrugged '…why don't you just get on with it?'

'We need a statement,' said Ross.

'Because?'

'The body was found here.'

'Christ almighty, that was just bad luck,' said Dragon.

'How can you be so sure?' asked Ross.

'How can you be so sure otherwise?' Dragon retorted.

'We're looking for evidence, Mrs Dragon,' said Wheeler. 'The body was specifically dumped here. Have you any idea why?'

'No.'

'Are you absolutely sure?'

'Yes.'

'Can we take a look around?'

'Bloody look where you want but don't involve me or the wean.'

Brilliant, thought Wheeler. If there was a pissing contest her money was on Sue Dragon. Never had a woman been so aptly named. 'Mrs Dragon.' Wheeler cleared her voice. 'Where were you when your husband discovered the body?'

'In bed.'

'And last night?'

'Watched a bit of telly with the wean, then an early night.'

'And your husband?'

'At work.'

'What time did he get home?'

'No idea. I was asleep.'

'I'll send in an officer to take your statement, Mrs Dragon,' said Wheeler.

'Right you are,' Sue Dragon glared at her. 'But can you tell them to hurry up? I've a busy day ahead.'

In the hallway, Ross muttered, 'She's all heart, isn't she?'

'You and she certainly hit it off. Let's get back to the station and have a word with Keith Dragon.'

At the station they took the stairs two at a time. Robertson met her at the door of the CID suite. 'Stewart wants a word in his office.'

'I'm just about to talk to Keith Dragon.'

'Boss said it can't wait.'

'Any ideas what it's about?'

'He didn't say but it's not good news by the look of him.'

'Go on.'

'I don't know anything. Honestly, Wheeler, I'd tell you if I did.'

'You go ahead, Ross. I'll only be a sec.' Wheeler crossed to DCI Stewart's door, knocked and waited a moment before going into the office.

'Wheeler,' Stewart was standing at the window, 'close the door.'

'Boss.' She took in the grey pallor, the sweat on his forehead. Involuntarily she glanced at the framed photographs on the desk. Stewart and his wife Adrianne. 'You wanted to see me?'

He cleared his throat. 'Adrianne's had a heart attack.'

'I'm sorry.' Useless words.

'She's stable at present but the consultant advised that…' He swallowed. 'Well, I need to be at the hospital. You need to take over the case.'

Wheeler's voice was calm. 'Of course. I'll get everyone up to speed on the latest developments.'

'Update me on what happened this morning at Muiryfauld Drive,' said Stewart.

'The victim was in her early twenties. Looks like she was a working girl. The pathologist says she was killed elsewhere and the body moved. Keith Dragon found her.'

'Shaved?'

'Yes. The back of her neck had been shaved, and there was a card similar to the one found beside Cameron Craig.'

'Are the wounds consistent? Not a copy-cat?'

'Dr Elliot says, on preliminary investigation, it's the same guy, but he'll have more for us after the post-mortem.'

Stewart stared out of the window. 'Any prints come back on that letter?'

'Nothing. Not even a postmark. It was left outside the station door overnight.'

'CCTV's shit,' said Stewart.

'I know, boss. And the weather didn't help.' Wheeler dropped her voice: 'You go on. Go to the hospital.'

Stewart hesitated for a second, and when he spoke, she heard the strain in his voice. 'Yes, I'm sure you've got it all in hand.'

'Go,' she repeated, opening the office door. She watched him walk towards the stairs. Gone was his usual determined stride. Stewart looked dazed.

Wheeler made her way to the interview room.

Chapter 45

The radiator in the interview room was still broken but someone had brought in a revolving halogen heater. It moved steadily, sending a small ray of warmth into the room, which just about kept the temperature above freezing.

Keith Dragon sat on the orange plastic chair at the pockmarked desk and kept his eyes on Wheeler when she entered the room. He held contact while she sat opposite him.

Ross was already seated.

Wheeler thanked him for attending, made the introductions and began: 'Can you talk me through the events leading up to when you called the police this morning?'

'I was coming back from my morning run and—' Dragon stared at the desk. Finally, he continued, 'And I found her.'

'And you didn't notice the body on the way out?' prompted Wheeler.

'I came back a slightly different route. I'm half asleep when I start my morning run – I usually wake up on the way. I wasn't paying attention. You don't expect to find a body outside your house.'

She kept her voice gentle: 'No. of course not. What did you do when you discovered her?'

'I called it in. Right away.'

She let him talk, going over the incident, leading them through what had happened until he had finished. Then she asked, 'Can you tell me where you were last night?'

'I was at the club.'

'The Equestrian Eatery?'

'Yeah.'

'Until what time?'

'I'm not sure, but it was late.'

'An approximate time?' Wheeler prompted.

'I'm sorry, my mind's gone completely blank. It must be the shock,' said Dragon.

'Of course,' said Wheeler. 'That's understandable, but I imagine that you have witnesses who can vouch for you being there?'

Dragon stared at the table.

'Were you with other staff members? Perhaps they can verify the time you left,' said Wheeler.

'Yes, I'd imagine they could.'

'Do you have their names and contact details?'

'Two of the door stewards were there when I left last night. Tommy Taylor and Maggie-May MacLaren were both still at the club. I can give you their contact numbers.'

'We already have Tommy Taylor's details, Mr Dragon,' said Wheeler.

'Sorry I can't be of any more help,' said Dragon. 'Can I go now?'

'Tommy Taylor's had a bit of a shock too.' said Wheeler.

Dragon traced his finger around some of the graffiti on the table. 'That right?'

'His ex-girlfriend Karen Cooper was murdered,' said Wheeler. 'Last Monday.'

'He never said.'

'Isn't that unusual?' asked Wheeler.

'What?'

'That he didn't mention it? I mean, your ex gets murdered and you don't say a peep about it at work?'

'Tommy's a professional. If it wasn't anything to do with work,' said Dragon, 'then why would he mention it?'

'There have been two murders. The ex-girlfriend of Tommy Taylor, who works for you, and now a young woman is found dead outside your house. Doesn't that look odd to you, Mr Dragon?' asked Wheeler.

'You tell me.'

'Is Tommy Taylor a new member of staff?'

'Yeah.'

'When did he start?'

'I'd have to check.'

'What do you know about him?'

'His references checked out. What else do I need to know?' said Dragon.

'Did you know the woman found dead outside your house?' asked Wheeler.

Dragon paused before he spoke. 'No, I didn't know her.'

Wheeler saw the sweat form on his forehead, heard his voice lose conviction. She knew that he was lying. 'Are you absolutely sure, Mr Dragon?'

'Yes.'

Again the tone. He was lying. 'Try to remember. Take your time. What time did you leave the club?'

A long silence. Then he answered, 'Sometime after we closed.'

'Which was when?'

'Around midnight.'

'And then?'

Dragon studied the floor. Finally he spoke: 'I guess I drove around.'

'You guess?'

'I drove around for a bit.'

'Where did you go?'

'I don't remember, nowhere in particular. I headed into the city centre and drove around.'

'Why didn't you go straight home?' asked Wheeler.

'I never do. I need to unwind. Sue and the kid are always asleep. I can't go straight from the vibe of the club to bed. I need to work in some downtime.'

'Were you on your own when you were driving around?' asked Wheeler.

'Yep.' Again, the glance at the floor.

Wheeler continued, 'Is there anyone who can corroborate your story?'

'As I said, I was alone.'

'Only uniform are checking CCTV at present, and of particular importance to them are cars seen in the area where the victim worked,' Wheeler bluffed. 'We know that she worked in the city centre.' Wheeler watched beads of sweat form on Dragon's forehead. And whatever it was on the floor was fascinating because Dragon stared hard at it.

'Why Glasgow, Mr Dragon?'

'Come again?'

'Why did you decide to move to Glasgow?'

'What does it matter?'

'I'm just curious.'

'Am I a suspect?'

'It's important that we eliminate you from our inquiries,' said Wheeler.

'And for that you need my résumé? You need to know why I moved here?'

'I just need a bit of background,' said Wheeler, 'and maybe a quick dusting of your car for prints.'

Silence.

Wheeler let it stretch.

Finally Dragon spoke: 'I didn't kill her.'

'Why don't you tell me what happened?' said Wheeler.

'She was a working girl, a prostitute. I picked her up sometimes when I was out driving.'

'And you picked her up last night?'

'Yeah.'

'And?'

'What do you think happened?'

'You tell me.'

'We drove into an alley. You know the score.'

'Which alley? Where was she?'

'It was around the Blythswood Square area. I don't know the name of the exact alleyway.'

'What happened when you'd finished?' said Wheeler.

'I paid her, she got out. Look, that's it. That's all it ever was. A financial transaction. I never touched her.'

'Was there anyone else in the alley?'

'What do you think?'

'So she was alive when you left her?'

'Yes, she was alive.' Dragon paused. 'There was a guy there when I picked her up. I only saw him from behind.'

'Can you describe him?'

'Never really paid him any attention. Figured he was there for the same reason I was.'

'What was the victim's name?'

'She called herself Irena.'

'Surname?'

'I never asked. Look, are we about done here?'

Wheeler's voice was low: 'Anything else you can tell us about Irena?'

Dragon sighed. 'A couple of times she mentioned a kid back home. I told her to save it, that I wasn't interested. She never brought it up again.'

'Where was home?'

'No idea,' said Dragon. 'it's not like I was there to chat to her.'

'Did she mention where she lived?' asked Wheeler.

'I wasn't interested. Look, DI Wheeler, if you intend keeping me here any longer, you're going to have to make it formal. I've done my bit. I've been as helpful as I could be and now I want to go. So what if I used a prostitute?' Dragon glanced at Ross. 'I'm sure a bunch of your male colleagues here at the station do, too. Okay, she wound up dead but—'

Wheeler cut him off. 'She wound up dead outside your house.'

Dragon stood. 'So go and find the psycho who killed her. I had nothing to do with it and, unless you can prove otherwise, you can't keep me here.'

'Sit down, Mr Dragon,' said Wheeler.

Dragon sat.

'Did your wife know that you were using prostitutes?'

'I see where this is going. You think Sue got wind of it,

tracked her down and dumped her outside as a wee warning to me?' Dragon snorted. 'Sue can be a prize bitch but she doesn't give a shit who I have sex with, as long as it's not her.'

'Did she know?'

'Not upfront but I don't imagine she thought I was living a celibate life.'

'Where was your wife last night?'

'She was in bed when I got back and she was there all night,' said Dragon, 'and if you think she paid someone to do it, you're nuts. Sue wouldn't waste that kind of money on me. Now, can I go?'

Wheeler stood. 'I may need to talk to you again.'

'Aye, I'm not going anywhere,' said Dragon. 'You know where to find me.'

Wheeler held open the door. 'I'll be in touch, Mr Dragon.'

'Feel free, Inspector.'

Chapter 46

The Devil's Waiting Room was located in Possilpark, in the north of the city. The two-storey building had been cutting-edge at the time of its construction. Unfortunately that was 1972 and the building hadn't stood the test of time. The nursing home was privately run and catered for a discreet clientele, mainly ex-cons and individuals who wished to remain below the radar. On occasions, the staff had had the opportunity to patch up injured gang members who, due to various degrees of criminal involvement, were unable to present themselves at their local Accident & Emergency.

Jake Whitestone's room was on the first floor. An hour previously he had been propped up in bed by Big Dougie Lennox, one of two burly workers on duty, but now he lay slumped on his side and chewed at the skin around his thumb, his small sharp teeth making rapid incisions. Soon he drew blood and watched it bubble before he sucked it dry. He saw the blood return and sucked again.

Later, a man arrived, stood for a second in the doorway and watched Whitestone gnaw at his thumb. By way of introduction he tutted loudly. Whitestone ignored him.

The visitor strolled casually into the room, grabbed a grey plastic chair, turned it around and straddled it, as if he was the hero in an old western.

'So, Grim,' Whitestone's voice was quiet, 'you've come in for a wee chat, eh?'

Graham Reaper smiled his slickest smile. 'Jake, it's been a long time. You're looking well.'

'You blind or just stupid?' said Whitestone.

Reaper took out a notepad, unscrewed the top from his pen. 'Jake, my man, let's try and keep this civil. You agreed to see me. I'm not forcing you to do this.'

Whitestone said nothing. He inhaled deeply and let the noise from his chest rattle around the room.

'I mean, this here's a chance for you to do some good.' Reaper's voice trilled with enthusiasm. 'You give me a wee scoop on Mark Haedyear and I'll see you right. You and me, we go way back, remember?'

Silence.

Reaper cleared his throat. 'Anyway, let's get started. You were inside with Mark Haedyear, weren't you?'

'Aye, but you already know that, Grim.'

'But now he's escaped and he's on the run. It would make a great wee story. Of course,' Reaper added hastily, 'there would be no threat at all to your personal safety. You're completely covered in here.'

'That's it decided, then. You're stupid.'

'What I meant is—'

'You think Haedyear would hesitate tae show his face in here? He could get in if he wanted tae. Even though the polis are after him. He's got nae fear, that one. None whatsoever. He's got tae be respected for that.'

'You've already spoken to the polis?'

244

'What do you think, Grim? They came in for a wee visit.'

'What did you tell them?'

'Ah told them nothing.'

'Great,' said Reaper. 'I'd pay good money, though, just for a bit of background about Haedyear. You know, what he was like inside.'

'He was a nutter.'

'I'd need a bit more than that, Jake, for any money to cross hands.'

'Thing is, Grim, if ah tell ye stuff about Haedyear, how can ye be sure he won't trace it back to me and come after me?' Whitestone drew a finger across his throat. 'Then it would be all over.'

'I'm a professional, Jake. I'll be discreet – there's no way he'll be able to trace any of it to you. He was inside with a lot of guys. He'd need to work his way through them all. And, given his present circumstances, I doubt he's got either the time or the inclination. If I was him, I'd keep my head down and get out of the country.'

'Right enough, Grim, and you think you're hard enough to give advice tae Mark Haedyear?'

Reaper squared his shoulders. 'I've seen enough action in my time.'

Whitestone hauled himself upright in the bed and turned his face to the reporter.

Reaper's mouth fell into an O. 'That happen inside?'

'Whit?' asked Whitestone.

'Your eye.'

Whitestone's left eye socket was empty. The delicate grey skin had stretched itself across the cavity like fragile crêpe paper. Whitestone smiled. 'Grim, this is what happens when you get into a disagreement inside. But I forgot – you're a man who's seen a lot. So, tell me, are you not scared that Haedyear will ignore me and come after you if you write up your wee article?'

Reaper tried for a casual shrug. Almost pulled it off.

'Well, seeing as how I'm taking a risk,' said Whitestone, 'what kind of money are you offering?'

'Depends on the amount of information you provide. If you give me enough in-depth material, something, perhaps, that would run over two or three pages – you know, like a psychological profile? That would be gold dust. And I already have a photograph of Haedyear.'

'How much money?' asked Whitestone.

'You give me the story and I'll tell you how much it's worth.'

'Aye, right.'

'See, Jake, my readers like to know what's happening in the city and just who's running around out there. The polis are saying very little on account of Haedyear being loose, which shows them up in a fucking bad light . . . and from what I hear, Jake, you desperately need the money.'

Whitestone stalled. 'It's not like I'm going anywhere, though. Is it?'

'But the money isn't for you, Jake, is it?' More of a statement than a question. 'It's for your boy, Dale.'

Whitestone sucked noisily at the air and took his time mulling over the proposition.

Reaper repeated his offer. 'There's good money in it, if it's the right information.'

'I'm trying to remember what he was like,' said Whitestone.

Reaper grinned. 'It would be an exclusive, mind. No talking to anybody else.'

Whitestone leaned back on his pillows. 'Aye, it's all coming back tae me now, just whit a bastard he wis.'

'This would be an insider's view of him. What did you know about the man they call a monster?' Reaper's voice rose. 'He must have talked about Amanda Henderson's murder? He must have boasted about it. Surely.'

'We were all inside and we all had stories to tell.' Whitestone's tone was sour. 'He wisnae the only one talking.'

'Go on, tell me.' Reaper's eyes flashed ambition. 'Was Amanda Henderson his first victim? Rumour has it that she wasn't.'

Whitestone turned his face away, considered the request and reviewed his choices. A smile traced over his lips. He faced Reaper. 'Tell you what, Grim, I don't think I will help you after all. I've changed my mind.'

'You're going to die with your secrets, then?' Reaper's voice was bitter.

'Thought you just said I looked well?'

'What's the point in not telling me what you know? Doing it this way means that Dale gets nothing. Is that the way you want to play it? The legacy you want to leave your boy?'

Whitestone leaned back into the pillows, his one eye blinking as he studied Reaper.

'Listen, Jake, it would be better for Dale if you talked to me about Haedyear. The word on the street is that your son's in deep shit.'

'That right?'

'He was sacked from his bar job for thieving.'

'A misunderstanding.'

'He's up on an assault charge against his ex-girlfriend.'

'She's a spiteful bitch.'

'His soul's in hock to the bookies and he's living in a scummy flat in Springburn.' Reaper tutted loudly. 'And now it looks like he'll be following in your footsteps, straight into the Bar-L. Whereas a spot of money from me would get the bookies off his back and he could make an offer of recompense to the lassie he slashed. That could impact on the assault case. Otherwise...' Reaper let the word hang in the air. Tapped his pen on his notepad.

Whitestone fingered the sheets, kept his voice to a whisper. 'That's it decided, then. What you said wis right.'

Reaper sat up.

'Looks like anything I know will go with me to the grave.'

Reaper swallowed his sulk and smiled thinly. 'Maybe given time you'll reconsider.'

'We both know there's nae chance of that happening.'

The door opened and Dougie Lennox stuck his meaty head into the room. 'Everything okay, Jake?' He glanced at Reaper. 'He annoying you?'

'Aye, he is. I need you to escort him out, Dougie.'

Lennox opened the door wide. ''Mon, Grim, your time's up.'

In the corridor Reaper said quietly, 'I don't suppose he ever talks to you about what he's done or who he knows?'

Lennox kept walking. 'What do you think?'

'And I guess you wouldn't tell me even if he did.' Reaper paused. 'Did I read it somewhere that it costs over twenty grand a year to keep someone like Whitestone in jail? And I imagine it must cost quite a bit just to keep him in here.'

Lennox shrugged.

'Isn't that galling for you on your salary?' He added, 'I'd imagine you're on the minimum wage, am I right?'

Lennox said nothing.

'Just between you and me, maybe you could keep an ear out and get back to me.'

Lennox pressed the code into the pad to release the door. Reaper offered Lennox his hand. There were two twenty-pound notes badly concealed in his palm. Lennox ignored them. 'I'll leave you here, Grim.'

Reaper stuffed the notes back into his pocket and walked through the open doorway. The door hadn't quite closed behind him when Lennox spoke: 'Cunt.'

Chapter 47

Monk's Dream was on the CD player and 'Bolivar Blues' drifted through the flat. A glass of Chardonnay sat on the kitchen worktop beside a bowl of black olives. Wheeler was pouring pasta into a metal colander when the intercom in the hall buzzed. 'Shit.' She wasn't expecting anyone. She balanced the colander over the sink and let the steam rise, then tossed the pasta back into the orange saucepan, dumped it on the stove and went through to the hall. She pressed the intercom. 'Yeah?'

A pause. 'It's me.'

She buzzed him in and a few seconds later Ross stood in the hallway holding a cardboard box and sniffing the air. 'You cooking?'

'I swear you have a radar for food, Ross. It's only pasta.'

'And?'

'Four-cheese sauce. A bit of garlic bread.'

'Throw in some fried halloumi?'

'Who invited you?'

He tried his wounded look, almost passed it off, thrust the cardboard box into her arms. 'I brought you this as a contribution.'

She looked inside. There was a bottle of Chardonnay, a bottle of Merlot, a thick wedge of Parmigiano-Reggiano, some olives and a baguette. 'Wonderful, Ross, thanks.' She walked back into the kitchen, dumped the box on the worktop, put the Chardonnay and cheese in the fridge and asked, 'Sparkling mineral water? It's a shame you're driving, Ross.'

'I don't have to drive. I've already parked up. I could leave it here and get a taxi back.'

'Red or white?'

'Red.'

'There's one already open, if that's okay?'

'Fine.'

She poured him a glass of wine and he took an olive from the bowl.

Wheeler crossed to the cooker, poured the sauce over the pasta, tipped the halloumi into a frying pan and checked the oven. 'Okay, dinner first or put it on hold and discuss the case?'

'Well, it's up to you but I'm starving and I can't work on an empty stomach.'

'When you put it like that, why don't we eat first?'

'Great, as long as I'm not taking up time you could be spending with your pathologist.'

'He's not my pathologist,' said Wheeler, 'so drop it and you can lose the smirk too.'

A few minutes later she dished up the food and carried the steaming bowls through to the table. Ross followed her with the wine bottles and their glasses. 'Have you heard from the boss?' he asked, between mouthfuls. 'Any update on his wife?'

'No change. She's still in intensive care.'

'That's good, though, in a way...' his voice faltered '...isn't it?'

'I hope so, Ross, I really hope so,' said Wheeler. 'Did we get anything back from the lab about the letter?'

'Nothing. There are no fingerprints on it. Nothing at all. It was printed on standard paper from a generic printer.'

'So, our killer gets to communicate with us and we just have to hold it.'

'I know. Another piece of the jigsaw puzzle.'

'What's your take on Keith Dragon?'

'I think he's a greasy fucker with no conscience about using Irena, but if you're asking me if he killed her, I reckon not.'

'Because?' Wheeler started on the garlic bread.

'Just my gut instinct. What was his motive? And he might be a sleazeball but he's not stupid enough to kill her and dump her body outside his home. Then call it in to us.'

'I agree. And, anyway, he's off the hook. CCTV backs him up. It has Irena on film close to Blythswood Square, a good hour after Dragon left her. Also, his car was caught on CCTV as he drove home. He left Irena when he said he did and scuttled home to his wife.'

'So, if we know it wasn't Keith Dragon, then how come she shows up dead outside his house?' Ross poured himself another glass of Merlot. 'And what happened to her after Dragon left her at Blythswood Square?'

Wheeler tore at a piece of garlic bread, mopped up some of the sauce and munched it before she spoke. 'Remember, Matt said she'd been killed elsewhere and her body moved. She could have been killed anywhere.'

'Okay, but let's say that she was killed around Blythswood Square, why dump her body outside Dragon's house in Muiryfauld Drive?'

'The killer wants to put Dragon in the frame?'

'Okay,' said Ross, 'then why not leave Cameron Craig's body there too?'

'And these cards from the Letum?'

'Did you call Ben Ramsey?'

'Yep. He claims not to have known Irena and had no idea why she would have a card.'

'Do you believe him?'

'The facts are that we have two deaths and two cards from the Letum,' said Wheeler.

'There was nothing found beside Karen Cooper's body?' asked Ross.

'Nothing, and Cooper wasn't shaved.' Wheeler sat back and sipped her wine. 'What are we missing?'

'Ben Ramsey?'

'There's nothing in Ramsey's background to suggest he's our killer. And uniform are working their way through the list he gave us. All those esoteric teachers just regurgitate the same old peace-and-love mantra. None of them has any previous.'

'Did the woman who did the past-life stuff ever get back to you?'

'Lotus Flower. Yeah, I spoke to her at length. Great length – I couldn't get off the phone. Very hippie-dippy, she needed to tell me her whole philosophy. I don't think we need to talk to her again.'

'So, on one side there's Ben Ramsey and his lot at the Letum, and on the other Keith Dragon, whose alibi holds up. And what links them? I can't see Keith Dragon going anywhere near the Letum. And I'd bet Ben Ramsey wouldn't be seen dead at the Equestrian Eatery.'

'Are they being targeted?' asked Wheeler.

'Who would gain from targeting them?'

'Let's look at the geography, in particular the area around Tollcross Park.'

'Cameron Craig was killed near the park and Irena's body was dumped outside Keith Dragon's house on the other side of it. At present our killer is focused on one area and both victims were vulnerable.'

'Karen Cooper was killed Southside,' said Wheeler.

'By Cameron Craig,' said Ross.

'Cooper's the odd one out. Both Cameron Craig and Irena worked the streets. Both existed on the periphery of society, while Cooper was a nurse. Both had a positive-thinking card left beside their bodies. Cooper didn't. I think our killer is mocking the Letum. Plus Cooper wasn't shaved. Our guy targets the vulnerable. They're easy prey.' Wheeler sipped her wine. 'Dragon must be connected in some way.'

'Our killer despises vulnerability, according to his letter.'

Wheeler stood, crossed to the far end of the room, lifted a folder, took out copies of the letter and brought one over to Ross. 'Let's have another look.'

They reread it in silence.

Ross spoke: 'What does it tell us? First, that he's well educated.'

'And he exhibits many of the traits of a psychopath. He has a grandiose sense of self, a complete lack of empathy about killing Cameron Craig, and he's glib.'

'And there's a total lack of remorse,' said Ross.

When they had finished the food, Wheeler cleared the table and brought over the cork notice-board, spread a map of Glasgow across it and began pinning notes to it.

Ross refilled their glasses.

'Cameron Craig was found here.' Wheeler pinned a name tag over Tollcross Road. 'Irena was found here.' She pinned one on Muiryfauld Drive. 'The card from the Letum Institute found in Cameron's pocket puts it here in Hyndland.'

'Is there a discernible pattern?' said Ross.

'Let's work through every angle,' said Wheeler.

'In that case,' said Ross, 'I'd better settle myself. It's going to be a long night.'

Chapter 48

In the West End for, at Hyndland, the Letum Institute was in darkness save for one room, which was illuminated by candlelight. In the centre of the room a red candle had been placed on the heavy oak table. As it burned, the candle emitted the deep earthy scent of vetivert. Around the table sat Ben Ramsey, Ms Dodds, Lotus Flower and Richard Henderson. Four other members of the Institute completed the group.

Lotus Flower closed her eyes and sat completely still, her short red hair standing in spikes around a sharp face. The phases of the moon had been tattooed across her left arm. Her fingernails were long, the varnish black. In front of her the candle flickered and snapped, although there was no draught in the room.

Eventually she opened her eyes and spoke, her voice clear and brittle: 'Spirit, you have served us well and we thank you. Tonight we wish to ask for guidance about a lost soul and I humbly ask that you speak through me to reveal your wisdom.'

The temperature in the room cooled.

'We know that at present there is much violence in our city and also that there are many lost souls.'

Richard Henderson shifted in his seat. Rearranged his damp fingers into a cat's cradle. Tried to still his shaking.

'We wish to ask you about Fiona Henderson,' said Lotus Flower.

The candle flickered and the light was almost extinguished. Shadows danced fleetingly on the walls, then died out. Lotus Flower's voice was steady. 'Is violence pursuing Fiona Henderson?'

Again the candle flickered.

Lotus Flower nodded. 'Very well. Speak through me. I am your vessel.' She cleared her throat twice and closed her eyes. When she spoke again it was in broken English, her voice masculine and hesitant. 'Fiona Henderson has been surrounded by darkness since she entered the world.'

Henderson's hands shook violently.

'She has connected with the dark energy of her father.'

Henderson spoke: 'Can you see where she is?'

Lotus Flower turned her head as if listening closely. 'The darkness is dispersing. I see Fiona. She lives among others who are afraid but she is fearless and—'

'Is she alone?' Henderson blurted out.

'Silence.'

'It's just that—'

'Silence!'

'I was only—'

Lotus Flower talked over him: 'The spirits are displeased. They will allow me only one message.'

The room was silent.

After a few minutes she spoke: 'Fiona's conception was through violence.'

The candle flickered and died.

Lotus Flower bowed her head, and when finally she spoke, it was in her own voice. 'The spirit has departed.'

Ben Ramsey rose and switched on the lights.

All eyes were on Henderson. His voice was hesitant: 'I don't know what to say.'

Ms Dodds said, 'You could begin by telling the truth, Mr Henderson. This is the second time that you have asked us to evoke the spirits' help.'

'I know.'

'In good faith I read the cards for you and now Ms Flower has channelled and yet you still conceal the truth from us. Well, no more, Mr Henderson. I'm asking you to leave the Letum for good.'

When Henderson spoke there was a tremor in his voice: 'I'm sorry, I couldn't tell you. I promised Amanda that I'd never admit Fiona wasn't my daughter. She insisted that it was to be kept secret.'

They waited.

'Amanda was pregnant when we met. I didn't care. I loved her from the moment I first saw her. We were married before Fiona was born.'

Ramsey spoke: 'Does Fiona know that you're not her father?'

'No.'

Ramsey nodded. 'And her biological father?'

'Someone Amanda knew vaguely at university. On the last day of term they were at a party and Amanda was very drunk...She told me that he raped her. She never saw him after that night. Later she found out that she was pregnant.'

'It is his darkness that I felt,' said Lotus Flower.

'What do you know about him?' asked Ramsey.

Henderson put both hands out in front of him, palms up. 'Nothing, really. Amanda didn't know him well and understandably she didn't want to speak about him. And we were so happy together, I didn't want to rock the boat. And then we got married and the baby was born. It didn't seem to matter – Fiona was mine. Then Belle came along and our family was complete.'

'Could he have found out about Fiona and made contact with her?'

'I don't know.'

'If we had a name, even, it would be something,' said Ramsey.

'She never mentioned him by name, and it was almost twenty years ago.' Henderson paused, closed his eyes. 'Let me think, there was something that came up.' He took time to remember, then continued, 'We were watching a programme on the TV and a character had a nickname. What was it?...Yes, that's it. It was Preacher. His nickname was Preacher. Amanda had quite a violent reaction to it, switched it off. When I asked her why, she said it triggered dark memories. The man who raped her had had the same nickname, the Preacher. Later she told me why but I can't remember. It was too long ago.' Henderson looked at them. 'Does the name mean anything to any of you?'

They all shook their heads.

'Do the police know that Fiona is not your biological daughter?' asked Ramsey.

'No one knew until just now,' replied Henderson.

'Will you tell them?'

'What does biology matter? Fiona is my daughter. I

can't see that it would make any difference to the police investigation.'

'You saw how DIs Wheeler and Ross viewed us,' said Dodds. 'They could hardly keep the smirks off their faces. If they knew that this detail came through while we are working with a spirit...'

'The detail is concrete enough,' said Ramsey.

'Leave the police to their enquiries and let us continue to work with the spirits and see what they tell us,' said Dodds.

Ramsey turned to Henderson. 'What do you want to do? It's your call.'

Chapter 49

The Smuggler's Rest was quiet. The twins, Shona and Heather, nursed their half-pints of shandy and surreptitiously glanced at the vodka optic every fifteen minutes. Business had not just been slow, it had been diabolical. The *Chronicle* was spread out on the table in front of them. A picture of Mark Haedyear stared back at them.

'We'd not be on the shandies if we'd found this fucker,' said Shona.

'I know, hen, we'd be in the money, but we've tried everything,' said Heather. 'Whit else can we dae?'

The door opened and Tuck approached the bar.

Sonny kept his voice low: 'Any news about Stella?'

'Nothing. Nobody knows nothing, Sonny. You hear anything?'

'Zilch. Even the twins have heard nothing. Absolutely sweet FA. It's like Haedyear's done a disappearing act.'

'We'll get him. I can feel it.'

'You want a drink?'

'No. Wanted to check if there'd been any developments.'

'Doyle not with you?'

'I work alone, Sonny. Doyle's on his way to see Jake Whitestone.'

'That auld bugger still alive? I thought he'd copped it years back when he wis still inside.'

'Seems he's still hanging on by a thread.'

'Where you off to the night, Tuck?'

'Driving out to walk the woods at Drumchapel.'

'The Drum?' said Sonny. 'I've not been out that way in years.'

'It's an ancient place, the auld Kilpatrick. I read that St Patrick was born there or thereabouts.'

'Aye. Mibbe he was,' said Sonny. 'Depends on who you believe.'

'It's like that for most of us in our lives, isn't it? We pick the folks or causes we believe in and we follow them. And even if we discover they're wrong for us, we sometimes never make the crucial U-turn.'

'Aye, and by the time we've decided on our course of action, all reason can fuck off.' Sonny glanced across at the twins. 'Like mibbe they should have reasoned that it was a mug's game tae follow their mammy intae the profession. Mibbe they should've made that crucial U-turn.'

Tuck looked at the twins and grimaced. 'But what the fuck else would they dae?'

'Mibbe something they'd be a wee bit more successful at, for a start. I worry that they'll starve,' said Sonny. 'I mean, look at them, skin and fucking bone. They're too old tae be on the game.'

Tuck averted his gaze. He nodded to Sonny and left.

Tuck drove the silver Volvo carefully through the sleet, heard the windscreen wipers beat their own quiet rhythm into the night. He followed the signs for Drumchapel, looked for the Garscadden woodland. He knew that the woods were really three woods in total. He had walked the land many times over, as he had all of Glasgow. He found the site and parked. Tuck pulled his coat collar up around his chin and walked between the bare trees. Oak, ash, rowan. Their twisted branches were naked and frozen. He stopped and looked at the sky. The moon was pale and the wind was loud. He listened closely, heard it shriek and howl around the bare trees. Nothing. There was nothing there. Tuck walked on.

Chapter 50

Doyle drove through Possilpark, turned into the car park and killed the engine. He walked into Reception, announced himself to Big Dougie Lennox and heard the buzzer sound, the door open. 'First floor, Mr Doyle. Jake's expecting you.' Doyle took the stairs.

Whitestone was sitting in a chair, two pillows bunched at his back. His one eye was alert and trained on Doyle.

Doyle sat in the plastic chair opposite him, kept his voice low. 'You know why I'm here, right?'

Whitestone nodded. His eye darted towards the closed door. His voice was hoarse as he whispered, 'I know it's not a courtesy call. Grim's already been in.'

'Wee shite.'

'Told him nothing.'

Doyle leaned forward, heard the breath rattle in Whitestone's chest. 'You'd better not be wasting my fucking time.'

'I'm sick, Mr Doyle.'

Doyle waited. There was no point in contradicting a man who already looked like death.

'And you know this is dangerous, me even talking to you. Haedyear'd kill me if he got wind that you were here. I'd be dead meat.' He looked at Doyle, saw the expression. Kept talking. 'See, I don't know whit it was between you two, what happened before, only he thinks someone in your organization... Well, let's just say he wis put inside on a tip-off. Anonymous. And he reckoned it was you or Weirdo who grassed on him.'

'Guy's a cunt. What do I care what he thinks?'

'Except now he's out and something's brought you here.'

'Did he mention what he would do by way of revenge?'

'Not outright but it makes sense that he'd go after the guy who grassed on him. You going to tell me what's brought you here?'

'Stella, my girlfriend, she's disappeared.'

'Fuck.'

'Tell me about it.'

'Since when?'

'Late Friday night, early hours of Saturday morning.'

'You think he's got her?'

'I wouldn't be here otherwise. What I need from you is information. The fucker must have said something all those years you and him were stuck together.'

'The polis were here.'

'So?'

'I told them sweet FA.'

'So, you're not talking to the polis or that wee shite Grim? You're letting me know that you've had other options. I get it, Whitestone. What do you want, a fucking medal?'

'I wis jist saying.'

'What do you know?'

'Haedyear's a psycho.'

'That much I knew already.'

'He wis originally just a psycho nut job and never said nothing, but bit by bit it seeped out. A wee comment here and there. He couldn't help himself.'

'Go on.'

'Hard to tell when it was exactly, but over time he started talking about a messiah. I thought he'd flipped and gone religious, but it was a nickname he had for the other guy.'

'Who?'

'The guy Haedyear reckons is the boss.'

'How does this help Stella?'

'I reckon this guy sprang Haedyear. If you find the guy, you'll find Haedyear. And Stella.'

'That it?'

'Haedyear talked about why he killed Amanda Henderson. He said it was kind of an initiation.'

'That right?'

'Sounded like it was a wee test for him.'

'To impress this boss guy?'

'Aye, tae prove that he wis hard enough tae work with the guy. That's why he kept her underground. He was waiting for the boss tae show up.'

'The Henderson woman died.'

'Starved tae death. Is that why you dobbed Haedyear in it?'

Doyle leaned forward. 'What else do you know about this other guy?'

'Just his nickname.'

'Yeah, you told me already, a messiah.'

'No, that was how Haedyear spoke about him, like he was a messiah. The guy has an actual nickname.'

Doyle waited.

'The Preacher.'

'The what?'

'That's it. The Preacher.'

'And he snatched Stella for this cunt Preacher?'

Whitestone shrugged. 'I'm not saying I know for sure, but if he has Stella, he might be holding her to show this Preacher guy. Like the last time. That's if my theory is right and Haedyear does have a score to settle with you.'

'If that bastard's got Stella in any kind of a box, he's dead.' Doyle's eyes blazed black.

'Did you grass to the polis about Haedyear?'

'Not my style. I'd have met him head on.'

'Weirdo?'

An imperceptible nod. 'There was something between them,' said Doyle. 'Weirdo hated him.'

'So this is all because of Weirdo? Haedyear's made a big mistake there.'

'Going up against me was his biggest mistake.' Doyle stood, made for the door.

'I need a favour, Mr Doyle.'

Doyle stopped.

Whitestone continued, 'I need to get some cash to my son, Dale.'

'Oh, aye?'

'I'm not going to be around for much longer…'

Doyle waited.

Whitestone licked his lips, pleaded, 'He's living in a flat in Springburn. I can give you his address.'

'I'll find him if I need to.'

'You know whit this is going tae cost me, if Haedyear finds out I gave you any info? You know whit he'll dae?'

Doyle stared at him. 'It was your call.'

Whitestone wiped the back of his hand across his face. 'I know that, Mr Doyle.'

Doyle put his hand on the doorknob. 'If this works out and I find Haedyear, I'll see your boy gets the cash. You want to say goodbye to him first or what?'

'Nae need. He disnae want tae have anything tae dae with me.'

Doyle kept his voice the right side of threatening. 'You'd better not be lying. If I find out you've been talking shite...'

The door slammed. Whitestone put his head in his hands and let the tears start.

Outside, Doyle walked to his car. He took out his mobile, made the calls and spread the word that they were looking for a guy nicknamed the Preacher. He threw the phone onto the passenger seat, switched on the engine. Then he heard it. A quiet, insidious chirp. He wrenched open his mobile and read the text.

GRASS. Now it's my turn to call the police. You can expect a visit. See how it feels. In the meantime, Stella's running out of air.

Chapter 51

It was late when Ross left. Wheeler went back through to the living room and put the CD on low. She sat down, relaxed, closed her eyes and let Dave Brubeck's 'Take Five' wash around the room. She woke up stiff and cold at 3 a.m. and padded through the silent flat as she switched off lights, brushed her teeth, poured herself a glass of water and climbed into bed. She closed her eyes and drifted towards a deep sleep, but there was something in the back of her mind, hidden in the recess of the foggy dreams. She slept fitfully and woke just before five. Still half asleep, she replayed her journey through the flat before she'd gone to bed. There was something about the door: something was wrong.

Wheeler sprang out of bed, hit the light switch, sprinted into the hall and there it was, the tip of an envelope protruding from under the front door. All mail, including flyers, was left in the main letterbox downstairs. Besides, it hadn't been there when she'd let Ross out, she was sure of it. She picked it up. On the front of the envelope, written in a neat script, was the phrase 'Meus par'. Wheeler ripped it open and her heart raced.

Dear Kat,

Tonight I close my eyes and allow myself to return to my secret place in the deserted fields of rye. Such a beautiful place! At night when there is no noise, no traffic, just the rustling of the trees, I can sit and think and enjoy the emptiness, the sense of isolation. At the top of the lane the deserted ground is where the Holy Trinity Church once stood. Today the air oozes with decay and past incantations but I remember when I first discovered it. I had been scouting for a special place and found the church. I loved the paintings on the walls, the gilded Madonna and her adoring angels. The frescoes depicted many biblical scenes including the three wise men on their camels bringing gold, frankincense and myrrh. And outside the church, as if to echo this, far in the distance the outline of a camel. But now let's venture into the woods. Look, over there, do you see? The space between the two trees? There are two thorn bushes? Yes, they do look old, but let me scrape away the earth. Do you see now? The wooden hatch? Yes, it's just big enough for two, if we are crouching. Ingenious, isn't it? Inside are the bones of Lena Varga and Katya Novak. Their greasy flesh gone, all gone. In our hypocritical world of morality, they were... What is the polite term? Sex workers? I had no sympathy for them: they were parasites.

But it was what was said after they had disappeared that really interested me, the nasty whispers.

Foreigners... There are crimes against honest taxpayers, law-abiding citizens... Resources are low, the police are overstretched. We all pay our taxes. What are they doing over here anyway? ... They should go back to their own country...They can't even speak our language...What do they expect?

Of course, there was some posturing, some shrugging of shoulders, some tut-tutting, in the liberal community, but the comments persisted. My personal favourite was: *Women like that – it was bound to happen one day.*

So, does society agree that the deaths of these women were inevitable? Tell me, is it better to die quickly, or exist in a living hell? I have merely accomplished the inevitable. I am an Angel of Fate. I put them out of their misery. And their existence was miserable, don't you see? Now, of course, they've become my little secret because, let's face it, they weren't particularly young and they certainly weren't beautiful. They were disposable, existing only on the periphery of your moral society and so easy to extinguish.

Kat, they were mere statistics. No one misses them, not even the vultures who prey on bodies, the police, the priests and ministers, the undertakers. The scavengers of death who squabble over bones. After they had disappeared, I heard a police spokesperson suggesting that the women had left the city. How wrong he was. They will remain here for eternity. And the women at the Centre, who were so concerned about Lena and Katya? Well, they have been silenced because their little Centre is now also gone through lack of funding. Well, boo-hoo. If society cared enough about the Centre, money would have been found.

But, Kat, you must be wondering about Cameron Craig? Our little intersex friend now belongs to both of us. He was my New Year's gift to you.

271

Wheeler wrenched open the door and raced down the stairs. She felt bile rise in her throat and curled the fingers of her right hand into a fist at the audacity of the killer trying to intimidate her. Wheeler felt her old army training kick in as she barged through the wrought-iron gates and out onto Brunswick Street. She sprinted to the end of the block. Nothing. She checked the alleyways, sprinted back in the other direction. Nothing. She jogged around part of the Merchant City. It was deserted. The city was still asleep. She walked back to her flat. There was no one around, no cars, no one waiting or watching. Wheeler walked through the courtyard garden, past the copper tubs of ivy and evergreens, and slammed the door. Once inside her flat she flicked open her mobile and dialled. It was answered on the second ring.

Chapter 52

The buzzer sounded. Wheeler pressed the intercom and unlocked the door. Seconds later Ross stood in front of her. 'I had a bloody good scout around outside. Nothing doing. It looks like the bastard's gone. I've called uniform – they'll scour the place and stop anyone they see.'

'I've already had a look. Whoever delivered the letter is long gone.'

'Are you okay?'

'I'm fine.'

'The bastard knows where you live, Wheeler.'

'So I noticed.'

'How did he get in?'

'The folk in the flat upstairs say they buzzed someone in sometime after midnight.'

'Because?'

'Because they'd been out partying and were drunk and thought it was a pal of theirs.'

'So they heard his voice?'

'Her voice,' she corrected him. 'They said they buzzed in a female. I talked to them but they're pretty out of it.'

'What about the people in the downstairs flat? Did they see anything?' said Ross.

'It's empty. They're in Italy.'

'You're not staying here. Come to mine.'

'You're overreacting. There was no chance of her getting into my flat, Ross. The stairway was as far as she got. I've spoken to upstairs and the main door will stay locked. If their buzzer sounds, they'll go down and answer it personally. And my door's securely locked.'

His mobile rang. Ross flipped it open, 'Yep, good.' He turned to her. 'The car's arrived. Uniform will stay outside.'

'Ross, she's not here. He got someone to dump it and leave, so he's obviously not working alone.'

'You don't think our killer could be a woman?'

'No. I think he's clever and playing a psychological game.'

'If you don't want to stay at mine, at least go to one of your friends. '

'You need to keep this in perspective, Ross.'

'And you need to remember what he did to Cameron Craig and Irena.'

The letter lay on the kitchen table between them. Wheeler kept her voice calm. 'I'll get it sent off to be dusted but I doubt there'll be anything on it.'

Ross pulled on a pair of gloves and picked up the envelope. '"Meus par"?'

'*Meus par* is Latin for "my equal",' said Wheeler.

He lifted the letter. 'Fields of rye?'

'According to Google, it's an old term for Auchenshuggle.'

'The Holy Trinity Church?'

'No idea.'

'The wooden hatch?' said Ross. 'It's Haedyear.'

'We need to get into the station, look up the old records, find out who Lena Varga and Katya Novak were and how they're linked to this case. Give me a second. I'll grab a quick shower and get changed.'

'I'll call the team, get them assembled.'

After her shower Wheeler dressed quickly, dragged a brush through her hair and was just about to pull on her boots when her mobile rang. 'Boss?'

She knew from the first word that it wasn't good news.

Chapter 53

The CID suite was full. Wheeler strode to the front of the room and kept her voice steady, composed. 'I spoke with the boss earlier this morning and I'm sorry to report that his wife Adrianne passed away during the night.' She waited until the room was silent again before she continued. 'I passed on our condolences and thoughts but as you can imagine DCI Stewart is distraught.'

'I'll bet,' said Ross.

'So, let's keep the boss in mind with this case, stay focused and get it wrapped up quickly.' She handed the copies of the letter and envelope to Ross to distribute.

'Last night another letter arrived from our killer,' she said. 'This time it was delivered to my home.'

'Fucksake.' Boyd shook his head. 'What we have here is one confident bastard.'

'Wheeler, did you get a look at him?' asked Robertson.

'No. The folk in the upstairs flat buzzed in a female and the letter was pushed under my door. No one saw her – she slipped in and out.'

'So he has an accomplice?'

276

'The bare facts are that he got someone to deliver a letter.'

Ross spoke: 'He addressed it to "Meus par", which means "my equal" in Latin. Our killer reckons that he and Wheeler are equals.'

'Does he now?' Tommy Cunningham stood at the back of the room. 'Well, he's delusional in more ways than one.'

'Let's look at the letter,' said Wheeler. 'First off, you'll see that it was handwritten.'

'So, more intimate,' said Boyd.

'Yep, and he's also mentioned a specific location, the "fields of rye", which is the old name for Auchenshuggle.'

'Do you think he's a local guy, then?' asked Boyd.

'Maybe, or he could have some knowledge of the area,' said Wheeler. 'Don't let's make the mistake of believing everything he tells us. This is what he wants us to think. It's not necessarily fact. Remember, this guy is playing a game with us.'

'An unreliable narrator?' said Cunningham.

'The Holy Trinity Church?' asked Wheeler. 'Does anyone have any idea where it was?'

'There was an old ruin of a church that sat in one of the far fields off Tollcross Road but it was demolished years ago,' said Boyd. 'I'm not sure exactly when, I'll look it up. The name rings a bell – it might have been Holy Trinity.'

'Boyd, you're a local guy, what's the camel?' asked Wheeler.

Boyd took a minute. 'Just past Auchenshuggle woods there used to be an area adjacent to the old iron works, which was called the Coosie. Presumably, historically, there would have been cows grazing there. There was a group of trees in the distance that were shaped like a camel, that's what it was known as, the Camel.'

'What about Lena Varga and Katya Novak?' asked Robertson.

'Both women disappeared five years ago,' said Wheeler. 'Although there was some suggestion that they'd simply left the area. According to records, they were both sex workers who disappeared. It was a women's centre that raised the alarm. It closed down three years ago.'

'Where were the women based?'

'They shared a bedsit in Partick.'

Ross read aloud, '"No one misses them, not even the vultures who prey on bodies, the police, the priests and ministers, the undertakers. The scavengers of death who squabble over bones. After they had disappeared, I heard a police spokesperson suggesting that the women had left the city. How wrong he was. They will remain here for eternity."'

'This will be his downfall,' said Wheeler.

'What will be?' asked Robertson.

'Arrogance,' said Wheeler. 'He got away with killing these two women. He didn't have to name them but he did. Then he killed Cameron Craig and Irena. He has to boast about how clever he is, how he's outsmarted the police. He's escalated and now he's making it personal. Cameron Craig was a gift. This guy needs our attention – he craves it.' She looked around the room. 'Anything else?'

Boyd spoke: 'Robertson, you did a course in handwriting analysis last year. What's your take on this guy?'

'It was only an online course, but from what I can tell...' Robertson cleared his throat '...the size of the letters, the large loops and whorls mean that the guy is outgoing, he's an extrovert. Also, the letters are open-ended, see the open *e* and *o*, which means he's creative and needs people to feed his energy.'

'His energy?' asked Boyd.

'We're all energized in different ways. For example, going to a party with lots of people might energize an extrovert, who'd come back feeling full of life.'

'Amen to that, brother.' Boyd high-fived an invisible friend.

Robertson continued: 'An introvert would come back from the same party feeling exhausted.'

'So our guy is an extrovert?' asked Ross.

'Yes. His handwriting suggests that he's an outgoing, open and charismatic type.'

'What else, Robertson?' asked Boyd.

'He is someone who feels morally superior to us all, apart from Wheeler. Also, he's using "soul-mate" to suggest intimacy. But that part is inauthentic.'

'Inauthentic because?' asked Wheeler.

'The term "soul-mate" is suggestive of a spiritual outlook. but our killer is the opposite. He despises those who believe in the spiritual side of things.'

'So, he's being sarcastic?'

'He loathes anyone he would think of as a believer,' said Robertson.

'And yet he leaves the cards,' said a uniformed officer at the back of the room.

'The cards are an affectation. He's not a believer. It's not just the tone of his letters, not even the words, it's the meaning behind the words.'

'So why leave the cards?'

'To mock. Think about the messages. *What will you create today that will make your tomorrow better?* was left beside Cameron Craig. But there was no tomorrow for Cameron. And *Seek the future you so desire* was left beside Irena. Again, there was no future for her. The killer made sure of that too. He played God,' said Robertson. 'He is mocking the spiritual while exhibiting his own power to administer death.'

'He thinks that he's this God-like person saving them from the degradation of their squalid human existence?' spat Boyd.

'In a grandiose manner, yes, he is releasing them from the servitude of being human.'

'By murdering them?' Boyd was incredulous.

'He thinks their lives are already a living hell,' explained Robertson. 'In his eyes, who would really choose to live as a homeless person or a prostitute? Life on the edge of our society to him is a cold, inhospitable Hell. To kill is to show a perverted mercy. In his eyes he is the compassionate one, he's their saviour. He saves them from a life of hardship, of misery, pain, exploitation. So he is a force for good.' Robertson finished quietly, 'In his eyes, he is their protector. Their God.'

Silence in the room as the team digested the information. Boyd chewed the end of his ballpoint pen. 'Well,' he said eventually, 'fuck me, what do I know? All that from a wee online course?'

'It's only my interpretation,' said Robertson.

'Christ almighty, this guy's a freak,' said Boyd.

'A freak who knows where Wheeler lives,' said Ross.

Wheeler was dismissive. 'It's easy enough for him to find out where I live, where any of us lives. He's trying to intimidate us. Of course, it's very flash of him to get a letter delivered to my house but, come on, really, is it that difficult? I'm on the TV, I'm in the phone book – I'm not even ex-directory.'

'He tracked you down,' said Ross.

'Yes, he did, and he also knows where I work, where we all work. Let's not get paranoid. Plus there's been a change in his pattern.'

'Go on,' said Ross.

'Lena Varga and Katya Novak were kept hidden. Cameron Craig and Irena were dumped in very public places. Why the change in behaviour?'

'He's upping his game,' said Ross.

'Exactly,' said Wheeler. 'That's why we need to keep an open mind. Right now we know three things. One, we have a killer on the loose in Glasgow and he has killed two people. Two, Mark Haedyear has escaped and is on the run. Three, someone is writing letters. These are the facts.'

'It's all part of the jigsaw,' said Ross.

'Yes. We need to stick to the facts and stay objective. Don't let assumptions or lazy thinking make us miss something crucial. You all know what you need to do. Let's get out there and do it.'

Chapter 54

Ross took the call from the front desk, and minutes later he was in the interview room, sitting across the table from Richard Henderson.

'I've been up all night.' Henderson's hands shook and his bloodshot eyes flitted from Ross to the graffiti on the desk. 'I can't sleep. I need to know what's happening to her. Do you have any news about Fiona?'

Ross could smell the whisky. 'There's been no new development, Mr Henderson.'

'Not even a sighting of her? Belle told you about the girl who was at the homeless unit in Salamanca Street?'

'Yes, the Rayner Association. We checked it out. Fiona left and there's been no other sighting. I'm sorry. We're still looking for her.'

Henderson's nose ran and he dragged a sleeve across his face. 'She's not mine, you know. Fiona's not my daughter.'

'Go on, Mr Henderson,' prompted Ross.

'Amanda was pregnant when I met her. It didn't matter to me. I loved her. She told me that she'd been at a party at university and that she'd been raped.'

'Did she report the attack?'

'No. She said they'd all been very drunk and that she felt…ashamed. It was only later that she'd found out she was pregnant.'

'Does Fiona know you're not her biological father?'

'No. Amanda made me swear never to tell anyone. I've kept my promise to her up until now. But things have changed.'

'What things?'

'I think her biological father has contacted her.'

'Do you think Fiona's with him now?'

'I do, Inspector Ross. I think that somehow he found out about Fiona and made contact with her. After Amanda died, Fiona began to pull back from me and Belle, and even when she was sleeping rough, she never returned dirty or unkempt. How can that be, Inspector? Don't you find that strange?'

'Shelters?'

'She hardly ever used them. I know, I searched them for her. She changed towards me – she began to despise me. Can you imagine how much that hurt, Inspector?'

'She would have been traumatized by her mother's death, Mr Henderson.'

'We were all traumatized. I lost my wife and Belle lost a mother she adored, but while it brought us closer, it made Fiona more distant.'

'Belle mentioned that Fiona developed a crush on Ben Ramsey.'

'Yes, and Ben was very sensible about it. But then Fiona began to turn away, to disown Belle and me. And now she's missing and Belle's out there searching for her.' Henderson's eyes filled with tears and he wiped a sleeve across his dripping nose. 'I don't drink but I bought a bottle of whisky. I thought it might numb the pain. But it doesn't, does it?'

'No,' said Ross. 'It doesn't.'

Henderson leaned forward and whispered 'I went to speak to the spirits.'

'Okay.'

'At the Letum Institute? The spirits said that Fiona was surrounded by death but that she wasn't afraid.' Henderson began to cry. 'Do you know what I'm scared of, Inspector?'

'Go on.'

'That Fiona is with her father and that he has turned her against me. Of course he wouldn't have mentioned that he raped Amanda – he'd leave that bit out. But he has her, I'm sure of it. Do you know what else happened at the Letum?' Henderson slurred.

'No, Mr Henderson, I don't, but if you'd like to tell me?'

'I remembered his nickname. Can you believe it? After all these years of burying it, of honouring Amanda's plea never to speak of it, I remembered his nickname. It was the Preacher. And the more I thought about it, the more I remembered.'

'Go on.'

'Do you know why the bastard was called the Preacher?'

'No, Mr Henderson, I don't.'

'He was brought up in a big old manse.' Henderson hiccuped loudly and frowned. 'I'm sorry, Inspector, but I think I'm going to be sick.'

'The toilet's this way.' Ross moved quickly to the door and opened it.

Too late.

Chapter 55

Despite the weather, Buchanan Street was crowded with shoppers. In the window of the pâtisserie, trays were laden with almond frangipane, chocolate éclairs, thick slices of gâteau, fruit tarts and profiteroles, fat with cream. Dawn stared at the display, her mouth watering. "Mon, hen, let's keep walking,' said Julie, taking her arm.

'I'm freezing,' said Dawn. 'Whit time's the soup run coming round?'

'Half an hour yet. Let's go intae the big place for a heat.' They walked towards the upmarket department store. Its windows were brightly lit, and behind the glass, designer shoes and handbags sat next to displays of heavy gold watches, while clusters of diamond rings and earrings sparkled in the reflected light. Julie pushed open the door and felt the warmth embrace her. The store was spread over three floors. They walked through to the fragrance department where immaculately coiffured women stood behind glass and chrome counters and rearranged bottles of expensive perfumes. At one counter Dawn reached for one of the testers and sprayed some on her neck. The assistant stared hard at her but did not offer assistance. When Julie and Dawn walked through to Handbags and

Accessories, a security guard followed closely. When Julie picked up a bag, the assistant trilled loudly, 'And just how may I be of assistance, madam?' The other shoppers turned to stare. Julie quickly put the bag back on its stand and hurried away.

Dawn joined her and the security guard hovered behind them. 'Let's go,' muttered Dawn, pulling her coat tight around her. 'That perfume was minging anyway.' They left the store, turned into Argyle Street and walked until they were sheltered under the bridge at the Central Station, known as the Heilanman's Umbrella. Julie's eyes welled. 'I wisnae going tae steal that bag, Dawn, honest. I jist wanted to touch it.'

'I know, hen, you jist wanted a look. That assistant wis a snotty cow. 'Mon, let's get some soup.' They carried on along Argyle Street, turned left and hurried towards the River Clyde. Dawn's stomach growled loudly. When they stopped to cross at the lights, a grey BMW slowed to a stop beside them. Dawn recognized the mohican.

The window slid down. 'Dawn, Julie. How goes it?'

'Okay, Weirdo?'

Weirdo nodded. 'You got anything for me?'

'Nothing. We've kept a good look-out but we've heard nothing about Haedyear.'

'We've got another wee bit of information.'

'About Haedyear?'

'About a pal of his, nickname the Preacher. Ring any bells with either of you two?'

'I never heard of the Preacher but one of the workers at the Duke Street hostel is called Monk,' said Julie. 'His name's Vincent Steele. I hate him.'

'Aye, I know about him, he's a bastard right enough,

but we'll get to him later. Can you think of anyone else?'

Dawn and Julie both shook their heads.

'Did you two know that the polis found a body up by Muiryfauld Drive?'

'We've not been back tae the East End yet. We've just been walking around, Weirdo. Keeping a look-out like you asked. '

'A wee foreign lassie was dumped outside Keith Dragon's place.'

Dawn swallowed. 'A foreign lassie?'

'Aye.'

'In our squat, in the back room, a wee foreign thing sometimes dosses down.'

'I heard the lassie that died was on the game,' said Weirdo. 'That sound about right?'

Dawn nodded. 'She kept herself tae herself. She didnae want tae talk or nuthin'. Just shut the door if we tried, but she wis on the game all right. It wis obvious.'

'She got a name?'

'Don't know nothing about her, Weirdo,' said Dawn.

'She wis dumped outside Keith Dragon's place?' asked Julie. 'His house or that Equestrian place?'

'His house. Why?' asked Weirdo.

'My cousin works for him at the Equestrian. You know Maggie-May?'

Weirdo thought for a second. 'Big fit lassie. Works as a bouncer?'

'She calls herself a door steward,' said Julie. 'Not that she talks tae me much.'

'Well, you two keep at it, keep looking for Haedyear. Mr Doyle wants him very badly and will pay good money for him,' said Weirdo. 'Where are you two going?'

'Soup van.'

'Christ almighty.' Weirdo dug into his pocket, pulled out a ten-pound note and handed it to Julie. 'But for fucksake, you two, sort yourselves out. Going tae a fuckin' soup kitchen at your age? You ought to be ashamed of yourselves. You're hardly out of school and you're living like dossers. Get a fuckin' grip, lassies. Have ye no ambition at all?' He drove off.

Julie pocketed the money. 'Wis that us got a wee motivational talk from Weirdo?'

'Aye, it wis indeed.'

'You feeling all motivated, Dawn?'

'Naw,' said Dawn.

They crossed the road and saw the van ahead. It was old and battered but the hatch was open and the smell of hot soup drifted into the cold air. There was a girl at the front of the queue. Dawn and Julie knew from the look of her that she wasn't homeless. This impression was reinforced when she spoke: 'Thank you, but I don't need soup. My name is Belle Henderson and I'm looking for my sister, Fiona.'

An elderly man stepped up behind her. 'If you don't need the soup, hen, then I do. I haven't eaten since this time yesterday. Move along now.'

Belle stood aside while the volunteer ladled the soup into a carton, saying, 'Aye, Hardie, here's your soup. You take care now and I'll see you tomorrow.' He handed the carton to the man, who took it and lifted a chunk of bread from a plate.

'God, but this smells great. I'll see you the morrow.'

The volunteer turned back to Belle. 'I heard folk were on the look-out for her. I saw her a couple of times, few

288

weeks back. She hung around with that Cameron laddie…' The man faltered.

'I know that Cameron Craig is dead, that he was murdered,' said Belle, 'but now Fiona's disappeared.'

'Go to the polis. They'll help.'

'I've already been to see them and they're trying to be supportive but they can't conjure her out of thin air and that's seems to be where she is at present.'

'She might have taken off. A fair few of them make their way down to London. They think that they can make a go of it down there.'

Belle shook her head. 'I don't think she's in London – she was spotted in the East End. I think she's still here in Glasgow but doesn't want to be found.'

'Well, that's understandable. She has a right to her own choices.'

Belle rubbed her forehead.

'You got a headache?'

'Migraine.'

'You don't look too well. If I were you I'd get back home and wait it out. It's not up to me but if you want my opinion you're no doing any good here, except getting yourself a headache. Hang about long enough and you could get pneumonia. And what good would that do?' He peered at her. 'Away home. You shouldn't be out and about in this sort of a place. It's not safe. Your sister's not here, and it's a waste of time you freezing to death waiting. When she wants to go home she will. They all do.'

'Cameron didn't,' said Belle. 'Neither did the woman they found in Muiryfauld Drive. They won't be going home again.'

'That right there is another reason you need to take off, some nutters cruising the city and carving up innocent folk. There's a fucking psycho on the loose.' His voice rose. 'So I'm telling you to get away home.' He glanced at the queue. 'Here, Julie, Dawn. A drop of soup to heat you up?'

Dawn and Julie reached up, took the soup and helped themselves to thick pieces of bread.

Belle walked away from the van and stood watching the queue. Julie and Dawn followed her.

Dawn's voice was tentative: 'Excuse me, but I heard you asking about Fiona. We saw Fiona the other night. She's the lassie that disnae speak, isn't she?'

'That's right,' said Belle. 'Where did you see her?'

'She was in a shop doorway talking to...somebody.' Dawn's voice shook.

'Who was she talking to, do you remember?'

'Guy name of Vincent Steele, works at one of the homeless units,' said Julie.

'Which one?'

'The Letum in Duke Street. He was talking to her but then he left.'

'And Fiona?'

'She stayed there.'

'When was this?' asked Belle, as her mobile chirped a text. She looked at the sender. Fiona. She quickly scrolled down. *I can see you talking to Dawn and Julie but I don't want to come to the van.* Belle scanned the area. She couldn't see her sister. She typed furiously, sent the text: *Where are you?*

Watching you but I won't come over. I'll text you tomorrow about a meet-up. But please don't tell anyone that we're meeting.

Not even Dad? He's beside himself with worry.

No one. Promise me or I won't meet you.

I promise.

I'll give you an address to come and see me tomorrow. Please just take it and keep it to yourself. I need to know I can trust you on this?

Of course you can. But why are we meeting tomorrow? Can't you talk to me today?

No. I'll explain everything tomorrow. You'll know it all then. I'll tell you everything. Promise. Fiona xx

'At last.' Belle spoke out loud. 'At long bloody last.'

'You want us to tell you when we saw Fiona?' asked Dawn.

'No, it's okay, she's finally made contact,' said Belle. 'Crisis over.'

Chapter 56

The board in the CID suite had been updated. Among the information and notes there were photographs of Cameron and Irena, maps of where the bodies had been found, information about Karen Cooper and copies of the letters that had been sent to Wheeler. The names of Lena Varga and Katya Novak had been circled and Fiona Henderson's name added to a separate list.

Wheeler was at her desk when she heard him.

'Bloody hell, what a nightmare,' said Ross, coming through the door.

'You get all the sick cleaned up?' asked Wheeler. 'How's Mr Henderson feeling?'

'He's on his way home in the back of a car. I just hope he doesn't throw up again.'

'This must be awful for him,' said Wheeler. 'Did he have any more information for us?'

'He's not Fiona's biological father.'

'Really?'

'Amanda Henderson was raped when she was at university and found out that she was pregnant later. By that time she'd met Richard Henderson. They got married and he brought Fiona up as his own. He believes that the biological father somehow found out about her and is now in contact.'

'And that's why Fiona's blanking Henderson and Belle?' asked Wheeler. 'Does he have any idea who's Fiona's biological father?'

'No, he just remembers a nickname, the Preacher. And that he got the nickname because he was brought up in an old manse.'

A female officer walked into the CID suite and handed Wheeler a piece of paper. 'This just came in.'

Wheeler read it aloud: '"Stella Evans is missing, presumed dead. Look at Andy Doyle."'

'Stella's missing?' said Ross.

Wheeler glanced at the message. 'And whoever called this in refused to give a name or number?'

'Sorry, DI Wheeler, he insisted on just leaving the message.'

Wheeler looked at the officer. 'Have you called Doyle?'

'I spoke with Mr Doyle just now and he insists that Stella's away visiting a friend.'

'So, did you get a number for the friend?' asked Wheeler.

'Apparently Stella never left either an address or a contact number.'

'Very convenient,' said Wheeler. 'I'll take it from here, thanks.'

'Missing, presumed dead?' said Ross. 'Could be bogus, or why wouldn't the caller leave a name?'

'Would you, if you were reporting Andy Doyle to the police?'

'I suppose not, but we're losing time here, Wheeler. This could be just another distraction.'

Wheeler glanced at the board. 'I'm not sure I agree, Ross. I think we need to investigate. Let's go pay Doyle a visit.'

'Because Stella Evans has gone to visit a friend?'

'Because she's been reported as missing, as has Fiona Henderson. And our killer mentioned Lena Varga and Katya Novak in his letter. So, four women reported as missing and Mark Haedyear on the run. Ross, we need to check this out.'

'Okay, but maybe Stella tried to do a runner and Doyle didn't like it,' said Ross, pulling on his jacket. 'Maybe it got ugly.'

Wheeler grabbed her coat and headed out of the door. 'Well, one thing we know about Andy Doyle is that he's capable of anything.'

Andy Doyle lived in a stone villa in Mount Vernon, close to Greenoakhill Quarry, which, at more than two hundred acres, was one of the biggest landfill sites in Europe. Wheeler parked at the top of the drive and saw a blue Mercedes, a black 4x4 and a silver Jaguar parked outside.

The door was opened before they rang the bell and Wheeler got a hit of expensive cologne. Doyle had just showered and his hair was damp. He wore a navy blue cashmere crew-neck and dark jeans. 'Saw you drive up.'

They flashed their ID cards. Doyle ignored them. 'I know who you are.'

Wheeler spoke: 'Mr Doyle, we'd like to ask—'

He cut her off: 'I've got nothing to say to you.'

'We'd like to have a word about Stella.'

'I already told one of your crew, she went to see a pal of hers. Did they not mention that to you?'

'My colleague did say that she'd spoken to you earlier but there are still concerns about Ms Evans,' said Ross. 'You have her pal's name?'

'No, and you already know that I don't. Stella didn't leave a name, an address or a number.'

'Isn't that odd?' said Wheeler. 'Wouldn't she normally have told you where she was going?'

Doyle smiled at Wheeler, leaned towards her and whispered, 'Do you always tell your boyfriend where you're going when you go out, Kat?'

'DI Wheeler.'

'She went off in the huff.'

'You had an argument?' asked Ross.

'Not a barny, just a wee difference of opinion about celebrating our anniversary. Apparently I didn't make it special enough.'

Ross nodded sympathetically. 'So, were you having relationship difficulties?'

'Not that I know of. It was only a disagreement.'

'She wouldn't have separated for good?'

Doyle stared hard at Ross. 'I doubt that very much.'

'It happens,' said Ross.

'Not to me it doesn't.'

'We have reason to believe Stella may have been abducted,' said Wheeler.

'So your colleague mentioned earlier. You got any evidence?'

'A phone call.'

'A phone call from …?'

'We can't divulge names but—'

'Anonymous. In which case you've got sweet FA.'

'Mark Haedyear,' said Wheeler. She watched Doyle

closely, saw his body tense and one eye darken. It blazed black.

'Who?' His tone was way too casual.

'He recently escaped from prison.'

'Is that right?'

'You must remember him,' said Ross. 'Big case on the telly and in the papers a few years back. He was convicted of the murder of Amanda Henderson, an art lecturer, over in the Southside. He buried her underground and she starved to death.'

'He sounds like a right bastard,' said Doyle.

'Agreed,' said Ross. 'But Mark Haedyear was only picked up after the police received an anonymous tip-off.'

Doyle shrugged. 'And this is my business, because?'

'I think Mark Haedyear has a grudge against you,' said Wheeler.

'Is that right?'

'I think you, or someone close to you, made that phone call and now Haedyear has Stella,' said Wheeler.

'Stella's at her pal's,' said Doyle. 'Now I need to go.' He began to close the door.

'If you change your mind,' Wheeler offered her business card, 'call us.'

Dark eyes blazed and the door slammed.

Wheeler put the card back in her pocket and walked down the driveway. She waited until they were in the car before she said, 'Haedyear has her and Doyle knows it.'

'Then why not tell us?'

'Because now it's personal. It's between the two of them. Doyle doesn't want us involved for two reasons. One, he thinks he can find Haedyear quicker than we can.'

'And so far he could be right.'

'And, two, he wants to find Haedyear for revenge. If we get to Haedyear, it means that he's going back inside and Doyle doesn't get revenge. But if Doyle gets to him first, then—'

'Then there will be no more Haedyear.'

'Exactly.'

'Should we tail Doyle?' asked Ross.

'Doyle's too clever for that. He's going to sit tight and let his crew fan out over Glasgow. Even if we knew who they were, and we don't, we can't possibly follow them all.'

'What about watching Weirdo?'

'Weirdo will just give us the run-around. Doyle has crew all over the city. We need to concentrate on our own investigation and make sure that we get to Haedyear first.' Wheeler's mobile rang. She answered it and listened carefully for a few seconds, then ended the call. 'Back to the station, Ross, we've got another communication.'

Chapter 57

They took the stairs to the CID suite two at a time and she was at her desk in seconds. Boyd stood beside her. 'It came in the post, usual delivery, Royal Mail.'

Wheeler recognized the handwriting.

'We're trying to trace where it was sent from,' said Boyd.

Wheeler pulled on gloves, opened the letter and began reading.

My dear Kat,

Are you and your team scrambling around looking for clues about who I am? How exciting. Who am I really? Well, perhaps we should go back to the beginning.

I was born into a universe of darkness, a prick of light in the hopeless abyss. When I was five my parents sent me away to school. At that time I was small, tiny even in comparison to the other boys, so they called me Hedgehog. Something to be kicked and if kicked hard enough would attempt to roll itself into a ball for safety. Which I did. This was a mistake. As a recoiled the bullies became more intrigued and a range of torments was devised to torture me. I was helpless. My parents were abroad, relieved to have finally offloaded their 'mistake'. Did it make me bitter? Of course. Plan to exact revenge? Naturally.

But it took time and I began small. I kept my diary entry from that time. Would you like to take a peek inside?

13 June 1990. Fourteenth birthday. Parents in Morocco.

Today was the rugby match. I'm not in the team, not even in the reserves. Instead of watching the stupid game I went for a walk. Guess what I found in the wood? A hedgehog. The filthy little creature was making slow progress dragging an injured hind leg and leaving a trail of slime behind it. I scooped it up, placed it carefully inside my plastic box, hid it in the undergrowth and raced back to my room. I thought it might die from a lack of oxygen, but when I returned it was still alive. Eagerly, I unpacked the scalpel from my bag. I pegged the creature on its back and studied the muscles heaving against the wooden stakes. Its eyes were watering against the afternoon sun. They looked soft and gentle. I would begin there.

Finally, the death of the creature came as a relief to us both. The anger against the other boys, and the tension I'd held in my head, receded. I shaved a little piece of flesh from the creature and carried it back to my room as a reminder. I knew then that I had found my vocation. I had tasted real power and it was delicious.

Eight days passed before I had the opportunity to progress.

'Bloody hell,' said Ross.

'He can't help himself,' said Wheeler. 'He needs to show off, and because of it we now have his age.'

They continued reading.

My guest was Joseph Mere, also fourteen. He was on a scholarship and this alone separated him from the rest of us. But lack of wealth or family influence did nothing to deter Joseph because he excelled at rugby. I loathed him. He inhabited a separate world to mine, one in which success on the rugby field was oxygen, which supported a lifestyle of excess while loosening the ties of accountability. I observed Joseph, as I did the other animals, from a distance and soon an opportunity revealed itself.

One night I was returning from one of my nocturnal visits. My box was empty. There had been no road kill for me to dissect and I had found nothing live in my trap. As I walked I caught sight of Joseph some way ahead of me. By his unsteady movement I realized that he was either drunk or stoned. He approached the stream and stopped. He appeared to be contemplating crossing the water using the fallen tree that extended to the other bank. Given his state, I knew that would be a mistake but, as ever, Joseph believed that he could make it. His type always did. I waited and watched. The moon was full and I could see clearly. Joseph was midway across the bough of the tree when he slipped. As he fell, his expression changed from incredulity to horror as the ice-cold water broke over him and his heavy winter coat began to curl itself around his torso and drag him under. Joseph began frantically clawing at the water until he had righted himself, then he slowly began to swim towards the bank, his face set in a grimace, as if every movement was excruciatingly painful. I imagine that it was. I watched his lips open and close like a goldfish's and saw his head bob above the water before it disappeared again. Joseph re-emerged a half-minute later, his goldfish mouth gasping for air. Joseph, once so arrogant, was now writhing clumsily in the water. He had become a cartoon character, one that might suddenly whirl up out of the water and laugh at the whole mess.

Perhaps not.

As I watched him panic, I began chanting childlike incantations and clapped as I sang. 'Joseph, you didn't like me. Joseph, you didn't need my friendship. Joseph, you never noticed me. *I bet you're regretting that now.*'

But Joseph refused to sink. Instead he latched onto the bough of the tree again and tried to haul himself out of the water. But he was exhausted. I'm unsure if he caught my eye as he lost his grip but for a brief moment his face lay at an angle in the water, as if by pure supplication he could charm death. Then all at once it was over and his body began to ebb and flow and became one with the water. I watched as he slipped under the surface. I was mesmerized by the beauty of his death.

'Fucking psycho,' said Ross.

'Maybe,' said Wheeler, 'but one who badly needs to communicate with us.'

'Christ, I feel like he's practically here in the room.'

'You're such a sensitive soul, Ross.'

'Aren't you feeling creeped out?'

'Energized, more like.' Wheeler fired up her computer, opened a search engine and typed in 'Joseph Mere'. A second later the links began to appear and she scrolled down until she found the reference. 'Got it.' She traced her finger along the top of the report. 'Our guy was a pupil at Oakwood School.'

'Go on.'

Wheeler read aloud:

'Glasgow Chronicle 14 June, 1990

'Tragic Death of Talented Student

'The body of Joseph Mere, 14, was discovered in the stream at Oakwood School yesterday. The head teacher of the school, Mr Kelvin Rowley, said, 'We are all devastated by this news and our thoughts and prayers go out to Joseph's family at this difficult time. Joseph was an extremely popular boy and a very gifted pupil.

'It is believed that Joseph had been with friends earlier in the evening and was returning to his room when he decided to take a short cut across the stream. It is believed Joseph tripped and fell into the stream and may have sustained a head injury when he fell. Reports suggest that Joseph was alone at the time.

'Police are investigating the incident but say they are not treating the death as suspicious.'

Wheeler scrolled down. 'Let's see what the final outcome was, here's a later report. Coroner decision...accidental death…1990,' she said, 'was when the accident happened.'

'When our guy watched the poor kid drown,' said Ross. 'So that would make our killer what? Around mid-thirties now? Mark Haedyear is thirty-eight and went to Oakwood School.'

'I know.'

'And now he's out there and sending us fan mail?' said Ross.

'As a pupil Haedyear would have known about the accident.'

'So, why confess now when he obviously got off with it?'

'He's only confessing that he witnessed the death, not that he killed him,' said Wheeler. 'He started with animals. He trapped them and cut them up. Once he had the taste for it he progressed to humans.'

'We need to get out to Oakwood and see what we can find on their former pupil.' Wheeler grabbed her coat. 'Let's go, Ross.'

Ross pulled on his leather jacket. 'I'd bet money Haedyear's still here in the city. I think he's watching us and waiting for his prize.'

'Which is?' asked Wheeler.

'You.'

Chapter 58

'I need you to drop me at Matt's office on the way back.'

'Why?'

'No, that it's any of your business but I'm going to the Arthouse to see the exhibition.'

'It's okay.'

'You've seen it? Any good?'

'I've seen better.'

'The turning for the school's up here on your left.'

'This a date, then?'

'It's a look at some pictures. A very quick look.'

'Sounds like a date.'

'You trying to match-make?'

'You could do better,' said Ross, as he indicated and turned towards the building.

Oakwood School stood in acres of manicured grounds. There were both rugby and football pitches, tennis courts and a running track. The stream was on the periphery of the playing fields. Ross nudged the car through the gates and read the signs as he passed them: 'Fencing Salle, Stables, Swimming pool. Not exactly like my school. What do you reckon for the fees?'

'A fair portion of our salary, I'd guess.'

'They must be so proud of producing an evil git like Haedyear,' said Ross.

'It's the old nature-versus-nurture argument,' said Wheeler. 'Are we born evil or do we become evil as a result of what happens to us?'

'Born,' stated Ross.

'You sound pretty sure.'

'Definitely. Lots of people have shitty childhoods or experiences and it doesn't make them kill, but what kind of a place produces Mark Haedyear? Did they even spot what he was like at school?'

'Obviously not,' said Wheeler, 'but then I'd imagine that he was cunning enough to conceal his real personality.'

Ross turned into the car park and pulled into a space. A notice read, *All Visitors Must Report to the Main Reception.*

Wheeler slammed the car door and looked up at the building ahead. 'Arts and Crafts. What do you reckon?'

'It's nice enough.' Ross strode across the gravel towards the school. Inside, the reception area was spacious. Polished parquet flooring glowed in the light from copper lamps, leaded stained-glass windows kept the weather at bay and an old oak staircase smelling of beeswax wound its way to the next level. Wheeler glanced at the patterned ceiling. It looked like an original William Morris design. A small woman in her mid-sixties with a tight perm approached. She was wearing a Harris tweed suit, thick black tights and sturdy brown leather brogues. Her only concession to jewellery was a gold ring, which she wore on the pinkie finger of her left hand.

'May I be of assistance?' Her smile was practised and professional, her voice high and clipped.

'DI Wheeler, and this is DI Ross,' said Wheeler, as they flashed their cards.

'And you are?' asked Ross.

'Miss Mackie, the school secretary.'

'We'd like to speak to the head teacher,' said Wheeler .

'I'm afraid that's not possible. Mr Farquar's off site at present. He's attending the Head Teachers' Conference in Perth.'

'When will he be back?' asked Wheeler.

'It's a two-day conference. Perhaps I can help?'

'Would it be possible to speak to a former head teacher, Mr Kelvin Rowley?' asked Wheeler.

'Unfortunately Mr Rowley passed away last year. Tragic, simply tragic. He was a very gifted man.'

'We've had a communication from someone describing themselves as a former pupil,' said Wheeler.

'I see. Do you have a name?'

'No, but he's someone we need to locate as a matter of urgency.'

'May I ask why?' Again the practised smile. 'We have a lot of very special alumni. We produce pupils who have...How should I say this? A certain cachet. I'd imagine that he may well be quite prominent. A politician or businessman. Perhaps a scientist? In which area is he connected?'

'We think he may well be connected to a murder,' said Ross.

'An ex-pupil of ours?' Mackie's smile disappeared.

'Yes,' said Wheeler.

'Then you must be referring to Mark Haedyear. A rogue of the highest order but one who can't possibly be seen as representative of our school. I do hope that you're not trying to undermine us because of that individual.' Mackie held up her hands, palms outward. 'He was simply an imposter, that was all.'

'He only pretended to be at the school?' asked Ross.

'I didn't say that. He did attend Oakwood but he does not represent our school.'

'Did you work here in 1990, Miss Mackie?' asked Ross.

'No, I started in 1995,' said Mackie. 'Is it important?'

'So you never met Joseph Mere?'

'The poor boy who drowned? No, I did not. It was a tragedy.'

'And you won't have known any of his classmates?'

'They would have left the school in 1994, so, no, I didn't know any of that year group. And, sadly, we have no teaching staff who would have been here in 1994. Our head teacher favours NQTs.'

'Why so keen on newly qualified teachers?' asked Ross.

'Financial prudence, Inspector, and also in response to the rapid changes in education. Our newly qualified staff are not only less expensive but they are up to date with all new initiatives, which saves a fortune on buying in outsiders for staff development days. I'm sure you understand.'

'We need a list of pupils from 1990,' said Wheeler.

'A whole school list?' asked Mackie. 'Well, I'm sure we'll have it on file somewhere.'

'We'd appreciate it if you could give us a printout of the pupils who were here in that year,' said Wheeler. 'In particular we need the pupils who were around fourteen years of age.'

'It'll be in storage, I expect. We don't keep anything live after seven years.' Mackie paused, 'And you need this information quickly, I'd imagine?'

'Is that a problem?' asked Ross.

'Logistically, yes.'

'But you do keep records?'

'Not on site. Our caretaker's off on holiday and I'm afraid the relief caretaker hasn't turned up. We're a little bit stuck. I would need to get the key myself and trawl through the old boxes. It would take time.'

'I'd appreciate it,' said Wheeler, handing Mackie her card, 'if you would call me when you locate them.'

Miss Mackie slipped the card into her jacket pocket, then showed them out.

'You still want me to drop you at Elliot's?'

'If you don't mind, Ross.'

'What if I do mind?'

'Tough.'

'He deals with dead people all the time. Corpses.'

'We deal with the same dead people, Ross, only we call them victims.'

Chapter 59

It was late afternoon but darkness had fallen over the city as Haedyear walked through Bridgeton, on past the red sandstone tenements and the ornate Templeton building with its turrets and circular windows. On his journey only a few people passed him, their heads bent into the sleet or under umbrellas. No one made eye contact with the man in rags. Haedyear walked on and finally reached his destination. Established in the fifteenth century, Glasgow Green was the city's oldest park. Haedyear walked to the far side, passing the largest terracotta fountain in the world, the Doulton Fountain. He walked until he saw him.

Tommy Taylor stood beside the dark green Mégane. 'Everything's in the boot. You need a hand?'

'No,' said Haedyear.

'No, of course not. You've done this before.'

'You know I have.'

'You're not the only one. You and me, we're the same.'

Haedyear stared at him. 'We're nothing alike.'

Taylor tried for a smile. 'Course we are. You and me are in the same line of work.'

Haedyear shook his head. 'You see, Tommy, that's where you are deluded. You are only good enough to be a runner. To bring your car out now and again. To deliver the odd message between myself and the Preacher. You're a go-between, that's all.'

'She said that I could move up in the organization.'

'There is no organization, Tommy. It's just the Preacher.'

'And her. And you and me.'

'You're second-rate, Tommy. You've no self-control, no finesse. You tried to rape your ex-girlfriend. Clumsy. Then you messed up and killed her instead. Very fucking clumsy. You're pathetic. Stick with the only talent you have, escorting drunks out of Dragon's club.'

Tommy Taylor balled his fists.

Haedyear moved towards him, leaned into his face and whispered, 'Don't ever try to play with the big boys, Tommy. You'll only get hurt.'

Taylor took a step back. 'Here, catch.' He threw the keys at Haedyear, then turned and headed back into Glasgow Green.

Haedyear caught them and quickly checked that a blanket and shovel were in the boot before he took out his mobile and punched in the familiar number. He spoke quickly: 'Tell the Preacher I'm going to collect her now. I'll call him later.'

'Don't bother, there's been a change of plan.'

Haedyear froze.

'You've been replaced. Your services are no longer required.'

The line went dead. Haedyear threw the mobile onto the seat. 'You little bitch, we'll see about that.' He turned the key in the ignition and pulled out.

Chapter 60

Elliot's office was in an old two-storey building on the opposite side of the car park to the morgue. Ross dropped her off and Wheeler made her way to the front door and rang the bell. A technician carrying a stack of files answered.

She held up her ID. 'DI Wheeler for Dr Elliot? He's expecting me.'

'He's not back from the lab yet – I think he was picking up some results – but you're welcome to wait.' Wheeler followed him into a small waiting area and sat in one of the plastic seats. The technician's footsteps echoed as he walked down the corridor and through the double doorway. Then there was silence. Wheeler checked her phone. There were no bars showing, so it was emergency calls only. Great. Five minutes later she heard the footsteps return and the technician burst through the doors.

'That's me off home, then. I'm sure Dr Elliot will be back soon.' He smiled. 'You okay to wait here by yourself? The building's empty but there are technicians on duty across at the complex.' Wheeler nodded, settled herself in her chair and heard the door slam behind him. After another five minutes she walked to the end of the corridor, saw the sign for the Ladies. It was on the second floor, as was Matt's office. Wheeler sprinted up the stairs and a few seconds later pushed through the swing doors on the first floor and up another flight. She was drying her hands when she heard it. The slam of the door on the ground floor. He'd arrived. Wheeler moved into the corridor and waited for Elliot to come up the stairs. After a few seconds she called, 'Matt?' There was no reply.

'Matt?'

The lights died. Wheeler stood in darkness and waited for the emergency generator to kick in. It didn't.

She called into the dark stairwell, 'Dr Elliot, it's DI Wheeler.'

Silence.

She identified herself again. Loudly. There was no response.

Wheeler reached out, touched the cold wall of the corridor and used it to steady herself in the dark. She began to feel her way towards the stairs.

She stilled when she heard the footsteps move across the hallway on the ground floor and stop at the bottom of the stairs. She tried again: 'DI Wheeler. Who's there?' She listened for a reply. Nothing. She inched her way down the stairs, testing every tread with her foot before stepping onto it. She paused again and listened for the other person's footstep. She heard only the distant roar of traffic. She reached the first-floor landing and heard the footsteps move towards the front door, heard it slam.

Wheeler turned back and felt her way to the window. She peered out into the car park but all she saw was her own reflection. She turned back towards the stairs and moved towards the swing doors. They flew open and Wheeler instinctively held her arms in front of her. The door swung back and slammed into someone. There was a sharp intake of breath as the door hit them, then the crash as they fell down the stairs.

Wheeler pushed open the doors, felt her way down to the bottom of the stairs and reached for the body. He was unconscious but still breathing. The generator kicked into life and the lights snapped on. Wheeler stared at the person lying at her feet.

Overhead the sky had turned black and the pale moon stared hard at Easterhouse as if in accusation. More than twenty-five thousand people resided in the Greater Easterhouse area but the forest was deserted. Tuck parked the silver Volvo and walked. He covered the frozen ground quickly. The forest was made up of five woodlands, Cardowan Moss, West Maryston, Todds Well, Bishop's Loch Local Nature Reserve, Lochend Burn. As he walked he listened to the night creatures call. He heard the earth shiver beneath a blanket of sleet. He listened to the wind shriek and howl, and thought that it carried a curse. He walked quickly and only stopped when he saw a broken branch, a scrap of material. Tuck pulled the scrap from the branch and closed his eyes, stilled his heartbeat, slow, slow, slow. Ssh. He listened for a few seconds. It was enough. Tuck knew that he was in the right place. He also knew that Stella was buried somewhere close by. What he didn't know was if she was still alive.

Chapter 61

The private hospital was situated on the outskirts of the city. It was a state-of-the-art facility and sat in its own grounds. The manager was a particular aficionado of modern sculpture, and a number of stainless-steel orbs had been installed in the grounds. Wheeler passed them as she pulled in and parked between a Mercedes and a Porsche. Her mobile chirped a text. It was Ross.

What do you think of Elliot's photographs?
She texted quickly: *Haven't seen them yet.*
Because?
We didn't make it to the Arthouse.
Why not?
He had an accident and is now in hospital.
The Royal?
Private.
Figures.
Sympathy?
Fresh out. Where are you?
Making a quick visit, I'll be back at the station soon.

Wheeler threw her mobile into her bag and walked towards the building. The reception area was spacious and she was directed to room eighteen. She knocked and heard, 'Come on in.' Matt Elliot groaned and sat up in bed, his ribcage bandaged.

'See you're still skiving in bed,' said Wheeler, by way of apology.

'Sorry about that, slamming myself into the door, then hurling myself down the stairs.'

'Kind of like an extreme sport, maybe.' She dumped her coat over the back of a chair. 'There was someone in the place before you came in. They didn't identify themselves. The staff on the other wing heard a car being driven away at speed.'

'Go on,' said Elliot. 'Did they have any idea who it was?'

'Nothing yet,' Wheeler made for the door, 'but we've got hold of CCTV. I'll get you a copy, see if you recognize the car. Just now, though, I'll let you rest.'

'Fine, but I've had a few thoughts about the case. Maybe we can meet up tomorrow for a chat? I'll call you.'

'Good.'

'You can't miss my exhibition – you'll have to see it at some point.'

'Of course, but for now, back to the station.'

There was a knock at the door and Philip Bishop came into the room. 'Oops, sorry, I didn't know you had visitors.'

'It's okay, I'm just leaving,' said Wheeler.

'DI Kat Wheeler, meet my old friend Philip Bishop.'

Wheeler smiled at Bishop as she made for the door. 'Good night, then.'

'Good night, Kat,' said Elliot.

'Good to meet you,' said Bishop.

Wheeler walked to the car park. Heard a text come through. *You done skiving?*

On my way.

She started the car.

Chapter 62

Haedyear drove the Mégane carefully and kept well within the speed limit: there was no need to draw any attention to himself. He was still shaken from the phone call. He hadn't made a rational decision when he'd gone to the office and had panicked when the woman detective had been there. He cursed himself for being clumsy. 'Fucking stupid,' he muttered, as he gripped the steering wheel and checked the road signs. He took the turn-off for Easterhouse. He felt a tension headache begin. 'Get a grip,' he muttered, while he checked his rear-view mirror. No one was following him: the road was deserted. He'd got away without being recognized. But, still, he'd been stupid. It wouldn't happen again. He'd make sure of that.

He turned off the road and drove the car into the wood. He parked it close to the hiding place, opened the boot and lifted out the shovel. He scanned the area and listened carefully, but there was nothing other than the wind. It was safe to continue. He placed the torch on the ground, hoisted the shovel and worked steadily until finally he found the hatch door. He cleared the last of the soil and heard the hatch creak as he opened it. He shone the torch into the space. Stella was unconscious, her body limp. Haedyear felt for a pulse. It was weak but she was still breathing. He forced his hands under her armpits, grabbed hold of her and hoisted her towards him. He dragged her towards the car, opened the boot and lifted her in. He covered her with the blanket and breathed deeply, inhaling the freezing air for a minute before closing the boot. He returned to the hatch, closed it and began shovelling the soil back into place. Finally, he stamped over the top soil. It didn't matter: the police could find his lair. He wouldn't use it again. And by that time Stella Evans would be long gone.

Haedyear threw the shovel onto the back seat and started the engine. The headlights flickered on and illuminated the bare tree trunks. The sleet fell in sheets and the wind howled as he gripped the steering wheel. He still fretted about the phone call. That fucking bitch was wrong: he was the disciple, the chosen one. 'I have every chance to be the disciple,' he muttered to himself. 'I have every chance.'

He had no chance.

The blow shattered the window. Fragments of glass showered Haedyear at the same time as a hand reached in, flicked the lock and grabbed him by the hair. Haedyear was hauled out of the car in one swift movement. Freezing cold air forced its way into his lungs as he was propelled head first into the bonnet. Blood. Throbbing pain. More blood. Haedyear felt his head being smashed against metal. His attacker paused. 'Who's the Preacher?'

Bright lights danced in front of Haedyear's eyes. He felt the blood run from his nose into his mouth and swallowed.

'Who is the Preacher?'

318

Haedyear felt his head being pulled back and then smashed once more against the car.

'For the last time, Haedyear, who is the Preacher?'

Haedyear closed his eyes. It was over. His mind told him that there was no point in begging for his life. Although he knew this, his lips tried to move, to form a silent plea. But he heard only a gurgle as blood escaped from his mouth. He consoled himself with the thought that he had been a true disciple. He smiled at the thought and felt the shards of cracked teeth tear through the soft skin of his bottom lip. He thought of the woman who had given birth to him and comforted himself with the thought that her ashes at the Rose Memorial Crematorium would have been scattered in the wind. If there was a Hell, they'd meet up again. As he faded into the sweet relief of darkness, he imagined that the crushing pain he felt had changed colour from grey to black. He understood that he would be dead in a second and that—

He hiccuped blood.

It was over.

Tuck watched Haedyear drool into death before he bent over the body and satisfied himself that the cunt was gone. He reached into the Mégane and flicked the release for the boot. Stella's body was cold. Tuck picked her up and carried her to the old silver Volvo, placed her on the back seat and tucked the blanket around her. He turned the heating up full. He walked back to the corpse, dragged it further onto the snow and dumped the heap of blood and snot. He wiped the blood and mess off his hands and walked away. He glanced back before he drove off and saw the mess of red, Haedyear's body. The ground around it was stained dark with blood. Tuck put the Volvo into gear, then drove out of the forest and towards the main road. He called Doyle.

'Is she alive?'

Tuck glanced at Stella. 'She's unconscious but still breathing. She's in a bad way, though. She needs attention.'

'Meet me back here. I'll take her into the hospital.'

'I'm on my way.'

'Where's Haedyear?'

'He's still on location. I left the Mégane and the body there.'

'Is Haedyear in bits?'

'He's shredded.'

'Good. I'll send Weirdo to collect him.'

'He'll need a bag. There are a few bits and pieces to collect.'

'Good work, Tuck.'

Tuck killed the call.

Chapter 63

Ross was at his desk when the call came in. He answered it on the second ring.

It was Laura Mearns. 'I've watched the CCTV of the car been driven away from the car park outside Elliot's office. '

'And?'

'I think I recognized the car. It's a dark green Mégane.'

'Go on.'

'It was definitely parked there about six months ago, on a fairly regular basis. The thing is, I remember it being parked in the staff car park.'

'It belongs to a member of staff?' asked Ross. 'Who?'

'A guy who used to be a porter at the morgue. I'm not sure of his name. I didn't know him – he was on night shift. I passed him in the corridor a few times.'

'Is there anything you remember about him? Think, Laura,' said Ross. 'This is important.'

'Don't you realize I get that?' Her tone was petulant.

'Sorry,' said Ross. 'Just take a minute, see what you can remember. Can you describe him?'

'I only saw him a few times when he was going off duty. He was maybe five five or five six, with cropped white-blond hair, white eyebrows. I think he might have been called Tommy, something like that.'

'Could it be Taylor?' asked Ross. 'Tommy Taylor?'

'Could be, I'm not sure.'

'Tommy Taylor,' said Ross. 'He's already known to us. If it was Taylor, is there any reason that he would be back visiting the place?'

'No idea.'

Ross thanked her and killed the call. He immediately redialled and the phone at the Equestrian Eatery was answered immediately. 'The Equestrian. Maggie-May speaking—'

Ross spoke over her, 'DI Ross, Carmyle police station. I need to speak with Tommy Taylor.'

'He's not here at the moment.'

'When do you expect him?'

'Just give me a second. I'll check the rota for you.'

Ross waited for a few minutes.

'He's not in again until Saturday.'

Five minutes later, Boyd and Robertson were driving to Strathbungo.

Weirdo edged the van into the outside lane and drove through the sleet, listening while the thrum of the windscreen wipers played a steady requiem for Mark Haedyear. He turned off at the sign for Easterhouse, drove into the forest and found the spot Tuck had described. Weirdo parked the van and pulled on gloves. He leaned into the back, pulled a heavy-duty body-bag from the selection, removed its plastic cover and unfolded it. He opened the door of the van, stepped out into the cold night air and took in the sight. The forest was beautiful. The wind had lessened and now only hummed a low, mournful melody through the naked trees as they twisted their branches towards the indifferent moon.

Weirdo walked towards what remained of Mark Haedyear. 'Right, you bastard. Trust you to ruin a lovely fucking night like this.' He reached the mess. 'Let's get you binned.' He bent over the corpse and began hauling it into the body-bag. He was careful to include everything, the bits of teeth and the handfuls of matted hair. There was an abundance of soft tissue and blood, which he scooped up and threw on top of the body. He smeared his gloves clean on Haedyear's coat, then zipped up the body-bag, dragged it to the van and hauled it into the back. He grabbed a petrol can and slammed the van door closed. He walked back to the car and carefully doused the seats in the dark green Mégane with petrol. Then he soaked a rag and stood back to survey the scene. He checked and double-checked that everything was gone, save the bit of blood on the ground, but it was already being diluted with sleet.

Weirdo lit the rag and threw it into the middle of the car before running back to the van, putting it in gear and hurtling towards the road. In the rear-view mirror he saw the explosion, the red of fire against the dark sky. He punched the numbers into his mobile and when the call was answered he spoke quickly: 'Crook? One body to be disposed of. Ashes to ashes.' He killed the call and drove along the deserted lane, then turned towards the main road.

Later, on the motorway, he moved into the outside lane and drove towards what would be Haedyear's final destination.

Chapter 64

Ross was on the phone: 'If Tommy Taylor's not at his flat, get over to the Equestrian Eatery, and if he hasn't turned up there, speak to his colleagues again. Find out where he drinks, if he goes to a gym, which one. Have uniform keep an eye on his flat and call me when you locate him.'

A call came through for Wheeler. She listened for a few seconds, then slammed down the phone. 'Stella Evans has just been admitted to Intensive Care at the Royal Infirmary.'

'Go on,' said Ross.

'The hospital says she's unconscious and suffering from hypothermia.'

'And Doyle?' Ross shut down his computer.

'They said her partner was with her,' said Wheeler. 'Let's go.'

Thirty minutes later they walked into the Royal Infirmary and made their way to Intensive Care. Andy Doyle was sitting in the waiting area.

Wheeler kept her voice compassionate: 'Mr Doyle.' Ross took a chair beside him.

Doyle ignored them both.

'We'd like a word about Stella,' said Wheeler.

Doyle looked at her, eyes blazing. 'Can you not leave me alone?'

'We just need to know what happened,' said Wheeler.

Doyle's tone was civil. 'When I found her she was unconscious, so I brought her straight here to the hospital.'

'You said she was off visiting friends, Mr Doyle.'

'Aye, well, something fucking changed in her plans, didn't it?'

'Do you have any idea what happened to her after she left your house?'

'Our house,' said Doyle.

'Any idea at all what happened?'

'No.'

'Where did you find her?' asked Ross.

'Tollcross Road,' said Doyle.

'Whereabouts?' asked Ross. 'It's a long road.'

'I found her across from Tollcross Park.'

'Was she walking along beside the park?'

'Yeah.'

'That was a lucky guess, that you found her just when she was walking along at that specific time,' said Ross.

'I had a hunch and took a look around the area. Found her walking on Tollcross Road.'

'It doesn't sound as if she was in any fit state to walk anywhere,' said Ross.

Doyle stared at him. 'Take it or fucking leave it. It's what happened.'

'And Haedyear?' asked Wheeler. 'Did you find him too?'

'I told you before, I don't know the guy.'

'Did he abduct Stella?'

'If he did, he's obviously scarpered. Reckon that would be the best thing for him.'

'Really? Why would that be?' asked Ross.

Doyle dropped the civil tone: 'You got a problem with me?'

'It just seems very convenient, Mr Doyle,' said Ross. 'You found Stella apparently strolling along Tollcross Road, when actually she's unconscious and, despite intensive press coverage, you've never heard of Mark Haedyear.'

'It's the truth. If your man Haedyear took Stella, the bastard must have scarpered. I grant you that it's not convenient – it would've been better for him to hang around and have a wee chat with us all but sometimes that's just the way it goes.' Doyle stared at Wheeler. 'Isn't it, DI Wheeler? It's kind of like when that wee student lassie died just before Christmas. She was only twenty-one. What was her name? Lauren something? She died and there was no one around to say what happened. Tragic.' Doyle tut-tutted. 'Fuckin' tragic. Don't you agree, Kat?'

Wheeler felt the heat rise in her face. Lauren Taylor had apparently died alone but she'd had gamma hydroxy-butyrate, or GHB, the date-rape drug, in her system. The young student had been a friend of Wheeler's nephew, Jason, and Wheeler suspected that Jason had been with her when she died. Jason, however, had denied it. Wheeler wondered how much Doyle knew and if this was a warning to back off from investigating Stella's abduction. 'Tell me again how you knew to go to Tollcross Road at this time of the night.'

'A hunch,' repeated Doyle.

'And why would Stella be walking on Tollcross Road when you live in Mount Vernon?' she asked.

'Who knows?' said Doyle. 'Mibbe you can ask her when she wakes up.'

Ross spoke: 'And you're absolutely positive you don't know anything about Mark Haedyear?'

'I only know what you told me. Guy escaped and is on the run. He could be off sunning himself abroad. Keeping himself nice and warm and toasty.'

'Right,' said Ross.

'If you think he was involved with Stella,' said Doyle, 'then you should be out there looking for him, instead of sitting here harassing me.'

'We're hardly harassing you,' said Ross.

'That's not the way I see it,' said Doyle. 'This conversation is over.' He stood and walked towards Stella's room. When he opened the door Wheeler heard the repetitive bleep from the life-support machine. Doyle paused. 'I've got enough on my hands. You do your job and I'll do mine.' The door closed behind him.

Ross turned to Wheeler. 'You think he had anything to do with Stella's disappearance?'

'No. You saw him – he's genuinely upset.'

'He could be faking it. Someone like Doyle is capable of anything.'

'True, but I'd bet you money Haedyear had her.'

'So you think Doyle's already got to Haedyear?'

'Yes. If we ever find him, it'll be a dead body we pick up.'

'You believe Doyle about Stella being found on Tollcross Road?'

'No, but I'll send uniform down there for a look around.

I think it will be a waste of time though.' Wheeler walked towards the door.

A nurse approached on her way into Stella's room. Wheeler flashed her ID. 'How is she doing?'

The nurse shook her head. 'Not at all well, but she's stable and the next twenty-four hours will decide how things will go.'

'What are her chances?' asked Wheeler.

'We're doing everything in our power to hold on to her but she needs to find the strength to pull through.'

'In your professional opinion?' prompted Wheeler.

The nurse's voice was low, discreet: 'Between us and these four walls, I don't know if she's too far gone. If it's already over and it's just a matter of time until she lets go.'

'Thank you,' said Wheeler. 'I appreciate it.'

'Then, again, she might have enough fight in her to pull through.' The nurse added, 'Do you know her?'

'I know of her,' said Wheeler.

'Is she a fighter?'

'Stella Evans is definitely a fighter.'

'Then she might be in with a chance.' The nurse nodded to them and opened the door to Stella's room and Wheeler caught sight of Doyle standing beside the bed. He was holding Stella's limp hand in his own. Wheeler saw tears. She heard the life-support machine bleep again, a solid, rhythmic promise of nothing, only that for the time being it would keep Stella's body alive. But what of the future? The door closed quietly.

Chapter 65

The Smuggler's was unusually busy. Sonny had pulled pints for six young men and had charged them tourist prices for the pleasure. He bared his teeth in a smile and addressed the leader of the group, 'This a dare then, son, or a bet? Which is it?'

'I'm not quite sure what you mean.' The customer in question was nineteen and wore denims and a heavy tweed jacket. His haircut was bold and asymmetrical but his voice was hesitant. 'It's a free country, isn't it?'

'Wee bunch of you college students taking a trip all the way over here to the wrong side of the tracks. Was it a wee bet and did ye lose?'

The boy backed away from the bar and joined his friends. They stood close together, too-loud voices contradicted by wide eyes and intermittent fidgeting, like nervous gazelles before an attack.

'At least it's warm in here,' said Julie. She sipped her vodka and looked at the group in the centre of the room. 'Whit are they doing here?'

'Sonny says there's a wee craze going on now at the college. They have loads of dares and bets. If you lose, one of the things is, ye have to come here and stay long enough for two drinks,' sniggered Dawn.

'That it? Ye lose and ye get to go drinking? How's that losing?'

'Thing is, it's here. They have tae come in here.'

'And?' said Julie. 'I don't get it.'

'We're not the sort of folk they normally hang around with, and this here's not the kind of pub they drink in. They think it's dead edgy tae come out here and have a drink. They think they're being edgy and dangerous.'

'Fucksake,' said Julie. 'They come here for a dare?'

'Aye,' said Dawn, sipping her vodka. 'Never mind them tossers. Did you say Maggie-May texted earlier?'

'You mind of her punk band?'

'CAC?'

'Well, they've got a regular slot in that Headfuck place.'

'That's great. Well done her. She going tae stop work the doors at the Eatery?'

'Naw, she says she can dae both. But, anyway, she says she's got enough deposit for a flat over by London Road.'

'That right?'

'Two bedroom,' said Julie.

'Posh.'

'She says we can have the other room.'

'You're kidding me?'

'Naw.'

'She's just going tae give us a room? For nothing?'

Julie shook her head. 'Nae chance, hen. There a wee list of conditions.'

'Right. Want tae tell me what they are?'

'Hold on.' Julie took out her mobile, scrolled down and read aloud, 'You two need to get real jobs and stop pissing about. You need to split the rent and food and you need to commit to it for a minimum of six months.'

'She's a bossy git.'

'Aye, but what dae I tell her?'

Dawn licked her lips. 'Whit's the option? End up like them two over there?' She nodded to the two women who had entered the bar. 'Shona and Heather look like they're casing the place.'

'I don't want tae be like them,' said Julie. 'This is no the way I thought my life would go after school.'

'Me neither,' said Dawn. 'This wisnae the plan, we just sort of fell intae it.'

'Aye, so we did.' Julie paused. 'Whit should I tell Maggie-May, then?'

'Tell her aye,' said Dawn, 'and also tell her ta very much for the offer. We'll take it and the conditions.'

'You sure?'

'Sure.'

Julie sent the text.

'Shit,' said Dawn. 'Look who's just walked in.'

Julie looked up and caught Vincent Steele staring at her. He smiled, baring a row of perfect teeth and oversized incisors. Steele ordered at the bar, took his pint from Sonny and sipped it casually. He watched Julie and Dawn.

'You want to go now, hen?' said Julie.

'Aye.' Dawn downed the last of her vodka.

Sonny waded over to collect the glasses. 'You two lassies off out the night?'

'Aye, Sonny.'

'Hope Vincent, a.k.a. the Monk, hasn't frightened you two off – that wouldnae be good for business. You a wee bit nervous around him?'

'A bit, Sonny.'

'Ah heard he wisnae very nice tae an old doll. Mashed her face up?'

Dawn stared at her hands. She kept an eye on Steele.

'You don't need tae say nothing. Weirdo told me already that you waited till he had left and helped her. See, that old doll had been very useful to Mr Doyle over the years on account of her hearing stuff and passing it along tae him via Weirdo. So, it was a wee bit disrespectful whit Steele did, plus there wis a boundary issue. You sit tight, I'll get ye another vodka. Weirdo's treat. Nae need tae worry about Steele. Him and me are going tae have words round the back jist as soon as they college boys have their second pint and leave.' Sonny tapped his nose with his forefinger. 'Take it from me, Vincent, or the Monk or whatever the fuck it is he calls himself, won't be bothering you again. He disnae know it yet, but this is his last pint in Glasgow. He's relocating first thing in the morning.'

Communication Four

When the nurse enters the room I pretend to be sleeping but I know *exactly* what she sees. A patient recovering. It's enough. She doesn't have to know the rest. How could she? There's nothing unusual about me. I open my eyes, glimpse her red hair, the snug rolls of fat under her tight uniform. Her name badge reads *Angela Fallon*. I smile at her but she ignores me, her mouth a thin, tight line. She wants out of here quickly. Quickly. When she bends over I smell her warm, sugary breath on my cheek. Doughnuts at tea break. Fatty Fallon. Fleshy Fallon. I move a fraction closer to her armpit to inhale the salt of her sweat. It is sour against the sugar on her breath. My senses are at their peak and I am trembling. I close my eyes in anticipation of her touch. I know she will notice my tremor.

She straightens the bedclothes. 'Are you cold?' She addresses the bed.

I ignore the question. I sense her at my side and feel the rough of her hands. She is impatient and harassed. No angel of mercy. I'd say she was around thirty and already hacked off with her Florence-fucking-Nightingale job.

I want to say, 'Only another thirty-five years of this left, bitch.' But I don't. I know better. Over the years I've taught myself well, remain docile and let them think I'm calm. Besides, with my eyes closed I can train my senses to tell me *precisely* where she is in the room. I open my eyes. She's exactly where I knew she would be, at the bottom of the bed, reading my notes. Unsuspecting, not paying attention, preoccupied with her menial tasks.

Not now. Not yet.

As she approaches me again I turn my face a fraction towards her. My mouth is level with her left breast. I address it, whispering in my best patient voice, 'Thank you, Nurse.'

She nods and heads towards the door.

'Nurse?'

'Yes?'

My timing is impeccable. Her tone is hostile: she's already thinking about the next patient.

'Nurse, I need a bedpan.'

I watch the roll of the eyes, hear the sigh as she wades towards the stack of sludge-grey cardboard bowls.

I force myself to take my time doing my business. Moving slightly, I allow the warm sticky smell to rise while watching her grimace.

'Almost done,' I whisper to her. It's almost a caress. After a few seconds I smile weakly. 'I'm finished now.'

She reaches for the bowl and as she does I let go, breaking wind into her face. Small, rapid farts escape like bullets. Coughing, she backs out of the room, the putrid bowl in her hand. I reach across to the cabinet, find the spray. Once. Twice. The air is filled with the scent of lemon.

I hear footsteps at the end of the corridor, muffled voices. I recognize her voice. I sit up, straighten the bedclothes. Wait.

Finally the door opens. It's my daughter – I see myself in her features.

She sits on the side of the bed. 'Mark Haedyear's disappeared.'

'You've called him?'

'He called and I spoke to him. I told him that he was redundant.'

'How did he take it?'

Fiona smiles. 'What do I care? Do you think Doyle got to him?'

'Maybe.'

'Would he have squealed? Would he have given them your name?'

'I don't think so, Fiona.'

'When are you coming home?'

'First thing in the morning.'

'Belle's coming over tomorrow after lunch.'

'I have a guest coming too.'

'Who?'

'DI Wheeler.'

'When?'

'Early evening.'

'Wonderful!' says Fiona. 'A party!' She claps her hands together in silent applause.

Outside the window the wind rages against the stainless-steel orbs and the sleet batters them.

Chapter 66

A bowl of cards from the Letum Institute stood on her bedside table. Fiona Henderson sat cross-legged on her bed and flicked through a photograph album. The original newspaper articles about Joseph Mere had been preserved under plastic. Fiona traced over it with her finger, then turned the page and saw photographs of ten other soulmates: Agnes Strang, Janet Brodie, Lucy McEwan, Danuta Kerr, Jackie McCurdy, Frances Merrick, Lena Varga, Katya Novak, Lizzie Ellis and Morag Bevan. Their bones had been scattered across the city and lay undiscovered still. The photographs showed the bodies in various stages of decay. Her father had photographed them using his usual understanding of chiaroscuro. They were works of art, thought Fiona. He had also included the shavings of soft down under each picture. A shared story, our story, he had told Fiona, when he had found her.

Fiona turned to the next page and Cameron Craig stared back at her. He was naked on the mortuary slab. Then she flicked to a similar picture of Irena. Fiona continued to look through the album until she saw the

pictures of her mother on the mortuary slab. He had recognized Amanda at the post-mortem, seen that she had
given birth and done the maths, then checked the records
from Rottenrow. Fiona glanced at the newspaper report
about Haedyear when he had killed her mother. Their
two faces stared out at her. United for life, was how
Richard Henderson had described it during one of his
breakdowns.

Fiona bent over the picture of Haedyear and spat on it.
She watched the saliva drip down the plastic and spoke
aloud: 'You were his disciple once but now it's my turn.
It's only right that I follow him. After all, blood is
thicker...' She grabbed her mobile, pulled up the search
engine and typed *suspension hanging*. A few seconds later
the information appeared on the screen and she scanned
it quickly. '...no need for long drop...Airway becomes
compressed, oxygen supply to brain cut off...'

She touched the right side of her neck, traced the curve
beneath her jawline, felt for the carotid artery, moved her
hand to trace where the jugular veins would be on either
side of her neck, then imagined the airways being
compressed. She returned to the information: 'If jugular
veins become blocked...pressure on the system...death
will...'

'Enough,' she said. 'I have enough.' She crossed to the
pile of cards, picked one up. 'This one's for you, Belle.'
She turned it over: *Happiness is when you learn to love
yourself.* She placed it in her pocket. She turned to the
photograph of Belle and traced a finger over her jaw line,
over where the jugular would be, just to make sure.

Fiona's phone chirped a text. She grabbed it and
scanned the message: *I'm on my way. Belle x*

Fiona scrambled from the bed and made for the stairs. A few minutes later the doorbell rang and she hurried to answer it. Belle stood on the step outside. Fiona stood back. 'Come in, Belle.'

Chapter 67

Wheeler pulled up outside the old stone mansion, turned the car into the drive and killed the engine. She locked the car, crossed quickly to the front door. Saw the inscription *1926 Manse*. She rang the bell and waited. Nothing. She stepped back and scanned the building. It was in darkness. Wheeler took out her mobile and checked Matt's text. Yes, she had the right time and the right address. Wheeler knocked hard on the door and heard the soft click. It had been left on the latch. It opened into a large hall and a lamp gave off a faint glow. Wheeler saw a tiled floor, an intricate pattern of geometric stars, red, black, grey, brown. She stepped onto the tiles and called, 'Matt?'

Silence.

'Matt?'

Wheeler glanced around her. An oak staircase led to the upper rooms. On ground level there were three oak doors, all closed. Wheeler walked to the nearest and pushed it open. She stood in the doorway of a library. The walls were panels of walnut, and a grandfather clock ticked the minutes off in a deep, rhythmic timbre. The air was scented with lemon. Wheeler closed the door.

The next door led to a sitting room. Framed photographs of decaying Airstreams and deserted buildings stared down at her. Wheeler stared at the photographs. They were all images of death and decay. She left the room.

She pushed open the third door and walked into an empty kitchen. It was Arts and Crafts. Oak cabinets ran the length of the room and copper wall lamps shone warmly across the space. The heat came from a dark green Aga. Stained-glass windows depicted green and red stars against a midnight-blue background. Wheeler walked into the hall. The wooden stairs creaked as she made her way to the top landing. It was in semi-darkness. 'Matt?' Silence met her as she made her way along the narrow corridor. She groped for a light switch, found one and flicked it, heard it click. Nothing. Only the soft, low glow from a wall sconce. Wheeler looked around her. Four oak doors. She tried the first, saw the empty bed neatly made, a table lamp, the window slightly ajar. Everything seemed ordinary. Wheeler stepped inside and saw a photograph album. She flicked through, glanced at photographs of Cameron Craig, Irena, Amanda Henderson and others. She stood in the darkness and listened. A lorry rumbled by in the distance, but there was no noise from the house itself.

Wheeler walked back into the corridor. She opened the second door. The room was empty and dust sheets shrouded the furniture. She stepped back into the corridor and felt the adrenalin course through her system. She opened the door to the third room and stepped inside. She felt her muscles tense. The third room was the one. She knew it – she could feel it.

And she was right.

The dimmed light came from the single lamp that shone over the silent tableau. Wheeler crossed the room quickly and knelt beside Belle Henderson's body. She loosened the silk scarf that had formed a ligature around Belle's neck and felt for a pulse. She detected a faint vibration but a deep wound to Belle's right temple oozed a dark stain that spread across the floorboards, creating a black halo around her head. The card lying beside Belle read, *Happiness is when you learn to love yourself.* Wheeler grabbed her phone and dialled furiously. He sprang from the shadows and pinned his arms around her, forcing the breath from her lungs. Wheeler wrestled and saw a flash of blade. She felt his arm press hard into her windpipe and the oxygen leave her. She tried to inhale air but her mind began to fog.

In a dark and hidden corner of the room, Fiona crouched, her eyes glittering. She made silent clapping gestures, which were gleeful and gloating. She mouthed one word over and over again: 'Dad. Dad. Dad.'

Chapter 68

The phone rang and Ross answered it. 'I need to speak with DI Wheeler.' Ross recognized the high, clipped voice of the Oakwood School secretary.

'I'm afraid she's not here,' said Ross.

'When will she be back?'

'Miss Mackie, it's DI Ross. We met at your school. Can I help?'

'I'd rather wait and speak to your superior if you don't mind.'

'I beg your pardon?' said Ross.

'DI Ross, I was led to believe that locating these files was a matter of urgency, so I took the time and energy to oblige and now DI Wheeler's not even around to take the call. Very well, then. I'll call back at a time more convenient to her.'

'Just read me the list of names, Miss Mackie,' said Ross.

'I certainly will not.'

'The list – now, Miss Mackie.'

'Young man, if you would be so kind as to inform—'

'Now.'

'I don't know who you think you are talking to, but may I remind you that honest tax-paying citizens such as myself pay your wages. I find that your sort conveniently forget that fact.'

His voice rose: 'This is a murder inquiry. Read me the list now or you will be obstructing a police investigation.'

There was a long silence. 'Very well, if you insist.'

'I do.'

'But when this is over, be sure that I shall make a formal complaint.'

'Fine.'

'How many names do you require?'

'All of them.' Ross grabbed a pen, started to write. He silently willed Mackie to give him a name he recognized. As she recited the list, he quickly wrote them down, circled any that were faintly familiar. 'Joseph Burns' – there was a petty thief of the same name who operated out of Altyre Street, but there was no way he'd gone to private school. Ross wrote them all down with the exception of Mark Haedyear and Joseph Mere. That much he knew already.

Eventually Miss Mackie paused. 'Well, just three left and then I take it I'm free to go? I have work to do.'

'Of course. Thank you for your time,' said Ross, pen poised mid-air. She recited the last three names and he scribbled them down – Anthony Clairmont and, underneath, Philip Bishop. Ross thought of what Richard Henderson had told him about the nickname 'Preacher' and underlined Bishop.

'The last one is Matthew Elliot. Is that enough for you? I need to get on.'

He stared at the last name.

'Well? At least tell me that this exercise was helpful?' Miss Mackie demanded.

Anne Randall

Ross heard her voice and realized he was still holding the receiver. He slammed down the phone, redialled quickly and heard Wheeler's voice message kick in. Two minutes later he was driving out of the car park. Beside him, Boyd was on the phone directing the nearest patrol car to Matt Elliot's address. Ross pulled into the road, veered straight into the outside lane and put his foot down. Light flashing, siren blazing.

Chapter 69

Wheeler felt the cool of steel against her throat. She closed her eyes and managed a shallow breath, then used her whole body to slam herself backwards and pin him against the wall. He staggered off balance for an instant before righting himself and tightening his grip. It was enough to let her get one deep breath and she inhaled quickly. He held her tightly and they swayed momentarily in a crazy, lurching dance, shadows pirouetting in the candlelight. In the distance a siren screamed. From the corner, a figure slunk out of the room. Wheeler glimpsed the shadow.

Wheeler felt his grip tighten. Her arms were pinned to her sides but she tucked her chin down as far she could and curled her head into her chest. Then she threw it back as fast and as hard as she could and caught him full in the throat. She heard him gasp, his grip on her loosened, then she felt him collapse behind her. She spun round and saw Elliot sink to the floor. She balled her fists and tensed but he was unconscious. She grabbed her phone and punched in the numbers.

999.

Before she had finished requesting the ambulance,

footsteps hammered on the stairs, the door flew open and Ross stood in front of her, panting. Wheeler felt her heartbeat begin to slow and the adrenalin leave her. She leaned into him. 'You took your fucking time, muppet. What kept you?'

Ross held her. 'The traffic. It was a fucking nightmare. You've no idea what I've gone through to get here.'

'I can imagine. Tough call?'

Ross kept his arms around her. 'The toughest.'

'Get an ambulance for Belle Henderson,' said Wheeler, moving towards the body on the floor, 'and one for Matt Elliot.'

Ross made the call.

Wheeler glanced at her feet, saw the card that had been meant for her: *Where is the bliss in your life? It's up to you to create it!*

In the West End, Fiona let herself in. The smell was unexpected. Whisky had been spilled. Richard Henderson didn't drink. 'But maybe you've turned to it, have you? Pathetic.' Fiona spoke out loud to the empty hallway. She made her way inside. 'Richard, are you here?' No answer.

She found him asleep in the bedroom, an empty whisky bottle beside him. Fiona went to the wardrobe. She already knew what she would find there. She rifled through the silk scarves and selected her mother's favourite design, red roses against a yellow background. 'Gaudy, Mother, just like you,' said Fiona, wrapping it around her fingers. She thought about her father's advice: the trick to any successful kill is speed and surprise.

Richard opened bloodshot eyes. 'Darling, you've come back.' He swung his legs over the side of the bed.

Fiona went to him. 'You're weak. Let me help you.' She knelt behind him, placed the scarf tight against his throat and pulled it hard. She felt his head jerk backwards as she increased the pressure. Henderson's fingers scrabbled furiously at the scarf but it was useless and finally his body sagged.

'Done,' smiled Fiona. 'All done now.' She reached into her pocket, pulled out a card and left it beside the body: *Think positive and you will attract positive experiences to you.*

She walked to the door, feeling the adrenalin surge through her. She was on a high. She went out onto Observatory Road and kept her head high. She barely recognized the flashing lights and the uniformed officers. But they were waiting for her. And it was over.

Chapter 70

Thursday, 6 February

The restaurant buzzed with diners and the waiter topped up her glass.

Ross sat across from her. 'This good enough for you, Wheeler?'

'Perfect, but you knew that already. I love this place.'

'Yep.'

'I still can't believe they're making me take time off.'

'You were attacked, Wheeler.'

'And I'm okay, Ross. Stop fussing.'

'A few days, that's all they said.'

'A waste of bloody time.'

A lengthy pause. Then Ross spoke: 'Matt Elliot.'

'Go on,' said Wheeler.

'He's been charged with Cameron Craig's murder and Irena's.'

'We know he did more, though, Ross.'

'Yes, we found a photograph album in his house. Uniform are working their way through it. There are at least ten unidentified victims.'

'Fuck.'

'But we've got him,' said Ross. 'Dr Matt Elliot's now residing in the secure unit.'

Wheeler touched the bruises on her neck. 'A very dangerous guy. Did they find his computer?'

'Yep, with his printer and examples of his handwriting. He sent all the letters to you, Wheeler. He stalked you.'

'And Fiona delivered them?'

'To the station and your flat.'

Wheeler sipped her wine. 'What brought Elliot and Fiona together?'

'Haedyear. He was at school with Elliot. They stayed in touch and he knew about the rape at university. Once he decided to claim a victim for Elliot, he tracked Amanda Henderson.'

'And, of course, the murder was in all the papers, along with the details of the family, including the ages of the two girls. So when Elliot did the post-mortem and saw that she had given birth he did the maths and knew Fiona was his daughter. He made contact and began to groom her.'

'And Fiona killed for him, first Belle and then Richard.'

'I thought Belle might have made it,' said Ross.

'I didn't.' Wheeler thought of the dark stain that had spread around Belle's head. 'Matt Elliot killed them all, one way or another. He's responsible.'

'Yes, but we have them, Wheeler,' said Ross, 'and both Elliot and Fiona are undergoing psychiatric assessment to decide if they're fit to stand trial. So,' he lifted his wine glass, 'a result?'

Wheeler raised hers. 'A result.'

'Plus Tommy Taylor confessed to killing Karen Cooper and, much as it pains me to say it, Mike Barr was right. It was an intended rape but ended with Taylor killing her.'

'Taylor worked at the mortuary before the Equestrian Eatery?' asked Wheeler.

'As a porter. So when he asked Elliot for help, Elliot contaminated the evidence and framed Cameron Craig,' said Ross.

'So Elliot pretty much owned Taylor?'

'Taylor owed him, so when Elliot told him Haedyear needed a car, Taylor provided one.'

'Bastards.' Wheeler sipped her wine. 'And Mark Haedyear. Any update?'

'He's still out there somewhere...apparently.'

'He's dead,' said Wheeler. It was more of a statement than a question.

Chapter 71

It was too bright. The walls in every corridor were white-washed. Even the metal railings were white. Only the rubberized flooring was dark. 'There's not enough contrast,' Dr Matt Elliot complained to the guard. 'There has to be chiaroscuro for it to work, for me to be inspired while I'm here. Do you even get that?'

The prison officer ignored Elliot and walked on.

'All this light lacks shadow and depth. How am I, as an artist, supposed to create in something this sterile?'

The officer stopped. 'This is your cell.'

Elliot smiled as the door slammed behind him. 'Finally,' he muttered, 'I welcome the silence. Now I can get back to work.' He sat at the desk, bent over the sheet of paper and began to write.

Communication Five

Hello Friend,

May I still call you friend?

I do hope so.

Have you enjoyed our shared story? Our adventure together? I am so pleased that we remain in contact.

We are still connected, even if only on the spiritual plane. But, then, you already know that, don't you? Despite what they say I have done, the enticing Inspector Wheeler and the revolting DI Ross, you and I are remain connected. We still vibrate at the same frequency. You and I remain soul-mates.

But I am temporarily incarcerated and they tell me that I will reside in a high-security psychiatric amenity. How wrong they are. They also suggest that I am criminally insane. Lazy thinking. You don't believe that of me, do you?

I do hope not.

Tiresome as infamy can be, I have attracted a certain species of fans. Women who are fascinated by me and wish to correspond. Perhaps they believe that communication with me will provide them with a frisson of excitement. That may be. Or danger? Most certainly.

And as for my daughter, Fiona? All she can conceivably be accused of is her youth. Loving those little cards from the Institute her poor, pathetic father so clung to. And, I ask you, shouldn't she be forgiven for having a childish love of them? As for the rest, she enabled our soul-mates to soar, to reach their spiritual destiny. But will we be revered? Congratulated? I think not.

And as for Glasgow itself? As ever, the city endures. Sweet, intense Glasgow. As dark as chocolate and twice as bitter.

To us all.

To our continued journey together.

Sláinte.

Chapter 72

In Carmunnock, inside the Rose Memorial Crematorium, the officiant, an emaciated man with a pencil moustache, prepared for the last four cremations of the day. Raymond Crook studied the pre-printed text in front of him, committing to memory what he could about the deceased.

Daphne Bateman had been ninety-one years old when she had passed away and had been a resident at the local home. Raymond Crook had known her slightly. His own mother had resided in the home until her departure the previous year. Unlike his mother, Daphne had been tiny, sparrow-like, and couldn't have weighed more than ninety pounds. She weighed far more now. As for the deceased scheduled for the following three cremations, Mr Gerald McGlone, aged ninety-two, Mrs Betty Sommerville, aged eighty-nine, and Ms Esme Meaden, aged ninety-one, well, they had all gained considerable weight since their demise. Like Daphne, they were all old and had either never married or had outlived their families. This had meant there would be no one to collect their ashes in an expensive urn to be placed on a sideboard or mantelpiece. They would be scattered in the garden of remembrance by the staff at the crematorium.

Crook looked out at the congregation. Two women sat in separate pews. One he knew to be a local social worker for the elderly. The other was a care worker from the home and she was taking it hard. Perhaps she had looked after Daphne Bateman for a long time. Tears were streaming down the woman's ashen face. Crook smiled compassionately and patted the notes in front of him. The care worker looked like she was in bits. Just like Mark Haedyear, whose body had been dissected into four equal parts after his blood had been drained and the parts spread equally among the four coffins. Weirdo had been right: ashes to ashes.

Crook stepped forward, gripped the side of the lectern, cleared his throat and began, 'We are gathered here today...'

Acknowledgements

Thanks to my agent Jane Conway-Gordon, Krystyna Green and all at Little, Brown. Also to Caroline Tonkyn, for providing support and inspiration.

N